FICTION   Gaines, Ernest J.,
GAINES   1933-

           A lesson before
           dying.

DATE			

Condition Notes 7/14 NCV

A LESSON BEFORE DYING

A
LESSON
BEFORE
DYING

ERNEST J. GAINES

ALFRED A.
KNOPF
NEW YORK
1993

THIS IS A BORZOI BOOK
PUBLISHED BY ALFRED A. KNOPF, INC.

Copyright © 1993 by Ernest J. Gaines
All rights reserved under International and
Pan-American Copyright Conventions.
Published in the United States by
Alfred A. Knopf, Inc., New York, and
simultaneously in Canada by Random House
of Canada Limited, Toronto. Distributed
by Random House, Inc., New York.

Library of Congress Cataloging-in-Publication Data
Gaines, Ernest J. [date]
A lesson before dying / by Ernest J. Gaines.
p.   cm.
ISBN 0-679-41477-0
I. Title.
PS3557.A355L47   1993
813'.54—dc20   92-20335   CIP

Manufactured in the United States of America

FIRST EDITION

For Dianne

A LESSON BEFORE DYING

1

I WAS NOT THERE, yet I was there. No, I did not go to the trial, I did not hear the verdict, because I knew all the time what it would be. Still, I was there. I was there as much as anyone else was there. Either I sat behind my aunt and his godmother or I sat beside them. Both are large women, but his godmother is larger. She is of average height, five four, five five, but weighs nearly two hundred pounds. Once she and my aunt had found their places—two rows behind the table where he sat with his court-appointed attorney—his godmother became as immobile as a great stone or as one of our oak or cypress stumps. She never got up once to get water or go to the bathroom down in the basement. She just sat there staring at the boy's clean-cropped head where he sat at the front table with his lawyer.

Even after he had gone to await the jurors' verdict, her eyes remained in that one direction. She heard nothing said in the courtroom. Not by the prosecutor, not by the defense attorney, not by my aunt. (Oh, yes, she did hear one word—one word, for sure: "hog.") It was my aunt whose eyes followed the prosecutor as he moved from one side of the courtroom to the other, pounding his fist into the palm of his hand, pounding the table where his papers lay, pounding the rail that separated the jurors from the rest of the courtroom. It was my aunt who followed his every move, not his godmother. She was not even listening. She had gotten tired of listening. She knew, as we all knew, what the outcome would be. A white man had been killed during a robbery, and though two of the robbers had been killed on the spot, one had been captured, and he, too, would have to die. Though he told them no, he had nothing to do with it, that he was on his way to the White Rabbit Bar and Lounge when Brother and Bear drove up beside him and offered him a ride. After he got into the car, they asked him if he had any money. When he told them he didn't have a solitary dime, it was then that Brother and Bear started talking credit, saying that old Gropé should not mind crediting them a pint since he knew them well, and he knew that the grinding season was coming soon, and they would be able to pay him back then.

The store was empty, except for the old storekeeper, Alcee Gropé, who sat on a stool behind the counter. He spoke first. He asked Jefferson about his godmother. Jefferson told him his nannan was all right. Old Gropé nodded his head. "You tell her for me I say hello," he told Jefferson. He looked at Brother and Bear. But he didn't like them. He didn't trust them. Jefferson could see that in his face. "Do for you boys?" he asked. "A bottle of that Apple White, there, Mr. Gropé," Bear said. Old Gropé got the bottle off the shelf, but he did not set it on the counter. He could see that the boys had already been drinking, and he became suspicious. "You boys got money?" he asked.

Brother and Bear spread out all the money they had in their pockets on top of the counter. Old Gropé counted it with his eyes. "That's not enough," he said. "Come on, now, Mr. Gropé," they pleaded with him. "You know you go'n get your money soon as grinding start." "No," he said. "Money is slack everywhere. You bring the money, you get your wine." He turned to put the bottle back on the shelf. One of the boys, the one called Bear, started around the counter. "You, stop there," Gropé told him. "Go back." Bear had been drinking, and his eyes were glossy, he walked unsteadily, grinning all the time as he continued around the counter. "Go back," Gropé told him. "I mean, the last time now—go back." Bear continued. Gropé moved quickly toward the cash register, where he withdrew a revolver and started shooting. Soon there was shooting from another direction. When it was quiet again, Bear, Gropé, and Brother were all down on the floor, and only Jefferson was standing.

He wanted to run, but he couldn't run. He couldn't even think. He didn't know where he was. He didn't know how he had gotten there. He couldn't remember ever getting into the car. He couldn't remember a thing he had done all day.

He heard a voice calling. He thought the voice was coming from the liquor shelves. Then he realized that old Gropé was not dead, and that it was he who was calling. He made himself go to the end of the counter. He had to look across Bear to see the storekeeper. Both lay between the counter and the shelves of alcohol. Several bottles had been broken, and alcohol and blood covered their bodies as well as the floor. He stood there gaping at the old man slumped against the bottom shelf of gallons and half gallons of wine. He didn't know whether he should go to him or whether he should run out of there. The old man continued to call: "Boy? Boy? Boy?" Jefferson became frightened. The old man was still alive. He had seen him. He would tell on him. Now he started babbling. "It wasn't me. It wasn't me, Mr. Gropé. It was Brother and Bear. Brother shot you. It wasn't me. They made me come with them. You got to tell the law that, Mr. Gropé. You hear me, Mr. Gropé?"

But he was talking to a dead man.

Still he did not run. He didn't know what to do. He didn't believe that this had happened. Again he couldn't remember how he had gotten there. He didn't know whether he had come there with Brother and Bear, or whether he had walked in and seen all this after it happened.

He looked from one dead body to the other. He didn't know whether he should call someone on the telephone or run. He had never dialed a telephone in his life, but he had seen other people use them. He didn't know what to do. He was standing by the liquor shelf, and suddenly he realized he needed a drink and needed it badly. He snatched a bottle off the shelf, wrung off the cap, and turned up the bottle, all in one continuous motion. The whiskey burned him like fire—his chest, his belly, even his nostrils. His eyes watered; he shook his head to clear his mind. Now he began to realize where he was. Now he began to realize fully what had happened. Now he knew he had to get out of there. He turned. He saw the money in the cash register, under the little wire clamps. He knew taking money was wrong. His nannan had told him never to steal. He didn't want to steal. But he didn't have a solitary dime in his pocket. And nobody was around, so who could say he stole it? Surely not one of the dead men.

He was halfway across the room, the money stuffed inside his jacket pocket, the half bottle of whiskey clutched in his hand, when two white men walked into the store.

That was his story.

The prosecutor's story was different. The prosecutor argued that Jefferson and the other two had gone there with the full intention of robbing the old man and then killing him so that he could not identify them. When the old man and the other two robbers were all dead, this one—it proved the kind of animal he really was—stuffed the money into his pockets and celebrated the event by drinking over their still-bleeding bodies.

The defense argued that Jefferson was innocent of all charges except being at the wrong place at the wrong time. There was absolutely no proof that there had been a conspiracy between himself and the other two. The fact that Mr. Gropé shot only Brother and Bear was proof of Jefferson's innocence. Why did Mr. Gropé shoot one boy twice and never shoot at Jefferson once? Because Jefferson was merely an innocent bystander. He took the whiskey to calm his nerves, not to celebrate. He took the money out of hunger and plain stupidity.

"Gentlemen of the jury, look at this—this—this boy. I almost said man, but I can't say man. Oh, sure, he has reached the age of twenty-one, when we, civilized men, consider the male species has reached manhood, but would you call this—this—this a man? No, not I. I would call it a boy and a fool. A fool is not aware of right and wrong. A fool does what others tell him to do. A fool got into that automobile. A man with a modicum of intelligence would have seen that those racketeers meant no good. But not a fool. A fool got into that automobile. A fool rode to the grocery store. A fool stood by and watched this happen, not having the sense to run.

"Gentlemen of the jury, look at him—look at him—look at this. Do you see a man sitting here? Do you see a man sitting here? I ask you, I implore, look carefully—do you see a man sitting here? Look at the shape of this skull, this face as flat as the palm of my hand—look deeply into those eyes. Do you see a modicum of intelligence? Do you see anyone here who could plan a murder, a robbery, can plan—can plan—can plan anything? A cornered animal to strike quickly out of fear, a trait inherited from his ancestors in the deepest jungle of blackest Africa—yes, yes, that he can do—but to plan? To plan, gentlemen of the jury? No, gentlemen, this skull here holds no plans. What you see here is a thing that acts on command. A thing to hold the handle of a plow, a thing to load your bales of cotton, a thing to dig your ditches, to chop your wood, to pull your corn. That is what you see here, but you do not see anything capable of planning a robbery or a murder. He does not even know the size of his clothes or his shoes. Ask him to name the months of the year. Ask him does Christmas come before or after the Fourth of July? Mention the names of Keats, Byron, Scott, and see whether the eyes will show one moment of recognition. Ask him to describe a rose, to quote one passage from the Constitution or the Bill of Rights. Gentlemen of the jury, this man planned a robbery? Oh, pardon me, pardon me, I surely did not mean to insult your intelligence by saying 'man'—would you please forgive me for committing such an error?

"Gentlemen of the jury, who would be hurt if you took this life? Look back to that second row. Please look. I want all twelve of you honorable men to turn your heads and look back to that second row. What you see there has been everything to him— mama, grandmother, godmother—everything. Look at her, gen- tlemen of the jury, look at her well. Take this away from her, and she has no reason to go on living. We may see him as not much, but he's her reason for existence. Think on that, gentlemen, think on it.

"Gentlemen of the jury, be merciful. For God's sake, be merciful. He is innocent of all charges brought against him.

"But let us say he was not. Let us for a moment say he was not. What justice would there be to take this life? Justice, gentlemen? Why, I would just as soon put a hog in the electric chair as this.

"I thank you, gentlemen, from the bottom of my heart, for your kind patience. I have no more to say, except this: We must live with our own conscience. Each and every one of us must live with his own conscience."

The jury retired, and it returned a verdict after lunch: guilty of robbery and murder in the first degree. The judge com- mended the twelve white men for reaching a quick and just verdict. This was Friday. He would pass sentence on Monday.

Ten o'clock on Monday, Miss Emma and my aunt sat in the same seats they had occupied on Friday. Reverend Mose Ambrose, the pastor of their church, was with them. He and my aunt sat on either side of Miss Emma. The judge, a short, red-faced man with snow-white hair and thick black eyebrows, asked Jefferson if he had anything to say before the sentencing. My aunt said that Jefferson was looking down at the floor and shook his head. The judge told Jefferson that he had been found guilty of the charges brought against him, and that the judge saw no reason that he should not pay for the part he played in this horrible crime.

Death by electrocution. The governor would set the date.

2

WHEN I CAME HOME from school that afternoon, I saw my aunt and Miss Emma sitting at the table in the kitchen. I was sorry now that I had come directly home, because Miss Emma was the last person I wanted to see. Just like everyone else in the quarter, I knew what the sentence was going to be, and I didn't want to have to look into her face. I hurried to my room with the satchel of papers that I had brought from school to work on that night. After laying the satchel on the table that I used as a desk, I sat down on the bed as quietly as I could. Neither my aunt nor Miss Emma had seen me come in, but they knew it was the time of day for me to be there. I tried to think of a way to make a quick appearance in the kitchen for courtesy's

sake and then leave. I didn't want to look into that face any more
than I had to.

It was late October, and though I wore a wool shirt under my
jacket, I was a little cold. I thought how nice it would be to sit
inside the Rainbow Club in Bayonne. I had a lot of work to do,
but I didn't feel like being here, not as long as Miss Emma was
in the house. I couldn't hear a sound from the kitchen. I wondered if I could sneak out of the house before my aunt saw me.
I got up from the bed, and I was near the door when I heard
footsteps in her bedroom. I hurried back to the table and took
some papers out of the satchel. When she came into my room,
I had sat down at the table and was pretending to read. She
stood looking at me.

"Ain't you go'n speak to Miss Emma?" she said.

"I was going to. I was just looking over some papers."

"She want talk to you."

"What about?" I asked.

"She can tell you."

"I have to go to Bayonne, Tante Lou," I said. "Something for
the school."

"I'm sure this won't take all day."

"The store closes at five, Tante Lou," I said. "It's almost four
now."

"You can spare a few minutes," my aunt said. " 'Specially
today."

She didn't say any more. She didn't have to. She was sure I
knew what had happened.

We looked at each other a moment, then I looked down at the
student's paper that I had taken from the satchel. The fourth-
grade writing was nearly illegible, but even if it had been typed
I would not have been able to concentrate long enough to read
it. My aunt, standing back watching me, knew I was not reading.

I pushed the papers away and followed her through her room,
back into the kitchen. Miss Emma sat at the kitchen table,

staring out into the yard. I started to speak to her, but I wasn't sure that she even knew I was there.

"Sit down, Grant," my aunt said.

"I can stand, Tante Lou."

"Sit down," she said.

She sat down first, next to Miss Emma, so that I would have to sit opposite both of them. In this way they could look at me at the same time, or take turns.

"How are you, Miss Emma?" I said.

"Making out," she said.

She stared out into the yard, my aunt looked down at the table, and I waited, afraid to even think what Miss Emma might want to speak to me about.

Miss Emma was in her early or mid-seventies; my aunt was in her seventies, and I figured they were pretty much the same age. Miss Emma's hair was gray and combed up and pinned on top. I had noticed her floppy brown felt hat and her overcoat on my aunt's bed on our way back into the kitchen.

Her name was Emma Glenn, but no one except her closest friends and the white people on the river ever called her anything but Miss Emma. Her husband, who was dead now, had called her Miss Emma, and she had called him Mr. Oscar, and that is how we on that plantation had grown up addressing them. Except for Jefferson. He called her "Nannan" and he had called Mr. Oscar "Parain"—godmother and godfather.

Miss Emma continued to stare into the yard, but I was sure she was not seeing anything out there. There was nothing out there to see but the jimsonweeds and crabgrass, and the rows of cane that ran parallel to the yard and about a hundred feet away from the kitchen where we sat. Miss Emma was not seeing any of that. She was remembering, she was thinking; she was not seeing.

"Called him a hog."

She said that, and it was quiet again. My aunt looked at me, then back down at the table. I waited.

"I know he was just trying to get him off. But they didn't pay that no mind. Still give him death."

She turned her head slowly and looked directly at me. Her large, dark face showed all the pain she had gone through this day, this past weekend. No. The pain I saw in that face came from many years past.

"I don't want them to kill no hog," she said. "I want a man to go to that chair, on his own two feet."

I waited, not knowing what was coming.

But she was finished talking. Now both she and my aunt looked at me as though I was supposed to figure out the rest of it. We stared at one another a few seconds before what they expected began to dawn on me.

"Wait," I said. "Wait."

Neither one said a thing until I started to get up, and my aunt told me to sit back down.

"Sit down for what?" I asked her.

"Just sit down," she said.

I settled back on the chair, but not all the way back. I was ready to get up at any moment.

"He don't have to do it," Miss Emma said, looking beyond me again.

"Do what?" I asked her.

"You don't have to do it," she said again. It was dry, mechanical, unemotional, but I could tell by her face and by my aunt's face that they were not about to give up on what they had in mind.

"What do you want me to do?" I asked her. "What can I do? It's only a matter of weeks, a couple of months, maybe. What can I do that you haven't done the past twenty-one years?"

"You the teacher," she said.

"Yes, I'm the teacher," I said. "And I teach what the white folks around here tell me to teach—reading, writing, and 'rithmetic. They never told me how to keep a black boy out of a liquor store."

"You watch your tongue, sir," my aunt said.

I sat back in the chair and looked at both of them. They sat there like boulders, their bodies, their minds immovable.

"He don't have to," Miss Emma said again.

"He go'n do it," my aunt said.

"Oh?" I said.

"You go'n do it," she said. "We going up there and talk to Mr. Henri."

"Talk to Henri Pichot? For what?" I asked her.

"So you have the right to visit Jefferson."

"What's Henri Pichot got to do with this?"

"His brother-in-law is the sheriff, ain't he?"

I waited for her to say more, but she did not. I got up from the table.

"And where you think you going?" Tante Lou asked me.

"To Bayonne, where I can breathe," I said. "I can't breathe here."

"You ain't going to no Bayonne till you go up the quarter," she said. "You go'n see Mr. Henri with me and Emma, there."

I had walked away, but now I came back and leaned over the table toward both of them.

"Tante Lou, Miss Emma, Jefferson is dead. It is only a matter of weeks, maybe a couple of months—but he's already dead. The past twenty-one years, we've done all we could for Jefferson. He's dead now. And I can't raise the dead. All I can do is try to keep the others from ending up like this—but he's gone from us. There's nothing I can do anymore, nothing any of us can do anymore."

"You going with us up the quarter," my aunt said, as though I hadn't said a word. "You going up there with us, Grant, or you don't sleep in this house tonight."

I stood back from the table and looked at the both of them. I clamped my jaws so tight the veins in my neck felt as if they would burst. I wanted to scream at my aunt; I was screaming inside. I had told her many, many times how much I hated this place and all I wanted to do was get away. I had told her I was no teacher, I hated teaching, and I was just running in place here. But she had not heard me before, and I knew that no matter how loud I screamed, she would not hear me now.

"I'm getting my coat, and I'll be ready to go," she said. "Em-ma?"

3

MY GRAY '46 FORD was parked in front of the house. Tante Lou, in her black overcoat and black rimless hat, and Miss Emma, in her brown coat with the rabbit fur around the collar and sleeves and her floppy brown felt hat, followed me out to the car and stood back until I had opened the door for them. Not only was I going up to Henri Pichot's house against my will, but I had to perform all the courtesies of chauffeur as well. After they had settled in the back seat, filling it completely, I slammed the door and went around to the other side and got in. I could feel my aunt's eyes on the back of my neck for shutting the door as I did. Miss Emma probably would have looked at me the same way, but her mind was on other things.

As I drove by the church where I taught school, I thought

about all the work I had to do. And I reminded myself that I had to see one of the men on the plantation about getting a load of firewood for the heater. I tried to remember who had brought us the last wagonload of wood. Fifteen or twenty families sent their children to the school, and I always made it a point—they expected it of me—to ask them to do something for the school during the six-month session. I would ask one of the older children to tell me who had brought in the last load of wood.

I stopped at the side gate to Henri Pichot's large white and gray antebellum house. When my aunt started to get out of the car to open the gate for me, I told her to keep her seat because I had nothing to do all that day but serve. I felt her eyes on the back of my neck again, then on the side of my face as I pushed open the gate, and on me directly as I came back to the car. After driving into the yard, I had to get out again to shut the gate. Since the side entrance led from the quarter to the house, Henri Pichot never used this gate. Only tractors, wagons, and trucks used this entrance, and over the many years, they had cut just as many ruts across the yard. I must have hit every one of them, driving up to the house. My aunt never said a thing, but I could feel her eyes on the back of my neck. I was not aiming for the ruts, but I wasn't avoiding them either. I could hear them bouncing on the back seat, but they never said a word. After parking under one of the great live oaks not far from the back door, I turned around to look at my aunt.

"Am I supposed to go in there too?"

She looked at me, but she didn't answer me. She thought I had hit those ruts on purpose.

"It was you who said you never wanted me to go through that back door ever again."

"Do I have to keep reminding you, Grant, this ain't just another day?"

"He don't have to go," Miss Emma said for about the hundredth time. She was looking at me but not seeing me, and not meaning what she was saying, either.

"He's going," my aunt said. She was definitely seeing me. "Mr. Henri won't come to him."

"Oh, yes, I keep forgetting that," I said. "Mr. Henri won't come to me."

After a minute of grunting and straining, they were able to get out of the car. I followed them into the inner yard, up the stairs to the back door. The maid, Inez Lane, had seen us come into the yard, and she opened the door for us. Inez was in her early forties, I suppose. She wore a white dress, white shoes, a blue gingham apron, and a kerchief on her head. She had a dark mole on her left cheek. She nodded to my aunt and me and spoke to Miss Emma.

"I heard," she said.

"I would like to speak to Mr. Henri if he's home," Miss Emma said.

"Talking to Mr. Louis in the library," Inez said.

"Like to speak to him if he don't mind," Miss Emma said.

Inez nodded and left us. I looked around the kitchen. I had come into this kitchen many times as a small child, to bring in wood for the stove, to bring in a chicken I had caught and killed, eggs I had found in the grass, and figs, pears, and pecans I had gathered from the trees in the yard. Miss Emma was the cook up here then. She wore the white dress and white shoes and the kerchief around her head. She had been here long before I was born, probably when my mother and father were children. She had cooked for the old Pichots, the parents of Henri Pichot. She had cooked for Henri and his brother and sister, as well as for his nieces and nephews; he did not have any children of his own. She cooked, she ran the house; my aunt washed and ironed; and I ran through the yard to get the things they needed to cook or cook with. As a child growing up on this plantation, I could not imagine this place, this house, existing without the two of them here. But before I left for the university, my aunt sat me down at the table in our kitchen and said to me, "Me and Em-ma can make out all right without you coming through that back door ever again." I had not come through that back door once since leaving for the university, ten years before. I had been teaching on the place going on six years, and I had not been in Pichot's yard, let alone gone up the back stairs or through that back door.

I saw both my aunt and Miss Emma looking around the kitchen. Some things had changed since they left, others had not. The big black iron pots still hung against the wall. But the wood-burning oven that I had known and that they had known had been exchanged for a gas range. And a big white refrigerator had taken the place of a smaller icebox. The war had changed all that. After so many of the young colored men had gone into military service or left the plantation, there was no one to chop the wood and haul the ice. And when they left, so did the old people, my aunt and Miss Emma.

I did not hear Inez knock on the library door or hear her call, but I did hear Henri Pichot's voice: "Yes, Inez, what is it?" Then, a moment later: "Who?" And a moment after that: "Did she say what she wanted?" And later: "Go back there and ask her what she wants."

Inez came back into the kitchen.

"Just tell him I like to speak to him," Miss Emma said. "It's important."

Inez started back up the hall, but Henri Pichot had already left the library. He was a medium-size man, of medium weight. He wore a gray suit, a white shirt, and a gray and white striped tie. He could have been in his mid-sixties; his hair was white and long. He held a drink. Louis Rougon, who followed him into the kitchen, was taller, heavier, and maybe a year or two younger. He wore a black pin-striped suit, and he also held a drink. Louis Rougon's people owned a bank in St. Adrienne, a small town about fifteen miles west of Henri Pichot's plantation.

"Mr. Henri, Mr. Louis." Miss Emma spoke to them. My aunt nodded. I didn't. I stood back near the door.

"What can I do for you, Emma?" Pichot asked her. He seemed annoyed that he had been disturbed while he had company.

"I want ask you a favor, Mr. Henri," Miss Emma said.

He drank from his glass and looked at her.

"It's Jefferson," she said.

"Yes, I heard," he said. And waited.

"I want ask you a favor."

"I can't change what has been handed down by the court," he said. "I spoke up before the trial; I can't say any more."

"Yes, sir," she said. "But that's not what I come to ask you for. I come to ask you something else."

Miss Emma looked tired. She was tired. She wanted to sit down at the table, but no one had offered her a chair. My aunt put her arm around her shoulders to comfort her and to help her stand. I looked at the two white men, who raised their glasses. Henri Pichot finished his drink and stuck out his hand. Inez knew what it meant, and she came forward to get the empty glass. Then she turned to Louis Rougon, who had stuck out his glass, empty of everything except two or three small cubes of ice. She took the glasses to a liquor counter to refresh the drinks.

"They called my boy a hog, Mr. Henri," Miss Emma said. "I didn't raise no hog, and I don't want no hog to go set in that chair. I want a man to go set in that chair, Mr. Henri."

He looked at her, but he didn't say anything. He was waiting for his drink.

"I'm old, Mr. Henri," she went on. "Jefferson go'n need me, but I'm too old to be going up there. My heart won't take it. I want you talk to the sheriff for me. I want somebody else take my place."

"That's up to you and Mr. Sam, isn't it?" Pichot said, and he took the drink off the tray that Inez held before him.

"I need you speak for me, Mr. Henri," Miss Emma said. "I want the teacher visit my boy. I want the teacher make him know he's not a hog, he's a man. I want him know that 'fore he go to that chair, Mr. Henri."

Henri Pichot glanced at me, then looked back at her.

"I done done a lot for this family and this place, Mr. Henri," she said. "All I'm asking you talk to the sheriff for me. I done done a lot for this family over the years."

"I can't promise anything," he said, and sipped his drink.

"You can speak to your brother-in-law."

"And say what?"

"I want the teacher talk to my boy for me."

He looked over her head at me, standing back by the door. I was too educated for Henri Pichot; he had no use for me at all anymore. But just as Miss Emma had given so much of herself to that family, so had my aunt. So Henri Pichot, who cared nothing in the world for me, tolerated me because of my aunt.

"And what do you plan to do?" he asked me.

I shook my head. "I have no idea." He stared at me, and I realized that I had not answered him in the proper manner. "Sir," I added.

"You think you can change him from a hog to a man in the little time he's got left?"

"I have no idea—sir," I said.

"But you're willing to try if I can get Mr. Sam to let you go up there?"

"That's what she wants, sir."

"But you didn't put her up to this?"

"No, sir, I did not," I said.

He was finished talking to me. Now he wanted me to look away. I lowered my eyes. When I raised my head, I saw his eyes on her again.

"I would forget all this if I were you," he said. "Let Mose visit him, and keep it at that."

"Reverend Mose will visit him," Miss Emma said. "But no, sir, I won't keep it at that."

"At this point, I would be more concerned about his soul if I were you," Henri said.

"Yes, sir, I'm concerned for his soul, Mr. Henri," Miss Emma said. "I'm concerned for his soul. But I want him be a man, too, when he go to that chair."

Louis Rougon, standing next to Henri Pichot, held his drink without drinking. He could not believe what he was hearing.

Henri Pichot looked at me again. He was sure I had put her up to this. I shifted my eyes, and I didn't look in his direction until I heard him speaking to her.

"Go on home, forget all this foolishness," he told her. "You have done all you could to raise him. Let the law have him now."

"The law got him, Mr. Henri," Miss Emma said. "And they go'n kill him. But let them kill a man. Let the teacher go to him, Mr. Henri. I done done a lot for this family over the years."

"I know what you've done for this family over the years," he told her. "And I also know what he did. Or have you forgotten that?"

"I ain't forgotten nothing, Mr. Henri," she said. "I know what they say he did."

"He did it," Henri said, leaving no doubt in his mind. "I spoke for him because of you, but all the time I knew he did it."

"If you say so, Mr. Henri."

"I say so," he said.

"That's not what I come up here for, Mr. Henri," Miss Emma said to him. "I'm not begging for his life no more; that's over. I just want see him die like a man. This family owe me that much, Mr. Henri. And I want it. I want somebody do something for me one time 'fore I close my eyes. Somebody got do something for me one time 'fore I close my eyes, Mr. Henri. Please, sir."

From where I stood, back by the door, I could see my aunt tightening her grip around Miss Emma's shoulders to give her comfort.

"I'll speak to him," Henri said. "But it's up to him, not me."

"Tell him what I done done for this family, Mr. Henri. Tell him to ask his wife all I done done for this family over the years."

"I said I would speak to him," Henri said, obviously becoming more and more impatient with her.

"When?" she asked.

Henri Pichot had started to raise his glass, because for him the conversation was over. But when Miss Emma spoke again, his hand stopped inches away from his mouth, and he lowered the glass.

"What?"

"When?"

"Whenever I see him, that's when," he said. "Now, if you don't mind, I have a guest."

He drank and turned away.

"Mr. Henri?" Miss Emma called him. But he kept walking. "I'll be up here again tomorrow, Mr. Henri. I'll be on my knees next time you see me, Mr. Henri."

But she was speaking to empty space. Henri Pichot and Louis Rougon were already in the library.

Miss Emma continued to stare up the hall for a moment, then she and my aunt turned away, and I held the door open for them to go outside. The sun had gone down, and it was getting colder.

4

I TOOK THEM BACK down the quarter. When I stopped in front of Miss Emma's house, my aunt got out of the car with her.

"I'm going to Bayonne," I told my aunt.

She had not shut the door yet.

"I'll be home to cook in a little while," she said.

"I'll eat in town," I told her.

Tante Lou held the door while she stood there looking at me. Nothing could have hurt her more when I said I was not going to eat her food. I was supposed to eat soon after she had cooked, and if I was not at home I was supposed to eat as soon as I came in. She looked at me without saying anything else, then she closed the door quietly and followed Miss Emma into the yard.

I turned the car around and started up the quarter again. There was not a single telephone in the quarter, not a public telephone anywhere that I could use before reaching Bayonne, and Bayonne was thirteen miles away.

After leaving the quarter, I drove down a graveled road for about two miles, then along a paved road beside the St. Charles River for another ten miles. There were houses and big live oak and pecan trees on either side of the road, but not as many on the riverbank side. There, instead of houses and trees, there were fishing wharves, boat docks, nightclubs, and restaurants for whites. There were one or two nightclubs for colored, but they were not very good.

As I drove along the river, I thought about all the schoolwork that I should have been doing at home. But I knew that after being around Miss Emma and Henri Pichot the past hour, I would not have been able to concentrate on my work. I needed to be with someone. I needed to be with Vivian.

Bayonne was a small town of about six thousand. Approximately three thousand five hundred whites; approximately two thousand five hundred colored. It was the parish seat for St. Raphael. The courthouse was there; so was the jail. There was a Catholic church uptown for whites; a Catholic church back of town for colored. There was a white movie theater uptown; a colored movie theater back of town. There were two elementary schools uptown, one Catholic, one public, for whites; and the same back of town for colored. Bayonne's major industries were a cement plant, a sawmill, and a slaughterhouse, mostly for hogs. There was only one main street in Bayonne, and it ran along the St. Charles River. The department stores, the bank, the two or three dentists' and doctors' and attorneys' offices, were mostly on this street, which made up less than half a dozen blocks.

After entering the town, which was marked by the movie theater for whites on the riverbank side of the road, I had to drive another two or three blocks before turning down an unlit road, which led back of town to the colored section. Once I crossed the railroad tracks, I could see the Rainbow Club, with its green, yellow, and red arched neon lights. Several cars were parked before the door; one of them, a big white new '48 Cadillac, belonged to Joe Claiborne, who owned the place. A man and a woman came through the door as I got out of my car to go inside. There were probably a dozen people in the place, half of them at the bar, the rest of them sitting at tables with white tablecloths. I spoke to Joe Claiborne and went through a side door into the café to use the telephone. The tables in the café had checkered red and white tablecloths. Thelma Claiborne was behind the counter. Thelma ran the café, and her husband, Joe, ran the bar. I asked her what she had for supper.

"Smothered chicken, smothered beefsteaks, shrimp stew," she said.

There was only one other person in the café, and he sat at the counter eating the stewed shrimps.

"Shrimps any good?" I asked Thelma.

"All my food's good," she said.

"Shrimps," I told her.

While Thelma dished up my food, I went to the telephone in the corner by the toilet. It took Vivian a while to answer, and she didn't sound too happy about it.

"Did I get you at a bad time?" I asked her.

"Getting these children something to eat," she said. "Where are you?"

"The Rainbow Club."

"Tonight?"

"I need to see you, baby. I need to talk," I said.

"Is something the matter?"

"I just need to talk to you, baby, that's all."

"You want to come over here? I can fix you a sandwich."

"No, I'm going to eat here at the café."

"I'll see if I can get Dora," she said. "If I can't, you'll have to come over here. I can't leave the children alone."

"I understand."

Thelma had the stewed shrimps, a green salad of lettuce, tomato, and cucumber, a piece of corn bread, and a glass of water on the counter, waiting for me.

"Anything else to go with that?" she asked.

"This'll do."

"Here or a table?" she asked.

"The counter is good."

"What you doing in town on Monday?" she asked. "Calling Miss Fine Brown?"

I nodded.

"Figgers," Thelma said, and smiled.

Thelma's mouth was full of gold teeth, solid gold as well as gold crowned. She also wore perfume that was strong enough to keep you a good distance away from her. I figured that's where most of their money went, on those gold teeth, that perfume, and payment on the new white Cadillac that Joe had parked before the door. But they were good people, both of them. When I was broke, I could always get a meal and pay later, and the same went for the bar.

I talked with Thelma awhile after I finished eating, then I paid her and went back to the other side.

"Usual?" Claiborne asked me. He knew what I drank, but he would always ask.

I nodded.

"What you doing here on Monday?" he asked, while pouring me a brandy.

"I needed a drink," I said.

"Sure," he said.

He poured a glass of ice water and set it on the bar beside the brandy.

"I think I know now," he said.

Car lights had just flashed upon the front of the club, and I could hear the tires on the crushed seashells just right of the door, and sure enough it was Vivian, and the men at the bar looked around at her when she came in. She was quite tall, five

seven, five eight, and she wore a green wool sweater and a green
and brown plaid skirt, and both fit her very well. She had soft
light brown skin and high cheekbones and greenish-brown eyes,
and her nostrils and lips showed some thickness, but not much.
Her hair was long and black, and she kept it twisted into a bun
and pinned at the back of her head. Vivian Baptiste was a
beautiful woman, and she knew it; but she didn't flaunt it, it was
just there. She came up to me, and a couple of the other men
at the bar nodded and spoke to her. One tipped his hat and
called her Miss Lady.

"You made it," I said.

"I got Dora."

"Usual?" Claiborne asked her.

She nodded toward my drink.

"Shirley can bring it to your table," Claiborne said.

"It won't tire her out, I hope."

Claiborne grunted at me.

It was a slow night. The few people at the bar were holding
on to their glasses and not buying any more. Shirley, the waitress, was sitting on a barstool at the far end, and she had not
moved once since I had been there. Vivian and I went to a table
far over into the corner, where we could be alone.

"I'm glad you came," I said, and kissed her.

Shirley brought the drinks and set them before us on paper
napkins. Before leaving, she looked at me out of the corner of
her eye to let me know she didn't like my remark at the bar.

Vivian and I touched glasses and drank.

"What is the matter, Grant?" she asked.

"I just had to see you."

"Is something the matter?"

"When was the last time I told you I loved you?"

"A second ago."

"I should say it more often," I said.

"What is the matter, Grant?" she asked me again.

"You want to leave from here tonight?" I asked her. "You

want to go home and pack your clothes and get the children and leave from here tonight?"

She looked at me as though she was trying to figure out whether I was serious or not.

"No," she said.

"Why not?" I asked her.

"Because the whole thing is just too crazy," she said.

"People do it all the time. Just pack up and leave."

"Some people can, but we can't," she said. "We're teachers, and we have a commitment."

"You hit the nail on the head there, lady—commitment. Commitment to what—to live and die in this hellhole, when we can leave and live like other people?"

"How much have you had to drink, Grant?"

"A whole fucking barrel of commitment," I said, and raised my glass.

"Do you want me to leave, Grant?" she asked. "You know I don't like it when you talk like that."

"No, I don't want you to leave. Please don't leave me," I told her.

She reached over and touched my hand, then she began to rub the knuckles with her fingers.

"I need to go someplace where I can feel I'm living," I said. "I don't want to spend the rest of my life teaching school in a plantation church. I want to be with you, someplace where we could have a choice of things to do. I don't feel alive here. I'm not living here. I know we can do better someplace else."

"I'm still married," Vivian said. "A separation is not a divorce. I can't go anywhere until all this is over with."

"That's not what's keeping you here. Even after the divorce, you'll still feel committed," I said.

"And you, Grant?"

"I'm tired of feeling committed."

"Then why haven't you gone?"

"Because of you."

"That's not true, Grant, and you know it," she said. "We met only three years ago. I was still married—pregnant with my second child. You told me then how much you always wanted to get away. And you did, once. You remember that? You went to California to visit your mother and father—but you wouldn't stay. You couldn't stay. You had to come back. Why did you come back, Grant? Why?"

"I want to go now, and I want you to go with me."

"I'm still married, Grant."

"After the divorce?"

She nodded. "After the divorce I'll do whatever you want me to do—as long as you're responsible for what you do."

"In other words, if I fail, I would have to blame myself the rest of my life for trying, is that it?"

"I'll leave all that up to you, Grant, if you still want me after the divorce."

"I'll always want you," I said, and touched her hand. "And if you don't know that by now, I don't know what you do know about me."

A couple from one of the other tables had gotten up and chosen a record on the jukebox. It was a blues, the tempo slow, and the two people danced close together. I needed Vivian closer to me than she was now, and I asked her if she wanted to dance.

We left the table, and I took her in my arms, and I could feel her breasts through that sweater, and I could feel her thighs through that plaid skirt, and now I felt very good.

We danced for a while. I didn't want to say it, but I had to say it.

"They gave him death," I said.

She and I had talked about it on the weekend, and I did not want to talk about it now, or even think about it now, but it was the only thing that stayed on my mind. I could feel her body go tense against me.

We danced awhile.

"They want me to visit him."

"That would be nice, Grant."

"They want me to make him a man before he dies."

She stopped dancing, and she stood back to look at me. Her face was twisted into a painful, questioning frown.

"The public defender, trying to get him off, called him a dumb animal," I told her. "He said it would be like tying a hog down into that chair and executing him—an animal that didn't know what any of it was all about. The jury, twelve white men good and true, still sentenced him to death. Now his godmother wants me to visit him and make him know—prove to these white men—that he's not a hog, that he's a man. I'm supposed to make him a man. Who am I? God?"

The record ended, and we went back to our table.

"I still don't know if the sheriff will even let me visit him. And suppose he did; what then? What do I say to him? Do I know what a man is? Do I know how a man is supposed to die? I'm still trying to find out how a man should live. Am I supposed to tell someone how to die who has never lived?"

Vivian lowered her head.

"Suppose I was allowed to visit him, and suppose I reached him and made him realize that he was as much a man as any other man; then what? He's still going to die. The next day, the next week, the next month. So what will I have accomplished? What will I have done? Why not let the hog die without knowing anything?"

Vivian raised her head to look at me, and she was crying. I took one of her hands in both of mine.

"I'm sorry. I didn't mean to do this to you. I don't want to do this to you. I just didn't know where else to turn."

"I want you to come to me, Grant," she said. "I want you to always come to me."

Shirley walked over to the table to pick up our empty glasses.

"Y'all want anything mo'?" she asked.

"Another round," I told her. She left.

"I want you to go up there," Vivian said.

"They make those decisions, sweetheart, I don't."

"If they say yes, I want you to go for me."

"For you?"

"For us, Grant."

I looked at her, and she looked back at me. She had meant what she said.

"I don't know if I can take it. I really don't."

"I know you can."

"I'll need you every moment."

"I'll be here."

Shirley came back with the drinks and set them on clean, dry paper napkins. She looked at me again that same way, to let me know she didn't like my remark at the bar earlier.

"Shirley is still mad," Vivian said, after she had gone.

"I'll leave her a good tip," I said.

Vivian raised her glass to me and smiled.

"You have the most beautiful smile," I said.

She smiled again.

"What are you doing this weekend?" I asked her.

"Homework and housework—what else?"

"Would you like to go to Baton Rouge one night, Friday or Saturday? I'll pay Dora."

"Friday sounds good," she said.

We had friends in Baton Rouge who knew about her pending divorce and knew about my aunt, and they let us stay awhile at their place while they went out to a bar. Sometimes we would join them at the bar later, other times we would just leave the key in an envelope with a thank you note. But we were both getting very tired of that.

We touched glasses and finished our drinks, then we left.

5

WE PLEDGED ALLEGIANCE to the flag. The flag
hung limp from a ten-foot bamboo pole in the corner of the
white picket fence that surrounded the church. Beyond the flag
I could see smoke rising from the chimneys in the quarter, and
beyond the houses and chimneys I could hear the tractors har-
vesting sugarcane in the fields. The sky was ashy gray, and the
air chilly enough for a sweater. I told the children to go inside
and begin their Bible verses.

After listening to one or two of the verses, I tuned out the rest
of them. I had heard them all many times. "In the beginning
God created the heavens and the earth." "The Lord is my
shepherd, I shall not want." "Let not your heart be troubled,
believe in God, believe also in me." "In my Father's house there

are many mansions." "Jesus wept." And on and on and on. I had listened to them almost six years, and I knew who would say what, just as I knew what each child would wear to school, and who would or would not know his or her lesson. I knew, too, which of them would do something for themselves and which of them never would, regardless of what I did. So each day I listened for a moment, then turned it off and planned the rest of the day.

My classroom was the church. My classes ranged from primer to sixth grade, my pupils from six years old to thirteen and fourteen. My desk was a table, used as a collection table by the church on Sundays, and also used for the service of the Holy Sacrament on the fourth Sunday of each month. My students' desks were the benches upon which their parents and grandparents sat during church meeting. The students either got down on their knees and used the benches as desks to write upon, or used the backs of their books upon their laps to write out their assignments. Ventilation into the church was by way of the four windows on either side, and from the front and back doors. Our heat came from a wood-burning stove in the center of the church. There was a blackboard on the back wall, and another on the right side wall. Behind my desk was the pulpit and the altar. There were three pictures on the wall behind the altar. One was a head-and-chest black-and-white photo of the minister in a dark suit, white shirt, and dark tie; the other two pictures were color prints of Jesus: *The Last Supper* and Christ knocking on a door.

This was my school. I was supposed to teach six months out of the year, but actually I taught only five and a half months, from late October to the middle of April, when the children were not needed in the field.

I assigned three of my sixth-grade students to teach the primer, first, and second grades, while I taught third and fourth. Only by assigning the upper-grade students to teach the lower grades was it possible to reach all the students every day. I devoted the last two hours in the afternoon to the fifth and sixth grades.

While the classes separated and moved to their respective areas, I asked my third and fourth graders to go to the back of the church to work on the blackboards. The third-grade class would do arithmetic on the board on the back wall, and the fourth graders would write sentences on the board on the right side wall. I moved from one blackboard to the other with my yard-long Westcott ruler.

I still felt bad about the problem I was having at home with my aunt. The night before, when I returned from Bayonne, I had gone to her room to say good night, but she pretended to be asleep, just to avoid speaking to me. And this morning, when I passed her on my way into the kitchen, she said over her shoulder, "Food there if you want it. Or you can go back where you had supper last night."

Breakfast was two fried eggs, grits, a piece of salt pork, and a biscuit. I ate at the kitchen table, looking across the yard. The crabgrass was wet from the night's heavy dew. I looked back over my shoulder a couple of times, but I couldn't hear my aunt anywhere in the house. After I finished eating, I washed my plate in the pan of soap water that she had left on the shelf in the kitchen window. I tried once more to speak to her before leaving for school, but to avoid me this time she pretended to make up her bed, which I knew she had already done two hours earlier. At a quarter to nine I left the house. She had gone out into the garden.

Every little thing was irritating me. I caught one of the students trying to figure out a simple multiplication problem on his fingers, and I slashed him hard across the butt with the Westcott ruler. He jerked around too fast and looked at me too angrily for my liking.

"Your hand," I said.

He held out his right hand, palm up. He still held the piece of chalk.

"Put that chalk down. I can't afford to break it."

He passed the piece of chalk to his left hand and held out the right hand to me again. I brought the Westcott down into his palm.

"You figure things out with your brains, not with your fingers," I told him.

"Yes, sir, Mr. Wiggins."

He turned back to the board and stared at the problem at least half a minute. It was cold in the back of the church, but standing two feet away from the boy, I could see that he was sweating. He raised his left hand up to his eyes to wipe away tears, then he stared at the problem again.

"Well, others have to work too, you know."

"Yes, sir, Mr. Wiggins."

The back of his neck shone with sweat. He wiped his eyes again. Then he wrote down an answer, large, awkward—and, of course, incorrect.

"You used enough chalk for five times that many problems," I told him. "Where do you think we're going to get more chalk when this runs out?"

He didn't answer.

"Well?" I said.

"I don't know, Mr. Wiggins," he said, staring at the board, not daring to look at me.

"I'd have to buy it," I said. "The school board doesn't give it away. They already gave me what they said was enough for the year. They're not giving us any more. Do you understand what I'm saying to you?"

"Yes, sir, Mr. Wiggins."

I jerked the piece of chalk out of his hand, corrected the problem, passed the piece of chalk on to another student, and walked away.

On the side board, one of the girls, wearing a gray dress and a black sweater, unpolished brown loafers and unmatching brown stockings, her head a forest of half a dozen two-inch plaits, had written a sentence of six words with a downward slant of nearly a foot.

"And what is that supposed to be?" I asked her.

She was so terrified by my voice that she jerked around to face me, then staggered back against the board.

"This-this-this," she stuttered, while gesturing toward the board with the piece of chalk. "That's a—that's a—a simple sentence, Mr. Wiggins."

"That's not a simple sentence," I told her. "That's a slanted sentence. A simple sentence is written on a straight line."

I reached for the piece of chalk, but in her fear of me she continued to hold on to it, and I had to pry it out of her hand. I drew three straight lines from one end of the board to the other.

"Those are straight lines," I said. "Do you notice the difference?"

She nodded her head while looking at me, not at the board.

I erased the three lines, as well as her slanted sentence.

"I want you to write me six simple sentences in straight lines," I said, and handed her the chalk. "You have until the end of the period to do it. The rest of the class, take your seats."

I left her standing there, trying to figure out where to begin. At the door, I turned back to look at the other classes. They all knew I was in a pretty rotten mood today, and they kept their heads down.

I went out into the yard, slapping the Westcott ruler against my leg hard enough to sting it. The cool air felt good on my face, and after standing in the yard awhile, I walked to the road. But there was nothing to see out there but a couple of automobiles— my gray Ford parked down the quarter in front of my aunt's house, and a car parked alongside the ditch farther up the quarter. Other than that, all there was to see were old gray weather-beaten houses, with smoke rising out of the chimneys and drifting across the corrugated tin roofs. Living and teaching on a plantation, you got to know the occupants of every house, and you knew who was home and who was not. I knew that the parents and the older brothers and sisters of the boy I had slashed on the butt with my ruler were out in the field, and that the old grandma, Aunt June, was at home cooking dinner for them to eat when they came in at noon. I could see the smoke rising from the kitchen chimney of the girl who stuttered, and I knew that she came from a family of twelve, and that she had a pregnant older sister, who was not allowed to come back to school but had to work in the field with all the others, and that she had an idiot brother and a tyrant father, and that the father beat the pregnant girl and any other member of the family, including the mother, but would never touch the idiot, whom he showered with love. I could look at the smoke rising from each chimney or I could look at the rusted tin roof of each house, and I could tell the lives that went on in each one of them.

I went all the way to the back of the yard, where I used the boys' toilet. Then I returned to my classes, but instead of coming in through the front door, as I had left, I entered through the back. Most of the students remembered the mood I was in and had their heads in their books. But one first grader had forgotten or didn't care, and he found time to play with a bug on the sleeve of his sweater. As I watched from the back door, he let the insect crawl an inch or two from his elbow toward his hand, then he picked it up and returned it up his arm to let it start all over again.

I looked at Irene Cole, my student teacher, to let her know not to warn him, and when I got in good striking distance of his nearly shaved head, I brought the Westcott down on his skull, loud enough to send a sound throughout the church. He jumped, hollered, grabbed at the already swelling knot. One or two of the students near him giggled nervously, but most remembered the mood I was in and seemed petrified. The boy, with his hand cupped over the welt, was crying now.

"Take that thing outside, get rid of it, and get back in here," I told him.

He left, crying quietly, the little red bug sitting on top of his extended arm.

"So it's bug-playing time, huh?" I asked the rest of the class. "You think that's why I'm here, so that you can play with bugs, huh?"

The boy came back and sat down. His hand was still cupped over his scalp, and he was still crying.

"The rest of you, back to your seats," I ordered.

They moved hurriedly, quietly, careful not to utter a word.

"Do you all know what is going on in Bayonne?" I asked them, back at my desk. "Do you all know what is going to happen to someone just like you who sat right where you're sitting only a few years ago? All right, I'll tell you. They're going to kill him in Bayonne. They're going to sit him in a chair, they're going to tie him down with straps, they're going to connect wires to his head, to his wrists, to his legs, and they're going to shoot electricity through the wires into his body until he's dead." I looked across the room at them. Some stared back at me, others down at the floor. But they were all listening. They knew Jefferson was supposed to die in the electric chair, but they hadn't known how this would happen. It had not been explained to them so vividly before, and maybe not at all. I could see how painful it was for most of them to hear this, but I did not stop. "Do you know what his nannan wants me to do before they kill him? The public defender called him a hog, and she wants me to make him a man. Within the next few weeks, maybe a month, whatever the law allows—make him a man. Exactly what I'm trying to do here with you now: to make you responsible young men and young ladies. But you, you prefer to play with bugs. You refuse to study your arithmetic, and you prefer writing slanted sentences instead of straight ones. Does that make any sense? Well, does it?"

No one answered. Most averted their eyes. I noticed that the girl whom I had criticized at the blackboard had lowered her head and was crying.

"Estelle, leave the class if you can't control yourself," I ordered her.

She shook her head, but she did not get up, or look at me.

"I'm-I'm-aw-aw right, Mr.-Mr. Wiggins. Bu-but-that's my cousin."

I knew that Jefferson was her cousin, but I didn't apologize for what I had said, nor did I show any sympathy for her crying.

"Either leave the class or stop crying," I told her again.

She wiped her eyes, but she did not look up.

"All right, the rest of the morning for studying," I told them. "And you'd better study, because I'm testing everybody this afternoon."

At two o'clock, I was at the blackboard with my fifth graders when we heard a knocking on the front door. I told the boy nearest the door to see who it was and ask him to come in. The boy went to the door and came back alone. He said that it was Mr. Farrell Jarreau, but Mr. Farrell didn't want to come in. I told the class to go on with their work, and I went to the door to see what he wanted. Farrell Jarreau was a small, light-brown man in his late fifties. He wore an old felt hat, a khaki suit, and worn work shoes. He was the yardman and all-round handyman for Henri Pichot. He fixed and sharpened tools for the big house, and he served as carpenter for the people in the quarter. He had made more benches, fixed more chairs and steps, than you could number.

He took off his hat as I approached him. He had known me all my life, and he knew my aunt and all my people before me, but since I had gone off to the university and returned as a teacher, he treated me with great respect. I went down the steps and into the yard.

"Professor."

"Mr. Farrell."

"He say it be all right if you come up by five this evening."

"Is this about Jefferson?" I asked.

"Didn't tell me. Just say it be all right if you come up there 'bout five."

"Thank you, Mr. Farrell."

"My pleasure, Professor," he said.

He put on his hat, and I noticed his eyes. He knew why Henri Pichot wanted me up there, all right. But Henri Pichot had not thought it was necessary to tell him. At his age, he was still only a messenger to run errands. To learn anything, he had to attain it by stealth or through an innate sense of things around him. He nodded to me, knowing that I knew he knew why Henri Pichot wanted to see me, and he walked away, head down.

6

INEZ WAS IN THE KITCHEN when I came up the back stairs, and she opened the door before I had a chance to knock. I could tell she had been crying. She had wiped the tears from her cheeks, but I could see the marks under her eyes.

"How are you, Inez?"

"I'm making out," she said, not looking at me.

"You know why he sent for me?"

"Mr. Sam coming here at five."

I glanced at my watch. It was ten minutes to five.

"Can I get you a cup of coffee?" Inez asked.

"No, thanks."

"You want to sit down?" She still did not look at me.

"I'm all right; I don't mind standing." I remembered how my aunt and Miss Emma had stood the night before.

"I don't know," Inez said, shaking her head. "I just don't know. Now Mr. Louis in there trying to get a bet."

"A bet on what?"

She looked at me directly for the first time. She had large eyes, brown and kind. I could see traces of tears that she had tried wiping away.

"You can't get him ready to die."

"Henri Pichot didn't take that bet, did he?"

"I left them in there talking. Mr. Louis say he got a whole case of whiskey he can bet on."

"Henri Pichot?"

"He ain't betting 'gainst you. He ain't betting on you neither."

"Smart man."

Inez looked at me sadly. I didn't know if it was because of my cynicism or the task I had facing me. She went back to the stove. With a dish towel she lifted the lid of one of the pots, and I could smell a strong scent of onion, bell pepper, and garlic. She raised the lids on two other pots, but still the odor of the onions, pepper, and garlic pervaded the room. Inez left the kitchen. I heard her knock on the library door, and I could hear her and Henri Pichot talking, then she came back into the kitchen.

"How's Lou?" she asked me.

"She's all right," I said. "I left her there with Miss Emma."

I thought about them sitting at the kitchen table at Miss Emma's house. I had gone home after school to drop off my satchel, and when I did not find my aunt at home, I figured she was keeping Miss Emma company. I found them at the kitchen table, shelling pecans into two big aluminum pans. I could see that neither my aunt nor Miss Emma had any intention of going up to Henri Pichot's house with me.

"But if you need me to hold your hand, I'd be glad to go," my aunt said.

"I don't want him doing nothing he don't want do." Miss
Emma repeated the old refrain I had heard about a hundred
times the day before.

I didn't answer them. I was angry already, and I knew things
would just have gotten worse if I said anything else. I went back
outside and got into my car and drove up to Pichot's.

Now I looked at my watch again. It was five-fifteen. No Sam
Guidry, and no one else, except Inez, had come into the kitchen
to say anything to me. Each time she returned from the library,
Inez seemed more agitated. I knew she was feeling sorry for me.

At five-thirty, we heard people entering the house off the
front gallery. Inez left the kitchen to meet them. She spoke to
Edna Guidry, then to Sam Guidry, and to one or two other
people. I could hear them talking as they came into the house.
Inez returned to the kitchen with two empty glasses to be
freshened. She added four glasses to her tray. She took that to
the library and came back.

"I'm sure it won't be too long now," she said. She knew how
I felt, and she was trying to encourage me.

It was quarter to six.

At six o'clock, Edna Guidry came back in the kitchen. A tall
woman in her early fifties, she had light-brown hair, a narrow
face, and gray eyes. She wore a shapeless black dress, gray
stockings, and low-heeled black shoes.

"Well, Grant—Grant, how are you?" she said, smiling and
coming up to me with her hand out. She stopped a good
distance back, and I had to lean forward to shake her hand,
which was long and bony, and cold from her glass. "Why,
Grant," she said, "I just do declare. I haven't seen you in God
knows how long. Been two, three years, I'm sure. Wouldn't you
say?"

"About that long, Miss Edna," I said.

"God, yes," she said. "Why, you're looking just as fine, like
you're living the good life. Doesn't he, Inez?"

"He's looking just fine, Miss Edna," Inez said from the stove.

"Well, tell me all about yourself," Edna Guidry said to me. "How've you been? No, no need to tell me; I can see you're doing just fine. But how is Lou? Why doesn't she come to see me? It's been how long? Oh, I bet you it's been six, no, eight months. And living so close. You tell Lou I say make you bring her to my house so we can sit down and talk. Lord, have mercy, do." She turned from me to Inez. "Mr. Henri says you may serve anytime now, Inez."

"Yes, ma'am," Inez said.

Edna turned back to me. "Grant, please tell Emma how sorry I am about Jefferson. I would do it myself, but I'm just too broken up over this matter. I ran into Madame Gropé just the other day; Lord, how sad she looks. Just dragging along. Poor old thing. I had to put my arms round her." Edna drank from her glass. "Tell Emma I'm sorry. I'm sorry for both families. I hear you would like the privilege of visiting Jefferson?"

"Yes, ma'am."

"Well, I'll leave all that up to you and the sheriff," she said. "He'll talk to you after supper." She turned to Inez. "Inez, is there anything that I may help you with?"

"No'm, I got everything under control," Inez told her.

"Well, in that case, I may as well help myself to another quick shot."

She poured about two ounces of bourbon into her glass and added ice cubes. After drinking half of it, she went back to the library.

Inez dished up the food. She had cooked a pot roast with potatoes and carrots, onions, bell pepper, and garlic. She also had rice and mustard greens, green peas and corn bread. She took the platters and bowls to the dining room.

"Can I fix you something?" she asked me when she came back to the kitchen.

"No, thank you," I told her.

I was hungry. I hadn't eaten anything but a sandwich since breakfast. But I would not eat at Henri Pichot's kitchen table.

I had come through that back door against my will, and it seemed that he and the sheriff were doing everything they could to humiliate me even more by making me wait on them. Well, I had to put up with that because of those in the quarter, but I damned sure would not add hurt to injury by eating at his kitchen table.

Inez went to the dining room and came back.

"They talking up there now 'bout him," she said. "Sheriff saying he don't like the idea at all. Saying nobody can make that thing a man. Saying might as well let him go like he is."

"I hope that's his final word," I said. "It sure would relieve my mind."

"Why don't you sit down," Inez said. "You'll feel better."

"I'd rather stand."

"You sure I can't fix you little something to eat?"

"No, thank you, Inez."

She went and came back.

"It won't be long now," she said. "They nearly through. Soon as I serve the coffee. You sure I can't get you a cup of coffee?"

"No, thanks. I appreciate it, though."

She poured coffee into half a dozen small white cups, and took the coffee, sugar, and cream to the dining room on a silver tray. She came back.

"He asked me if you was still here," she said. "I think he go'n let you see him, but he say he still against it. I'm sure it's Miss Edna making him do it. Well, all the time Miss Emma done spent with this family, that ain't asking too much."

At a quarter to seven, Inez cleared off the table in the dining room and brought the dishes into the kitchen. Then she took a bottle of brandy back with her. A half hour later, while she was putting away the dishes she had just finished washing, Sam Guidry, Henri Pichot, Louis Rougon, and another fat man came into the kitchen. I had been standing there nearly two and a half hours.

Sam Guidry was a tall man, well over six feet, and he was well tanned. His hair was dark brown, his sideburns and mustache showed some gray. His face was narrow, well-lined, and strong. His hands were large and hairy. He wore a brown suit and a tie. He usually wore a Stetson hat and cowboy boots. He had probably left the hat in the library or the dining room, but he had the boots on.

The four white men split into pairs. Sam Guidry and Henri Pichot stood on one side of the table, while Louis Rougon and the fat man stood over by the dish cabinet. They had brought their drinks with them.

Inez left the kitchen as soon as the white men came in. I tried to decide just how I should respond to them. Whether I should act like the teacher that I was, or like the nigger that I was supposed to be. I decided to wait and see how the conversation went. To show too much intelligence would have been an insult to them. To show a lack of intelligence would have been a greater insult to me. I decided to wait and see how the conversation would go.

"Been waiting long?" Sam Guidry asked me.

"About two and a half hours, sir," I said. I was supposed to say, "Not long," and I was supposed to grin; but I didn't do either.

The fat man glanced knowingly at Louis Rougon, but Louis Rougon was looking directly at me. I could see in their faces that they had talked all this over and Sam Guidry had already made up his mind what he was going to do.

"What can I do for you?" he asked.

Louis Rougon and the fat man waited for my answer. I knew it didn't matter what I said, since Guidry had made up his mind. Henri Pichot, standing next to Guidry, looked more tired than he had the day before. He seemed more sympathetic. Maybe he had been thinking about all the services Miss Emma had provided for his family over the years.

"It's about Jefferson, Sheriff Guidry," I said. I knew they had discussed it, still I had to go through the motions. "His nannan would like for me to visit him."

"What for?" Guidry asked.

They had discussed this too. I could tell from the way the fat man drank from his glass. I could see in his face that he was amused. So was Louis Rougon. I knew they were both betting against me.

"She's old," I said. "She doesn't feel that she has the strength to come up there all the time."

"She doesn't, huh?" Sam Guidry asked me. He emphasized "doesn't." I was supposed to have said "don't." I was being too smart.

"Yes, sir," I said. "She doesn't feel that she can."

I used the word "doesn't" again, but I did it intentionally this time. If he had said I was being too smart and he didn't want me to come to that jail, my mind would definitely have been relieved.

"What about that preacher in the quarter? Can't he visit him?"

"I asked her the same thing."

"You did, huh?"

"Yes, sir."

"And what did she say?"

"She said there'll be time for the preacher."

"She did, huh?"

"Yes, sir."

"So she feels that he has that much time, time for teacher and preacher?"

The fat man grunted. Louis Rougon's eyes showed that he was amused. Henri Pichot, next to Sam Guidry, looked uncomfortable.

"What you plan on doing when you come up there—if I let you come up there?" Guidry asked me.

"I have no idea, sir," I told him.

"You're not trying to play with me, now, are you?" Guidry asked.

"No, sir, I'm not. But I have no idea what I'll talk to him about."

"I hear from people around here you want to make him a man. A man for what, at this time?"

"She asked me to go to him, sir. Her idea. Not mine."

"That was not the question," Guidry said. "Make him a man for what?"

"To die with some dignity, I suppose. I suppose that's what she wants."

"You think that's a good idea?"

"That's what she wants, sir."

"What do you think?"

"I would rather not have anything to do with it, sir. But that's what she wants."

"So you think he ought to go just like he is?"

"I don't know how he is, sir. Believe me, Mr. Guidry, if it was left up to me, I wouldn't have anything to do with it at all," I said.

"You and I are in accord there," he said. "But my wife thinks different. Now, which one you think is right, me or her?"

The fat man snorted. He thought Guidry had me.

"I make it a habit never to get into family business, Mr. Guidry."

The fat man didn't like that quick maneuver. I could see it in his face.

"You're smart," Guidry said. "Maybe you're just a little too smart for your own good."

I was quiet. I knew when to be quiet.

"I don't like it," Guidry said. "And I want you to know I don't like it. Because I think the only thing you can do is just aggravate him, trying to put something in his head against his will. And I'd rather see a contented hog go to that chair than an aggravated hog. It would be better for everybody concerned.

There ain't a thing you can put in that skull that ain't there already."

I remained quiet.

"You can come up there," Sam Guidry said. "But the first sign of aggravation, I'm calling it off. You understand?"

"Yes, sir."

"You have any questions?" he asked me.

"Yes, sir. When can I see him?"

"You can come anytime you like. Not before ten in the morning, not after four in the evening. Any other questions?"

"Any idea how much time he has left?"

"That's entirely up to the governor, not me," Guidry said. "But I wouldn't plan on a diploma. Okay?"

The fat man and Louis Rougon seemed impressed by the sheriff's questions and answers to me. Louis Rougon, who had light-blue eyes, stared at me to make me look back at him, but I refused to pay him that courtesy. The fat man, drinking, rattled the ice cubes in his glass. Henri Pichot appeared to wish all this was over with.

"Anything else?" Guidry asked me.

"When can I start coming up there?"

"Not for a couple of weeks," Guidry said. "Let him get used to it. Report to Chief Deputy Clark if I'm not around. Don't bring anything up there you don't want taken away from you— knife, razor blade, anything made of glass. Not that I expect him to do anything—but you can never be sure. Anything else?"

"No, sir, nothing else."

Guidry nodded. "Good luck. But I think it's all just a waste of time."

"Thank you, sir."

I waited until they had left the kitchen, then I went out to my car and drove away.

7

TWO THINGS HAPPENED at the school during the weeks before I visited Jefferson in jail. The superintendent of schools made his annual visit, and we got our first load of wood for winter.

We heard on Monday by Farrell Jarreau, who had gotten the news from Henri Pichot, that the superintendent was going to visit us sometime during the week, but we didn't know what day or time. I told my students to take baths each morning and wear their best clothes to school. After the Pledge of Allegiance in the yard and the recitation of Bible verses inside the church, I would send a student back outside to look out for the superintendent. If the student saw a car, any car, turn off the highway down into the quarter, he or she was supposed to run inside and tell me.

The superintendent didn't show up until Thursday. By then we had had many false alarms. The minister of the church, who didn't live in the quarter, had made a couple of visits to church members. A doctor had come once, a midwife had visited a young woman twice, an insurance man had shown up, a bill collector from a furniture store had appeared, Henri Pichot had driven through the quarter at least once each day, and family and friends of people in the quarter had also visited. On Thursday, just before two o'clock, the boy I had watching for cars ran into the church.

"Another one, Mr. Wiggins, another one."

"All right," I said to the class. "Keep those books opened and look sharp."

I passed my fingers over my shirt collar and checked the knot in my necktie. I felt my jacket to be sure both flaps were outside the pockets. I had three suits—navy blue, gray, and brown. I had on the blue one today. In the yard, I passed the tips of my shoes over the backs of my pant legs. Now I was ready to receive our guest.

This time it was the superintendent. He stopped his car before the door of the church. A thick cloud of gray dust flew over the top of the car and down into the quarter. The superintendent was a short, fat man with a large red face and a double chin, and he needed all his energy to get out of the car.

"Dr. Joseph," I said.

"Hummmm. Stifling," he said.

I thought it was a little cool myself, but I figured that anyone as heavy as he was must have felt stifled all the time. He wheezed his way across the shallow ditch that separated the road from the churchyard. He looked up at me, but I could tell he didn't remember my name, though he had visited the school once each year since I had been teaching there.

"Grant Wiggins," I said.

"How are you, Higgins?"

"Wiggins, sir," I said. "I'm fine."

"Well, I'm not," he said. "All this running around. More schools to attend."

Dr. Joseph visited the colored schools once a year, the white schools probably twice—once each semester. There were a dozen schools in the parish to visit, if that many.

"We're honored that you took this time for us, sir."

He grunted and looked around the yard. There was a good breeze coming in from the direction of the cane fields, and it wavered the flag on the pole in the yard.

"Place looks about the same," Dr. Joseph said.

"Things change very slowly around here, Dr. Joseph," I said.

"Hummmm," he said.

I motioned for him to precede me into the church. He needed all his strength to go up the three wooden steps, and as he entered the doorway, I heard Irene Cole, the sixth-grade student in charge, call out to the class: "Rise. Shoulders back."

I followed Dr. Joseph down the aisle, and on either side of us, the students from primer through sixth grade stood as still and as straight as soldiers for inspection.

I nodded toward my desk for Dr. Joseph to take my chair. He grunted, which meant thanks, and pulled the chair farther from the desk before he sat down. He needed the extra distance for comfort.

Irene was watching me all the time, and when I nodded to her, she called out to the classes: "Seats." And the whole school sat as one. We had been rehearsing this, morning and afternoon, for the past three days.

"Students, I'm sure you all know Dr. Joseph Morgan," I told them. "Dr. Joseph is our superintendent of schools here in St. Raphael Parish. He has taken time out of a very busy schedule to visit us for a few minutes. Please respond loudly: 'Thank you, Dr. Joseph.' " Which they did, loudly.

Dr. Joseph acknowledged their greeting: "Hummmm."

"Dr. Joseph, we're at your service," I said, and sat down on one of the benches against the wall.

Dr. Joseph leaned back in the chair, and still his large stomach nearly touched the edge of the table. He looked over the classes from one side of the aisle to the other, as though he was trying to catch someone doing something improper.

"Primer, on your feet," he said.

They stood up, seven or eight of them. Dr. Joseph looked them over for a moment, then he told the little girl at the end to come forward. She took a deep breath and looked at the girl standing beside her before coming up to the desk. She was afraid, but she came up quickly and stood before the table with her little arms tight to her sides. She would not look up.

"Nothing to be afraid of, child," Dr. Joseph said to her. "What is your name?"

"Gloria Hebert," she said.

"I can't hear you if you keep your head down," Dr. Joseph told her.

She looked up, timidly. "Gloria Hebert."

"That's a pretty name," Dr. Joseph said. "Hold out your hands."

She must have thought she had said or done something wrong, because as she held her hands out across the table, palms up, I could see them trembling.

"Turn them over," Dr. Joseph told her.

She did.

"Uh-huh," he said. "Relax."

She did not know what he wanted her to do.

"Lower your arms, child," Dr. Joseph said.

She brought her arms back to her sides and lowered her eyes as well.

"Did you say your Bible verse this morning, Gloria?"

"Yes, sir, Dr. Joseph."

"Well, what did you say?" he asked her.

"I said, 'Lord is my shepherd, I shall not want,' Dr. Joseph."

"Hummm," Dr. Joseph said. "Seems I've heard that one

before. But you're a bright little girl. You tell your folks Dr. Joseph said they ought to be proud of you. Go back to your seat."

"Thank you, Dr. Joseph," she said, bowing and turning away quickly. She smiled as she faced forward again. But no one else was smiling.

"Primers, take your seats," Dr. Joseph said. "First graders, on your feet."

And he called on the one boy in class who I wished had stayed home today. He was without doubt the worst child in the school. He came from a large family—thirteen, fourteen, fifteen: I don't know how many—and he had to fight for every crumb of food he got. At school he did the same. He fought if he played marbles, he fought if he played ball, he fought if he played hide-and-go-seek, he fought if he played hide-the-switch. In class he fought with those who sat in front of him, beside him, behind him. I had punished him as much during the last month as I had all the other children put together.

Dr. Joseph asked his name, and he ran together three words even I couldn't understand. His name was Louis Washington, Jr., but what he said didn't sound anything like that.

"Your hands," Dr. Joseph told him.

The hands had been cleaned an hour before, I was sure, because I had checked each pair when the students came in from dinner. But now the palms of those same hands were as black and grimy as if he had been pitching coal all day.

"Did you pledge allegiance to the flag this morning?" Dr. Joseph asked him.

"Yazir," he said. Not "Yes, sir," as I had told him a hundred times to say. "Yazir."

"Well?" Dr. Joseph said.

"Want me go stand outside and s'lute flag?" the boy asked.

"You don't have to go outside," Dr. Joseph said. "You can show me in here."

The boy raised his hand to his chest.

"Plege legen toda flag. Ninety state. 'Merica. Er—er—yeah, which it stand. Visibly. Amen."

Dr. Joseph grunted. Several students giggled. Dr. Joseph seemed quite satisfied. I would have to do a lot more work.

For the next half hour it continued. Dr. Joseph would call on someone who looked half bright, then he would call on someone whom he felt was just the opposite. In the upper grades— fourth, fifth, and sixth—he asked grammatical, mathematical, and geographical questions. And besides looking at hands, now he began inspecting teeth. Open wide, say "Ahhh"—and he would have the poor children spreading out their lips as far as they could while he peered into their mouths. At the university I had read about slave masters who had done the same when buying new slaves, and I had read of cattlemen doing it when purchasing horses and cattle. At least Dr. Joseph had graduated to the level where he let the children spread out their own lips, rather than using some kind of crude metal instrument. I appreciated his humanitarianism.

Finally, when he felt that he had inspected enough mouths and hands, he gave the school a ten-minute lecture on nutrition. Beans were good, he said. Not only just good, but very, very good. Beans, beans, beans—he must have said beans a hundred times. Then he said fish and greens were good. And exercise was good. In other words, hard work was good for the young body. Picking cotton, gathering potatoes, pulling onions, working in the garden—all of that was good exercise for a growing boy or girl.

"Higgins, I must compliment you. You have an excellent crop of students, an excellent crop, Higgins. You ought to be proud."

He had said the same thing the year before, and he had called me Higgins then too. And the year before that he had said the same thing, but he had called me Washington then. At least he was getting closer to my real name.

"Rise," Irene called to the class.

They came to their feet, their heads up, their arms clasped to their sides. But instead of feeling pride, I hated myself for drilling them as I had done.

Dr. Joseph and I went down the aisle. Outside, he looked up at the flag waving on its bamboo pole in the corner of the fence. I thought for a moment the superintendent was about to salute it, but he was either too tired or too lazy to raise his hand.

"Doing a good job, Higgins," he said.

"I do the best I can with what I have to work with, Dr. Joseph," I said. "I don't have all the books I need. In some classes I have two children studying out of one book. And even with that, some of the pages in the book are missing. I need more paper to write on, I need more chalk for the blackboards, I need more pencils, I even need a better heater."

"We're all in the same shape, Higgins," he said.

I didn't answer him.

"I said we're all in the same shape, Higgins, the white schools just as much as the colored schools. We take what the state gives us, and we make the best of it."

"Many of the books I have to use are hand-me-downs from the white schools, Dr. Joseph," I said. "And they have missing pages. How can I—"

"Are you questioning me, Higgins?"

"No, sir, Dr. Joseph. I was just—"

"Thank you, Higgins."

He started to get back into his car. It was harder to do than getting out, because he was upset with me now.

"More drill on the flag, Higgins," he said, through the rolled-down window. "More emphasis on hygiene."

"Some of these children have never seen a toothbrush before coming to school, Dr. Joseph."

"Well, isn't that your job, Higgins?"

"Yes, sir, I suppose so. But then I would have to buy them."

"Can't they work?" he asked me. "Look at all the pecan trees." He waved his hand toward the yards. "I wager you can count fifty trees right here in the quarter. Back in the field, back in the pasture, you can count another hundred, two hundred trees. Get them off their lazy butts, they can make enough for a dozen toothbrushes in one evening."

"That money usually goes to helping the family, Dr. Joseph."

"Then you tell the family about health," he said, looking out of the rolled-down window to let me know that his visit was over. "I have another school to visit. All this running around 'nough to give a man a heart attack."

He drove away. I stood there until he had turned his car around and started back up the quarter. I waved at him, but he did not wave back.

8

THE WEEK AFTER the superintendent paid his visit to the school we got our first load of wood for winter. Two old men brought the wagonload about eleven o'clock that morning. We did not have a gate wide enough for the wagon to come through, so the men came into the yard next door to the church. One got down off the wagon to open the gate, and the other drove the wagon into the yard. I could not see them, but I could hear them. They were joking about the mules, the wood, and the weather. One of them said, "Don't let Bird hang us up in that ditch, now. I don't feel like unloading all this wood 'way out here and got to put it on that wagon again."

"She go'n pull," the other one said. "Hi, there, Bird, get them shoulders in there."

I heard the wagon cross the ditch and enter the yard.

"All right," I said to the class. "The first one who looks outside will spend an hour in the corner. They can do pretty well without you."

The wagon came farther into the yard on the other side of the fence, passing the church windows. I could see the two mules—one big and red, the other small and dark brown with long, droopy ears—pulling hard into the chains. Then I saw the long poles of wood stacked high upon the wagon, with one of the old men riding atop the wood while the other, the one who had opened the gate, walked alongside the wagon. They were still joking and laughing.

"Louis Washington junior, get back into that corner and face the wall."

"But, Mr. Wiggins, now you was looking out that window too, now. I seen you."

"Just out of the corner of my eye," I said.

"Now, I was just looking out the corner of my eye too, Mr. Wiggins."

"In that case I won't punish you for looking out the window," I said. "But I'm going to punish you for using bad grammar. You were supposed to say, 'You *were* looking out the window, Mr. Wiggins,' not 'You *was* looking out the window, Mr. Wiggins.' Get back in that corner and face the wall and stay there. One more word out of you, and you'll spend the rest of the day standing on one leg."

Sitting at my desk, I could hear the old men unloading the wood, throwing the long poles across the fence and into the churchyard. They were still kidding each other.

"Show me them grits, show me them grits you had this morning."

"I got my end up."

"Well, I got the heavy end."

"You sure got that right." They both laughed. And I heard the wood come across the fence.

This went on for half an hour, then one of the men knocked on the back door. I went to see what he wanted.

"Professor," he said, and smiled.

Henry Lewis was a short black man with hardly any teeth. His hands were the color and texture of the legs of a snapping turtle. He wore an old straw hat, a green and brown plaid shirt, khaki pants, and rubber boots. He had grandchildren in the school.

"Some wood there," he said. "I'm leaving the saw and couple them axes. Your boys can chop it up."

"Appreciate it, Mr. Lewis," I said.

"Glad to be of service."

I spoke to Amos Thomas, who sat on the wagon. The thin, brown-skinned man nodded at me.

"That ought to hold you awhile," Mr. Lewis said to me. "Just call 'fore it run out. Somebody get you another load."

"Thanks," I said.

"Bye, Professor."

"Goodbye, Mr. Lewis. Mr. Thomas."

I returned to my desk.

"All right," I said to the class. "It's a quarter to twelve now. I'm letting you out early because you'll have to chop wood this afternoon. I want you all back up here by twelve-thirty."

That afternoon, I stood by the fence while the fifth- and sixth-grade boys sawed and chopped the wood. The smaller boys and all the girls were inside. They wanted to know why they had to study while the older boys were outside having fun. I told them that they could have fun the next day picking up chips and stacking wood while the older boys were inside studying. They did not see this as quite the same, but when I didn't give them any other choice, they grudgingly relented. I gave them assignments and left Irene Cole in charge.

Standing by the fence, I watched the five older boys saw and chop the wood. Two would saw while another would straddle the wood pole to keep it steady. The other two boys split logs and chopped up small branches with the axes. They laughed and kidded each other while they worked.

And I thought to myself, What am I doing? Am I reaching them at all? They are acting exactly as the old men did earlier. They are fifty years younger, maybe more, but doing the same thing those old men did who never attended school a day in their lives. Is it just a vicious circle? Am I doing anything?

After a while, they exchanged the saw and axes. The ones who had been sawing were now splitting logs, the other two were pulling on the handles of the saw. The smallest boy still held the log as steady as he could with his hands and knees.

With my back to the fence as I watched them, I remembered when it was I who had swung that ax and pulled my end of the saw. And I remembered the others, too—Bill, Jerry, Claudee, Smitty, Snowball—all the others. They had chopped wood here too; then they were gone. Gone to the fields, to the small towns, to the cities—where they died. There was always news coming back to the quarter about someone who had been killed or sent to prison for killing someone else: Snowball, stabbed to death at a nightclub in Port Allen; Claudee, killed by a woman in New Orleans; Smitty, sent to the state penitentiary at Angola for manslaughter. And there were others who did not go anywhere but simply died slower.

The big mulatto from Poulaya had predicted it, hadn't he? It was he, Matthew Antoine, as teacher then, who stood by the fence while we chopped the wood. He had told us then that most of us would die violently, and those who did not would be brought down to the level of beasts. Told us that there was no other choice but to run and run. That he was living testimony of someone who should have run. That in him—he did not say all this, but we felt it—there was nothing but hatred for himself as well as contempt for us. He hated himself for the mixture of his blood and the cowardice of his being, and he hated us for daily reminding him of it. No, he did not tell us this, but daily he showed us this. As clearly as anything, he showed his hatred for himself, and for us. He could teach any of us only one thing, and that one thing was flight. Because there was no freedom here. He said it, and he didn't say it. But we felt it. When we told our people how we felt, they told us to go back and learn all we could. There were those who did go back to learn. Others who only went back. And having no place to run, they went into the fields; others went into the small towns and cities, seeking work, and did even worse.

But she told me that I would not be one of the others, that I would learn as much as he could teach me, then I would go away to learn from someone else. But that I would learn as much as he could teach me. And when he saw that I wanted to learn, he hated me even more than he did the others, because I challenged him when the others did not. The others believed what he said. They went out into the fields, went into the small towns and into the cities and died. So you think you can? he said. So you think you can? No, he did not say it with words, only with his eyes. You will be the loser, my friend. Maybe he did not say "friend"; he probably didn't say "friend"; "fool," more likely. Anyway, you will be the loser, he said. Yes, I will teach you. You want to learn, I will help you learn. Maybe in that way I will be free, knowing that someone else has taken the burden. Good, good, you want to learn? Good, good, here is the burden.

Even after I had gone away for further education, on returning to the plantation to visit my aunt I could still see the hatred in him. And after he had retired from teaching because of ill health and I would visit him at his home in Poulaya, I would still feel his hatred for himself, for me, for the world. Once, as I sat at the fireplace with him, he said to me, "Nothing pleases me more than when I hear of something wrong. Hitler had his reasons, and even the Ku Klux Klans of the South for what they do. You don't believe me, do you?" he asked me. "No, sir, I don't," I said. "You will one day," he said. "I told you what you should have done, but no, you want to stay. Well, you will believe me one day. When you see that those five and a half months you spend in that church each year are just a waste of your time, you will. You will. You'll see that it'll take more than five and a half months to wipe away—peel—scrape away the blanket of ignorance that has been plastered and replastered over those brains in the past three hundred years. You'll see." Then he would be quiet for a long time, while we both stared into the fire.

"I'm cold," he said one day while we sat there looking into the fire. I got up to put on another piece of wood. "That's no good," he said. "I'll still be cold. I'll always be cold." He looked at me. "You'll see, you'll see." "I must," I said. "No, you don't must," he said. "You want to. But you don't must." "You did," I said. "Yes, I did," he said. "But I told you not to. I told you to go. God has looked after them these past three hundred years without your help. He won't—" "God?" I said. Because I had never heard him say God before. Because when we had said our Bible verses for him, he seemed to have hated the very words we spoke. "Sir, did I hear you say—?" "I'm cold"—he cut me off. "I stay cold. You better go. Come back some other time if you like. I made a mistake." I came back a month later. I remember that it was cold that day too.

Now, about that mulatto teacher and me. There was no love there for each other. There was not even respect. We were enemies if anything at all. He hated me, and I knew it, and he knew I knew it. I didn't like him, but I needed him, needed him to tell me something that none of the others could or would.

I brought some wine that day. He sent me into the kitchen to get two glasses. "This will warm you up," I said. "Nothing can warm me up," he said. He sat in the rocker, gazing down at the fire, with the blanket tight around him. He was a big-boned man, but very skinny now. "To flight," he said, raising his glass. "But you didn't go," I said. "I'm Creole," he said. "Can't you tell?" "Was that it?" I asked him. "That was it," he said. "I'm Creole. Do you know what a Creole is? A lying cowardly bastard. Did you know that?" "No, I didn't know that," I said. "I was afraid," he said, looking into the fire. "I was afraid to run away. What am I? Look at me. Where else could I have felt superior to so many but here?" "Is that important?" I asked him. "It is," he said. "For everyone. Especially for the whites and the near whites. It is important." "Do you feel superior to me?" I asked him. "Of course," he said. "Don't be a damned fool. I *am* superior to you. I am superior to any man blacker than me." "Is that why you hate me?" I asked him. "Exactly," he said. "Because that superior sonofabitch out there said I am you." "Do you think he is superior to you?" I asked him. "Of course," he said. "Don't you?" "No," I said. "Just stay here long enough," he said. "He'll make you the nigger you were born to be." "My only choice is to run, then?" I asked him. "That was your choice. But you won't. You want to prove I'm wrong. Well, you'll visit my grave one day and tell me how right I was." "Tell me more," I said. "What's wrong with that university?" he asked. "Don't they tell you?" "They tell me how to succeed in the South as a colored man. They tell me about reading, writing, and arithmetic. I need to know about life." "I can't tell you anything about life," he said. "What do I know about life? I stayed here. You have to go away to know about life. There's no life here. There's nothing but ignorance here. You want to know about life? Well, it's too late. Forget it. Just go on and be the nigger you were born to be, but forget about life. You make me tired, and I'm cold. The wine doesn't help."

I visited him again only a month or two before he died, in the winter of '42. He was forty-three years old. That was my first year as a teacher. I had been teaching two or three weeks when I visited him. We had just gotten our first load of wood for winter. Maybe that's why I had gone to see him. I could always remember that first load of wood for winter, how we older boys had chopped the wood into smaller pieces while he stood back against the fence, overseeing us. He looked terribly frail that day. I hadn't seen him in several months. He was being looked after by a relative, who did not care too much for anyone visiting him, and especially darker people. She admitted me into the room and left us. He sat at the fireplace. Summer or winter, he always sat at the fireplace when he was inside. We shook hands. His hand was large, cold, and bony. He was coughing a lot. "We got our first load of wood last week," I told him. "Nothing changes," he said. "I guess I'm a genuine teacher now," I said. He nodded, and coughed. He didn't seem to want to talk. Still, I sat there, both of us gazing into the fire. "Any advice?" I asked him. "It doesn't matter anymore," he said. "Just do the best you can. But it won't matter."

9

AT ONE-THIRTY I left school to take Miss Emma into Bayonne. She came out on the porch with Tante Lou, and she had a basket hung over one arm and a handbag in the other hand. Tante Lou closed the door to keep the heat in the room, and she and Miss Emma came down the walk and out to the car. Miss Emma wore her brown overcoat with the rabbit fur around the collar and cuffs. Tante Lou wore only a sweater, so I figured she was not going to Bayonne with us. She opened the door for Miss Emma to get into the back seat, and after shutting it, she leaned against the door to continue their conversation. I am sure they had been talking all day, but still they had things to talk about.

"This way is best," she said.

Miss Emma may have nodded, but I am not sure. I refused to look into the mirror at them.

"Anything else he need, let me know," my aunt went on. "They got plenty old socks and shirts round the place."

"I think we're supposed to be there around two," I said, without looking back at them.

I could feel both sets of eyes on the back of my neck.

"Tell him I'm praying," my aunt said. "Y'all better go. I'll see you when you get back."

She was talking to Miss Emma, not to me. She knew how I felt about the whole thing. I drove farther down the quarter and turned around. My aunt was standing where we had left her; she was waving now. You might have thought we were going to China instead of the thirteen miles to Bayonne.

Driving along the St. Charles River, I could feel Miss Emma not looking at me, not looking at anything—just thinking. Maybe once or twice she glanced in my direction, but most of the time she was lost in thought. Like my aunt, she knew how much I hated all this.

So the thirteen miles to Bayonne were driven in silence. I didn't say anything to her, she didn't say anything to me. I never looked at her in the rearview mirror. I never turned my head to the river on my right or to the houses on the side of the road to my left. As far up the highway as you could see were stalks of sugarcane that had fallen off the trailers on their way to the mill. The people were gathering pecans on either side of the road, but I looked at them only from a distance. If they waved, I did not wave back. I didn't want Miss Emma to think for a moment that my mood had changed.

The courthouse, like most of the public buildings in town, was made of red brick. Built around the turn of the century, it looked like a small castle you might see in the countryside somewhere in Europe. The parking lot that surrounded the courthouse was covered with crushed seashells. A statue of a Confederate soldier stood to the right of the walk that led up to the courthouse door. Above the head of the statue, national, state, and Confederate flags flew on long metal poles. The big clock on the tower struck two as I parked opposite the statue and the flags. It took Miss Emma a while to get out of the car, so by the time we came into the sheriff's office, the clock on the wall there said five after two.

Two deputies, dressed in gray chinos, and a colored prisoner, in green coveralls with the letter "p" on the back, were in the office. The deputy behind the desk was giving the prisoner instructions. The younger deputy, who stood beside the desk, looked at us.

"I come to see Jefferson," Miss Emma said.

The young deputy nodded to the deputy who was giving orders to the prisoner. It had something to do with the floor of the outside toilet. This toilet was for colored people who came to the courthouse, and it was down in the basement. You entered it from the courthouse parking lot. I had gone in there once or twice myself, but it was always filthy, and like everyone I knew, I tried to avoid going down there. But that was the only place to go. The toilets inside were for whites only.

"I want that done 'fore I leave from here," the deputy told the prisoner. "I mean that, you hear?"

The prisoner, fifteen or sixteen years old, bowed his head and left.

"I come to see my boy, Jefferson," Miss Emma told the deputy behind the desk.

"What you got there?" he asked her.

"Just some food, some clean clothes for him," Miss Emma said.

"Paul," the older man said.

The deputy who stood beside the desk came toward us.

"How's he been?" Miss Emma asked the deputy in charge.

"Quiet," the deputy said.

"Yes, sir," Miss Emma said.

The deputy grinned.

"Jefferson's been quiet," Paul, the young deputy, told Miss Emma.

"Thank you, sir," Miss Emma said to him.

The deputy went through the basket of food. Fried chicken, bread, baked sweet potatoes, tea cakes. Then he went through the handbag of clothes. There was a pair of old blue jeans, an old overwashed brown shirt, a pair of long johns, and two pairs of my socks, which my aunt had given Miss Emma for Jefferson.

"Empty your pockets," he said to me.

I had nothing but a wallet, a handkerchief, and some loose change. I had left my keys in the car. I laid the things on the desk.

"Is that it?" the deputy asked me.

He had brown hair and gray-blue eyes, and he appeared to be a couple of years younger than I was. He looked pretty decent. The one behind the desk didn't look decent at all. His eyes were the color of cement. He had a big neck and a fleshy face. He was much older and much heavier than Paul.

Paul patted me down to see if I had taken everything out of my pockets. Then he told me that I could put my things back.

"Sheriff explained everything to y'all?" the chief deputy asked us.

"Sir?" Miss Emma said.

The chief deputy could see that I didn't like him, and I could tell he didn't like me. But he knew who was in charge and that I would have to take anything he dished out.

"No knives, no forks, no plates. Pans," he said to Miss Emma. That was after he had looked at me a long time to let me know what he thought of me. "No hatpins, no pocket knives, no razor blades, no ice picks," he said, looking at me again.

"Jefferson won't never do nothing like that," Miss Emma said.

"You can't ever tell," the deputy said. "Take them on up, Paul."

"Follow me," the young deputy said.

We followed him down a long, dark corridor, passing offices with open doors, and bathrooms for white ladies and white men. At the end of the corridor we had to go up a set of stairs. The stairs were made of steel. There were six steps, then a landing, a sharp turn, and another six steps. Then we went through a heavy steel door to the area where the prisoners were quartered. The white prisoners were also on this floor, but in a separate section. I counted eight cells for black prisoners, with two bunks to each cell. Half of the cells were empty, the others had one or two prisoners. They reached their hands out between the bars and asked for cigarettes or money. Miss Emma stopped to talk to them. She told them she didn't have any money, but she had brought some food for Jefferson, and if there was anything left she would give it to them. They asked me for money, and I gave them the change I had.

There was an empty cell between Jefferson and the rest of the prisoners. He was at the end of the cellblock and was lying on his bunk when we came up. The deputy unlocked the door for us, and Miss Emma and I went in. The deputy told us that he would have to lock us in, and that he would return within an hour. Miss Emma thanked him, and he locked the door and left. Jefferson still lay on his bunk, staring up at the ceiling. He didn't look at us once.

"How you feel, Jefferson?" Miss Emma asked him.

He didn't answer, and kept his eyes on the ceiling. The cell was roughly six by ten, with a metal bunk covered by a thin mattress and a woolen army blanket; a toilet without seat or toilet paper; a washbowl, brownish from residue and grime; a small metal shelf upon which was a pan, a tin cup, and a tablespoon. A single light bulb hung over the center of the cell, and at the end opposite the door was a barred window, which looked out onto a sycamore tree behind the courthouse. I could see the sunlight on the upper leaves. But the window was too high to catch sight of any other buildings or the ground.

"I come to see you and brung you something," Miss Emma said.

We were standing, because there was no place to sit.

"You been all right?" she asked him.

He lay there looking up at the ceiling. His hair had grown out since the trial, but I am sure he had not combed it once. I told myself that I would bring him a comb next time I came.

"I brought Professor Wiggins," Miss Emma said. "I brought you some fried chicken, some good old yams, and I brought you some tea cakes too."

He looked up at the ceiling.

"Ain't you go'n ask me to sit down, Jefferson?"

He looked up at the ceiling, but he wasn't seeing the ceiling.

Miss Emma put the handbag of clothes and the basket of food on the floor and sat down on the bunk beside him. I should say that she sat as much of herself on the bunk as she could. About half, I would say. She passed her hand over his forehead and over his hair.

"Ain't you go'n speak to me, Jefferson?" she asked.

He remained quiet. She stroked his hair again.

"You want to just talk to me? You want Professor Wiggins to leave?"

He didn't answer her.

"You want me to go, and you just talk to Professor Wiggins?"

He still didn't answer.

She looked up at me. She was ready to cry. And I wished I were somewhere else.

"Hand me that basket, Grant," she said.

I passed her the basket, and she took out a piece of chicken wrapped in brown paper. She unwrapped the drumstick and held it before Jefferson.

"Look what I brought you," she said. "I knowed how much you like my fried chicken. Brought you some yams and some tea cakes, too. Ain't you go'n try some of it?"

"It don't matter," I heard him say. He was looking up at the ceiling.

"What don't matter?"

He didn't answer.

"What don't matter, Jefferson?"

"Nothing don't matter," he said, looking up at the ceiling but not seeing the ceiling.

"It matter to me, Jefferson," she said. "You matter to me."

He looked up at the ceiling, not seeing it.

"Jefferson?"

"Chicken, dirt, it don't matter," he said.

"Yeah, it do, Jefferson. Yeah, it do. Dirt?"

"All the same," he said. "It don't matter."

"My chicken?" she said. "I'm tasting it right now." She took a small bite. "You always liked my chicken. Every Sunday."

He was quiet.

"You like a yam?" she asked him.

He didn't answer her.

"You want a tea cake? You don't have to eat no chicken if you don't want. You don't have to eat no old yam neither. But I know how much you like my tea cakes. I didn't bring no clabber, but— Jefferson?"

"When they go'n do it? Tomorrow?"

"Do what, Jefferson?"

He was quiet, looking up at the ceiling but not seeing it.

"What, Jefferson?"

He turned toward her. His body didn't turn, just his head turned a little. His eyes did most of the turning. He looked at her as though he did not know who she was, or what she was doing there. Then he looked at me. You know what I'm talking about, don't you? his eyes said. They were big brown eyes, the whites too reddish. You know, don't you? his eyes said again. I looked back at him. My eyes would not dare answer him. But his eyes knew that my eyes knew.

"You with 'em?" he asked me.

"With who?" I said.

His eyes mocked me. They were big brown eyes, and the whites were too reddish, and he had been thinking too much the past few weeks, and the eyes mocked me.

"You the one?" he asked me.

"The one for what?" I said.

His big brown eyes with reddish whites mocked me.

"Go'n jeck that switch?" he said, looking at me.

"What switch?" Miss Emma said.

He was looking at me, not at her. His eyes told me that I knew what switch he was talking about.

"That's Professor Wiggins, your teacher—what switch?" she asked.

He turned his head and began staring up at the ceiling again.

The deputy came back and stood just outside the cell. Miss Emma still sat on the bunk. But now Jefferson had turned his back to her and was facing the gray concrete wall. Miss Emma passed her hand over his hair again, then she pushed herself up from the bunk.

"I'm leaving, Jefferson," she said. "I'll come back soon."

The deputy opened the cell door to let us out.

"Can I leave the food?" Miss Emma asked him.

"Sure," the deputy said.

"If he don't eat it all, can you give it to the rest of them children?"

"Sure," the deputy said.

He locked the cell door.

"I'm leaving, Jefferson," Miss Emma said, looking back into the cell.

He faced the gray concrete wall and didn't answer her.

"Oh, Lord Jesus," she cried. "Oh, Lord Jesus, stand by, stand by."

The deputy and I exchanged glances. With his eyes and a nod, he told me to put my arms around her. Which I did.

10

OUR NEXT TWO VISITS went pretty much as the first one did. I picked up Miss Emma at her house at around one-thirty—my aunt was always there with her—and after she had settled down into the back seat of the car, we drove in silence all the way into Bayonne. Each time, we arrived five or ten minutes before the hour. The food was searched, I was asked to take everything out of my pockets, then told to put everything back into my pockets, and we were led down the narrow dark-wood corridor, passing opened office doors where white men and white women carried on their daily routines. The deputy walked a step ahead of us, with Miss Emma directly behind him, and me beside her. At the end of the corridor we would climb the steps to the first landing, where the deputy would wait a minute to allow Miss Emma to catch her breath, then we would continue on up to the next floor and through the heavy steel door to the cellblock. The prisoners would hear us coming, and they would stand at the cell doors with their hands stuck out between the bars. As she had done the first time, Miss Emma promised that they could have the food Jefferson did not eat. As I had done the first time, I gave them the change I had in my pockets, which was always less than a dollar. Then we would move down the line to the last cell. Jefferson always lay on the bunk, either looking at the ceiling or facing the wall. Each time, the deputy opened the door and locked us in. Jefferson had no more to talk about the second or third time than he did the first, and after we had spent an hour with him, we were let out. Each time, Miss Emma left the cell crying, and both times she told the young deputy to give the food to the other children.

On Friday, our fourth visit, I left Irene Cole in charge of the school and instructed her to let the children go at three. If she felt that they had done all their schoolwork before three, she could dismiss them early, because it was getting colder and most of the children would have work to do at home. I had to go down to my aunt's house to get my car, then I drove back up the quarter to Miss Emma's. Usually she was waiting for me, but not today. I sat out there in the car a good five minutes, but no Miss Emma. I didn't want to blow the horn; I thought that might show impatience and disrespect. But still no Miss Emma. The door was shut and the only thing to give the place any sign of life was a trickle of white smoke rising occasionally out of the chimney.

After sitting out there another couple of minutes, I put patience and respect aside. I pressed on the horn hard and long enough for everybody in the quarter to hear it. I had given up my class to take her to Bayonne, and she was not ready, and I wanted them all to know about it.

Finally, the door did open. My aunt came out on the porch and pushed the door shut behind her. She stood there watching me. I knew that stand, I knew that look. I knew that she was not coming one step farther and that I would have to come to her. She still watched me as I got out of the car and came up the walk. I stopped short of the porch.

"Something wrong with you?" she asked me.

I wanted to ask that same question about Miss Emma, but I held my tongue.

"Don't you know if she was able she would be out here?"

"Then why didn't she tell me she wasn't going? I could be teaching my class."

"Nobody said you wasn't going."

"You're saying I'm supposed to visit him alone? He's no kin—"

"Come on in here, boy, and get that bag," my aunt said.

She watched me come up on the porch and go by her, then she followed me into the house. Miss Emma was sitting at the fireplace in a rocking chair. She had on two sweaters, a black one over a green one. She had some kind of rag, possibly a baby's diaper, tied around her head. I stood in the center of the room near the hanging light bulb. I had the feeling that Miss Emma was not nearly as sick as she was pretending to be. For one thing, I had seen her that morning picking up chips in the yard, and she didn't look sick at all. And now I could smell fried chicken and baked potato, and I knew she could not have done all that if she was dying.

My aunt sat down in the rocker next to Miss Emma's. Now, both of them peered into the fireplace, at the two half-burned logs that gave about as much fire as a candle would. Neither said a thing, as if they were sitting alone in deep thought. Then Miss Emma coughed twice—short and dry—to let me know that she was on her deathbed. Then silence again.

There was smoke in the room, and I must have cleared my throat or something, because my aunt used that moment to speak.

"That food waiting."

I didn't know where the food was waiting for me; I didn't look
for it. I just stood back looking at them.

"He don't have to go," Miss Emma said. She coughed again,
reminding me that she was still on her deathbed. "Not if it go'n
be a burden."

My aunt looked back at me. "I said that food waiting."

"Miss Emma's dying. But you can go with me," I said.

"I don't have on my good dress," my aunt said.

"I can wait," I said.

"No you won't," she said.

"Don't force him," Miss Emma said. "When I'm able to get
on my feet—God willing—I'll get somebody else to take me up
there. I don't want to be a burden on nobody."

As I stood there listening to her, I realized that this had been
planned from the beginning. All that other stuff I went through
was to lead up to this day. Going up to Pichot's house, meeting
the sheriff, the three visits to the jail with her—all that was
nothing but preparation for today. Didn't she say it that first
night at Pichot's? "I'm old. My heart won't take it. I want
somebody else to take my place." Didn't she say it? Sure she did.
Because it was planned even then. But she had had help. My
aunt.

She coughed again—quick, dry, faked as before.

I told myself that what she needed was more wood on the fire.
I went to the corner of the room where the wood was stacked,
and I piled as many logs on my arms as I could stand up with,
then I threw them all into the fireplace. Sparks of fire shot across
the hearth into the room, and smoke and ashes shot up the
chimney. I brushed off my clothes and stood there until the
wood had started burning.

"Can I do anything else, Miss Emma?" I said. "Maybe some
cough syrup?"

"You can watch your tongue, sir," my aunt said.

"I just want Miss Emma to get better," I said.

"He don't have to go," Miss Emma said.

"He's going," my aunt said.

"If it's a burden," Miss Emma said.

"Maybe I'll go halfway," I said. "Maybe I'll dump the food out there in the river. Fishes don't get much to eat in winter. Maybe they like fried chicken."

"You better get that food and get out of here if you know what's good for you," my aunt said.

I went back into the kitchen and snatched the bag off the table. There was enough food in it to feed everybody in the jail.

"Everything you sent me to school for, you're stripping me of it," I told my aunt. They were looking at the fire, and I stood behind them with the bag of food. "The humiliation I had to go through, going into that man's kitchen. The hours I had to wait while they ate and drank and socialized before they would even see me. Now going up to that jail. To watch them put their dirty hands on that food. To search my body each time as if I'm some kind of common criminal. Maybe today they'll want to look into my mouth, or my nostrils, or make me strip. Anything to humiliate me. All the things you wanted me to escape by going to school. Years ago, Professor Antoine told me that if I stayed here, they were going to break me down to the nigger I was born to be. But he didn't tell me that my aunt would help them do it."

She got up slowly, heavily, and went to Miss Emma, who had begun to shake her head and cry. Miss Emma sincerely did not want me to go now, but my aunt had not changed her mind for a moment.

"I'm sorry, Mr. Grant, I'm helping them white people to humiliate you. I'm so sorry. And I wished they had somebody else we could turn to. But they ain't nobody else."

11

THE SHERIFF WAS in his office when I came into
the courthouse. I could see him behind his desk, talking to
another man, who had just opened the door to leave. They
talked awhile longer, then the man came out into the corridor.
I caught the door and went into the office with the bag of food.

"Help you?" Guidry asked me.

He sat with his cowboy boots propped up on the desk. He
wore an open-collar light-gray shirt and dark-gray pants. His
necktie, his cowboy hat, and his coat hung on a rack by the file
cabinet next to his desk. This was the first time he had been in
his office since I started coming up there, but I didn't doubt that
he knew who I was.

"I came to see Jefferson," I said.

"How y'all getting along?"

"This'll be my first time alone with him."

"What's in the basket?"

"Food his nannan sends him."

"Paul?" Guidry called, while still looking at me.

The young deputy came into the office from a side door.

"Called, Sheriff?"

Guidry nodded toward me.

"How you doing?" the deputy asked.

"Fine, and yourself?"

"I can't complain," he said.

We went through the usual routine. I had to take everything out of my pockets and put it all back. The deputy went through all the food, unwrapping one piece of chicken, checking it, putting it back. He unwrapped two or three pieces of candy, checked out the bag of sweet potatoes, then, finished, he wiped his hands on a pocket handkerchief.

"Still think you can get something into that head of his?" Guidry spoke across the tips of those cowboy boots.

"I don't know, sir."

"Just remember what I said," Guidry said. "Any sign of aggravation, I'll stop all this."

I nodded my head. Then I remembered that I had to speak out. "Yes, sir."

He looked at me awhile, then he nodded to the deputy, and we left the office. Since Miss Emma was not with us this time, I walked beside the deputy instead of behind him. We went by all the familiar opened doors where people pecked on typewriters, we climbed the familiar stairs up to the big steel door that led onto the cellblock. By now I could probably have done this with my eyes shut. The prisoners came to the cell doors as before. If they were not the same ones, they were the same ages—in their late teens or early twenties. I gave them the change I had. Nobody got more than a dime. Two could put their money together and get a pack of cigarettes, or one could get a pack of gum and a candy bar.

Jefferson sat on his bunk with his head bowed and his arms hanging down between his legs. The deputy opened the door for me to go in, and he reminded me that he would be back within the hour. In case I wanted to leave before then, I could call a trusty, and the trusty would come to get him.

"Jefferson," I said.

He didn't look up.

"Your nannan couldn't make it today," I said. "She has a bad cold. But she sent you something. How are you feeling, Jefferson?"

After a while he raised his head, but he didn't look at me; he looked at the barred window. From the cell, all you could see were the yellow leaves on the sycamore tree and the pale-blue sky between the leaves.

"You hungry?" I asked.

"You brought some corn?" he said.

"Corn?"

"That's what hogs eat," he said, turning his head now to look at me.

He had not washed his face or combed his hair for days. He wore one of my old khaki shirts and a wrinkled pair of brown pants. He didn't have on shoes. They were stuck under the bunk.

"I didn't bring any corn," I said. "And you're not a hog."

He looked at me as if I was patronizing him.

"When was the last time you ate?" I asked him.

"I don't know."

"Today?" I asked him.

"I don't know."

He was playing with me, and I knew it.

"Some chicken in there," I said. "Biscuits and sweet potatoes. Even some candy she made. You ought to try it. It'll make her happy."

"Hogs don't eat no candy," he said.

"You're not a hog," I said. "You're a man."

He grunted deep in his throat and grinned at me.

"Mind if I have a piece of your chicken?" I asked him. "I left before dinner."

He acted as though he had not heard me.

Since the deputy had already gone through the paper bag, I didn't have to do too much unwrapping to get to the food. I took out a drumstick and a biscuit and started eating.

"Your nannan can sure cook," I said.

"That's for youmans," he said.

"You're a human being, Jefferson," I said.

"I'm a old hog," he said. "Youmans don't stay in no stall like this. I'm a old hog they fattening up to kill."

"That would hurt your nannan if she heard you say that. You want me to tell her you said that?"

"Old hog don't care what people say."

"She cares," I said. "And I do too, Jefferson."

"Y'all youmans," he said.

"You're a human being too, Jefferson."

"I'm a old hog," he said, more to himself than to me. "Just a old hog they fattening up to kill for Christmas."

"You're a human being, Jefferson. You're a man."

He kept his eyes on me as he got up from the bunk.

"I'm go'n show you how a old hog eat," he said.

He knelt down on the floor and put his head inside the bag and started eating, without using his hands. He even sounded like a hog.

I stood back watching him, while I continued to eat the biscuit and piece of chicken.

"That's how a old hog eat," he said, raising his head and grinning at me. He got up from his knees and went back to his bunk. "That's how a old hog eat."

"All right," I said. "But when I go back, I'm going to tell her that you and I sat on the bunk and ate, and you said how good the food was. I won't tell her what you did. She is already sick, and that would kill her. So I'm going to lie. I'm going to tell her how much you liked the food. Especially the pralines."

He said nothing. He just grinned at me.

"Are you trying to hurt me, Jefferson?" I asked him. "Are you trying to make me feel guilty for your being here? You don't want me to come back here anymore?"

His expression didn't change—as though someone had chiseled that painful, cynical grin on his face.

"That man out there doesn't want me up here either," I told him. "He said I will never be able to make you understand anything. He said I'm just wasting my time coming up here now. But your nannan doesn't think so. She wants me to come up here. She wants us to talk. What do you want? You want me to stay away and let him win? The white man? You want him to win?"

His expression remained the same—cynical, defiant, painful.

I could not think of anything else to say to him. But since I had been there less than half an hour, I knew it was too early to call for the deputy. The sheriff would have known that Jefferson and I were not getting along, and that was the last thing I could afford, at least for Miss Emma's sake.

The rest of the hour just dragged along. Jefferson was not looking at me anymore; he had lain back down on the bunk, facing the wall. I gazed out the window, at the yellow leaves on the sycamore tree. The leaves were as still as if they were painted there. Between the leaves I could see bits of pale-blue sky. I looked at Jefferson, with his back to me. I looked at his pair of laceless shoes under the bunk. I looked down at the bag of food, trying to remember how many pieces of chicken, biscuits, potatoes, or pieces of candy were still in there. I went to the washbowl and got a handful of water to drink. I tried turning the faucet off completely, but it continued to drip. The water had left a brown stain from the top of the bowl to the drain. I turned to Jefferson again. He was facing the wall, his back to me. I wanted to ask him what he was thinking about.

When I heard the deputy come down the cellblock, I went to the bunk.

"Anything you want me to tell your nannan?" I asked him.

He didn't answer. His eyes were open and staring at the wall.

"I'll tell her how much you enjoyed the food," I said. "That would make her happy."

The deputy came up to the cell and let me out.

"Y'all doing all right?" he asked, as we walked away.

"He was glad to get some home cooking," I said.

"I can't blame him for that," the deputy said.

12

I KNEW MISS EMMA expected me to come back
and tell her all about Jefferson, but I had not thought of a good
lie yet. I couldn't go there and tell her what had really happened;
that would have hurt too much. I couldn't go there and say that
we had had a good talk; she probably wouldn't have believed it,
not after the way he had acted when we were there together. I
needed time to think, to think of something. Not a big lie, just
a little lie or a number of little lies, but a lie it had to be. Maybe
I could tell her he was concerned about her health. She would
like that. Maybe I could tell her he had begun to use the brush
and comb I had bought for him. Or maybe I could say that the
deputy had told me what a good prisoner he was, and that the
sheriff himself had said he was a good boy. I needed time, time

to get my lies straight. And the best place for that was at the Rainbow. I got into my car and drove back of town.

The Rainbow Club was quiet, dark and quiet. There were only two old men in the place, besides Joe Claiborne, who was behind the bar. All three stood talking baseball. Jackie Robinson. Robinson had just finished his second year with the Brooklyn Dodgers.

"What's happening, Prof?" Claiborne said to me.

"A Jax," I said.

He brought the bottle of beer to me.

"A little business in town," I said.

Claiborne could see that I didn't want to talk about the business, or maybe he realized what the business was. He nodded his head and went back down the bar where the other customers were. The two old men had continued their conversation, and Claiborne joined them again as if he had never left.

From where I stood, about halfway down the bar, all I could hear was Jackie this and Jackie that. Nothing about any of the other players, nothing about the Brooklyn Dodgers as a team. Only Jackie. Jackie this and Jackie that.

I sipped my beer slowly while listening to them. And they were very good. They could recall everything Jackie had done in the past two years. They remembered when he got his first hit, and who it was against. They remembered the first time he stole two bases in one game and the first time he stole home. One of the men backed away from the bar to demonstrate how slow the pitcher was in throwing the ball, which gave Jackie the opportunity to steal home plate. The old man looked over each shoulder, as pitchers do when there are runners on bases. He raised his leg as high as he could, which was only about a foot off the floor, to show how much time the pitcher took to throw the ball to the plate. While the pitcher went through the motion of raising his leg and winding his arm, Jackie was on his way home. Now the old man became Jackie—not running, but showing the motion of someone running at full speed. His arms were doing what the legs could not do. He showed you the motion of Jackie sliding into the plate, the motion of the umpire calling Jackie safe, and the motion of Jackie brushing off his clothes and going into the dugout. The old man nodded his head emphatically, with great pride, and went back to the bar. Claiborne and the other old man told him that he was exactly right.

Listening to them, I could remember back to the time before Jackie came to the major leagues, when it was Joe Louis that everyone talked about. Yes, I could remember, I could remember when he was the only one. Especially the big fight with Schmeling, that German. I could still remember how depressed everyone was after Joe had lost the first fight with Schmeling. For weeks it was like that. To be caught laughing for any reason seemed like a sin. This was a period of mourning. What else in the world was there to be proud of, if Joe had lost? Even the preacher got into it. "Let us wait. Let us wait, children. David will meet Goliath again." And everyone told everyone else: "They go'n meet again. Just wait."

And we waited and waited, and finally the big fight did come. There were two radios in the quarter, one at the Williams's house, down the quarter, another at the McVays', up the quarter. I was down the quarter. I was seventeen then. I was not the youngest, nor surely the oldest. I was just one. Praying and hoping for the only hero we knew. There was much noise, much talking, while the people waited for the fight to begin. Once the announcer said that the fighters were in the ring, everyone became silent without anybody having to tell them to do so. There were small children there too, but even they had quit playing and were silent. We held our breath, remembering the first fight. Could God let it happen again? Would He let it happen again?

Then it was over. And there was nothing but chaos. People screamed. Some shot pistols in the air. There were mock fights. Old men fell down on the floor, as Schmeling did, and had to be helped up. Everybody laughed. Everybody patted everybody else on the back. For days after that fight, for weeks, we held our heads higher than any people on earth had ever done for any reason. I was only seventeen then, but I could remember it, every bit of it—the warm evening, the people, the noise, the pride I saw in those faces.

Now, while I stood there listening to the old men in their praise of Jackie Robinson, I remembered something else. The little Irishman. I was at the university then. The little Irishman was giving a series of lectures at white universities, but some way or another, our university got him to visit us. How? Only God knows. But we were all gathered in the auditorium—and there stood this little white man with the thick accent, talking to us about Irish literature. He spoke of Yeats, O'Casey, Joyce— names I had never heard before. I sat there listening, listening, trying to remember everything he said. And a name he repeated over and over was Parnell. And he told us how some Irishmen would weep this day at the mention of the name Parnell. Parnell. Parnell. Parnell. Then he spoke of James Joyce. He told about Joyce's family, his religion, his education, his writing. He spoke of a book called *Dubliners* and a story in the book titled "Ivy Day in the Committee Room." Regardless of race, regardless of class, that story was universal, he said.

For days after the lecture, I tried to find that book. But it was not in our library and not in any of the bookstores. I went to Mr. Anderson, my literature teacher, and asked him if he knew how I could get a copy. He said he would see what he could do. A week later, he kept me after class and handed me a collection of stories. It was not Joyce's *Dubliners* but an anthology of short stories, with "Ivy Day in the Committee Room" included as one of them. Mr. Anderson had gotten a professor at the white university to check the book out of his library for him. "He's a pretty decent fellow," Mr. Anderson said about the white pro- fessor. "Some of them are, you know. And always remember that. Now take care of that book. You can keep it a week. And it had better come back to me in the same condition in which it left. You do understand me, don't you, Wiggins?"

I read the story and reread the story, but I still could not find the universality that the little Irishman had spoken of. All I saw in the story was some Irishmen meeting in a room and talking politics. What had that to do with America, especially with my people? It was not until years later that I saw what he meant. I had gone to bars, to barbershops; I had stood on street corners, and I had gone to many suppers there in the quarter. But I had never really listened to what was being said. Then I began to listen, to listen closely to how they talked about their heroes, how they talked about the dead and about how great the dead had once been. I heard it everywhere.

The old men down at the end of the bar were still talking about Jackie Robinson. But I was not thinking about Jackie now, or Joe Louis, or the little Irishman; I was thinking about that cold, depressing cell uptown.

I raised my hand for Claiborne to bring me another beer. He gave me the bottle and looked into my eyes, and he could tell that I didn't feel like talking. So he went back down the bar to where the old men were still talking baseball.

I didn't want to think about that cell uptown; I didn't even want to think about Miss Emma and the lies I had to tell her. I wanted to think about more pleasant things. I thought about Vivian. Now, there was not a more pleasant thing in the world to think about. Today was Friday, wasn't it? And wouldn't it be nice if the two of us could go somewhere and spend the entire weekend? Wouldn't that be nice? I would be able to forget the whole thing, the whole thing for at least a couple of days.

Damn it, it would be so good if we could go away and never come back. I knew I could find a job doing something else, and so could she. If we could just get the hell away from here. Just go away.

The old men down the bar continued to hit the ball, throw the ball, and slide into bases.

And my mind went back to that cell uptown, then to another cell, somewhere in Florida. After reading about the execution there, I had dreamed about it over and over and over. As vividly as if I were there, I had seen that cell, heard that boy crying while being dragged to that chair, "Please, Joe Louis, help me. Please help me. Help me." And after he had been strapped in the chair, the man who wrote the story could still hear him cry, "Mr. Joe Louis, help me. Mr. Joe Louis, help me."

And down the bar the old men went on hitting the ball, running the bases, and sliding home. And I wondered if the one in that cell uptown would call on Jackie Robinson as the other one had called on Joe Louis.

"Taking off, Prof?" Claiborne asked me.

"I have to find my lady," I said.

"Take it easy, Prof."

I waved my hand to the old men. They nodded to me.

The school was three or four blocks away, on the main street. But everything back here was pretty close to everything else. The school was on the same street as the Catholic church, the movie theater, the mortuary, a café, and the ice cream parlor. The grocery store was not far from the church, but on another street. The barbershop and a gas station weren't too far from the mortuary. Everybody knew everybody, everybody knew everybody else's business.

I parked in front of the movie theater and watched one of the teachers direct the children onto the school bus. When the bus drove away, I got out of my car.

"What's happening, handsome?" the teacher said.

"What's going on, Peggy?"

"Thank God it's Friday," she said. "She's still inside."

"Having a drink later?"

"A couple," Peggy said.

As we walked up to the entrance of the school, I saw two boys taking in the flag. Peggy told me she would see us at the club later, and I went to Vivian's classroom. The school had only five rooms, and in some the classes were doubled. Vivian taught the sixth and seventh grades. The children had all gone, and she sat behind her desk, looking over papers. She wore a brown woolen suit and a white blouse. She didn't raise her head until I was near the desk. Then she smiled. She had the most beautiful and most even teeth I had ever seen. But I thought every bit of her was perfect.

"What are you doing here?" she asked.

"You ever known a Friday I could stay away from you?" I went around the desk and kissed her.

"Last boy stood at this desk wouldn't dare do that," she said.

"I better not ever catch anyone else doing it," I said.

"What *are* you doing here?" she asked.

"To see you, what else?"

She looked up at me, and she could read my face, and she knew that I had been at the jail.

"Still working?" I asked.

"Nothing I can't do later."

"I saw Peggy. They were going over for a drink."

"Sounds like a good idea," Vivian said. She put some papers into a briefcase and stood up. "I have to see the principal before she leaves. Do you know how to clean a blackboard?"

"I've done a few."

"If you do a good job I'll give you an apple," she said.

"Thanks, teacher."

She kissed me lightly on the lips and walked away. At the door she looked back and smiled again.

A vertical line had been drawn down the blackboard. On one side of the line were French sentences, on the other side English translations. They were simple sentences: "Where is the book?" "Where is the tablet?" "Where is the pencil?" I wiped both halves clean, but you could still see the imprint of the sentences.

I drew another vertical line, and on one side I wrote, "Je t'aime. Je t'aime. Je t'aime." And on the other side I wrote, "I love you. I love you. I love you."

Vivian came back into the room and saw what I had done.

"You naughty boy," she said. "Suppose Daisy sees that?"

"Doesn't she already know?"

"I ought to make you stand in the corner on one foot."

"If you stood there with me, I wouldn't mind."

"Naughty, naughty boy," she said. "Erase that."

"Only if you kiss me first."

She had picked up the briefcase, and I took it from her and laid it on the desk and I pulled her into my arms.

"Let's go somewhere, just the two of us," I said, after kissing her. "Let's go somewhere and spend the night. Baton Rouge, New Orleans—anywhere."

"My babies," she said.

"Dora will look after them. Come on, let's go somewhere."

"We're having a drink with Peggy, remember?"

"Let's forget Peggy and everybody else. Let's go somewhere."

I could see that for a moment she was thinking about it. Then she shook her head.

"No," she said. "I can't take that chance."

"Don't you want to?"

"More than anything."

"Then let's take the chance."

"No," she said. "I can't give him an excuse to take my babies."

"You think he would?"

"I don't know. I can't take that risk."

"I hate going to Robert and Helen's, then leaving in the middle of the night."

"I hate it too," she said. "But staying overnight somewhere—I can't take that chance."

"Where is he now?"

"Last I heard, in Houston."

"When's he coming back?"

"I don't know."

"Until he makes up his mind, we just do nothing."

"I thought we did a lot."

"You know what I mean."

"Come on, let's go find Peggy and them and have a drink."

"Not until I get another kiss."

"What is the matter?" she said, after we had kissed.

Maybe it was the way I had held her. Maybe it was the look in my face.

I told her what had happened at the jail, how Jefferson had gotten down on his knees to eat the food out of the paper bag. I saw her frown, and she brought her hand up to her mouth.

"I have to go back to that old woman. But I couldn't go back then. I couldn't face her then. I needed some time to think of a lie to tell her."

With her hand still over her mouth, Vivian was looking at me.

"I wish I could just run away from this place."

Vivian shook her head. "You know you can't."

"Why not?"

"For the same reason you haven't done it yet."

"I've wanted to."

"But you haven't."

"Why?"

"You know the answer yourself, Grant. You love them more than you hate this place."

"Is it love or cowardice? Afraid to take a chance out there."

"You have your folks in California. You can always go to them."

"I have thought about it many times."

"Sure," she said. "You even did it once, but you came back. This is all we have, Grant."

"I want more."

I turned away from her and erased the blackboard.

"Well, let's go have that drink," I said.

"Wait," Vivian said. She went up to the board and wrote in large letters: "Je t'aimerais toujours, Je t'aimerais toujours, Je t'aimerais toujours."

"And suppose old Daisy comes in here before you get back on Monday?"

"She already knows about it," Vivian said. "So do all the rest—teachers and students."

13

▶

NOT LONG AFTER the second bell rang at the church, I heard Miss Eloise Bouie out in the road, calling my aunt. I went onto the porch and told her that my aunt was in the back. Miss Eloise, tall and thin, stood in the road, leaning on her bamboo walking stick. She wore a long black overcoat and a black hat with a white band. She was looking up the quarter. She said she thought there was a new chill in the air, and I agreed with her. While she waited for my aunt, she continued to look up the quarter, toward the church. I didn't feel like standing out on the porch, but I thought it would be rude to go inside and leave her in the road with no one to talk to.

I heard my aunt come into the house from the backyard. She was in her room only a moment before she walked out on the porch. She wore the black coat over a black dress, white stockings, and low-heeled black shoes.

"Hey, there, Elou," she called.

"Hey," Miss Eloise called back. She really stretched it out. "Haaaaaaaay."

"Ain't been waiting too long, I hope," my aunt said.

"Just getting here," Miss Eloise said.

"Be sure you shut them doors if you leave from here," my aunt said to me.

She was already halfway down the steps when she said it. She had not looked at me. Years ago, she had quit looking at me when she was on her way to church. When I came back from the university, I told her that I didn't believe anymore and I didn't want her to try forcing it on me. If she did, I told her, then I would have to look for some other place to live. She didn't want me to leave, so she let me alone. Only occasionally, when she had some other church member at the house, would she bring it up. Even then she wouldn't press it too far.

She and Miss Eloise started up the quarter, one tall and slim, the other short and much heavier. They stopped in front of Miss Emma's house, and I heard my aunt calling her. "Em-ma? Hey, there, Em-ma?" Miss Emma came out of the house, and the three of them continued on up to the church together.

I went back inside. I had started correcting papers a couple of hours earlier, but I hadn't done very much. On Sunday, my aunt began getting ready for church as soon as she woke up, which was around six o'clock. Until eleven o'clock, there was nothing I could do but listen to her singing her 'Termination song.

Determination Sunday was the third Sunday of each month, when members of the church would stand and sing their favorite hymns and tell the congregation where they were determined to spend eternity. My aunt started warming up at six in the morning, whether it was 'Termination Sunday or not, and didn't quit until eleven, when she walked out of the house. So I would be forced to put away the work until after she had gone, or I would go for a walk through the quarter and back into the field.

I sat at my table trying to correct papers, but my mind kept drifting back to Friday. It had been dark when I returned to the quarter from Bayonne. It was colder too; I could see sparks of fire rising out of chimneys. When I stopped in front of Miss Emma's house, Farrell Jarreau, who lived across the road, told me she had gone to my aunt's house. I said good night to him and went down the quarter. I recognized Reverend Ambrose's car, parked before the door. Now I felt a little guilty for getting back so late.

The three of them were in the kitchen drinking coffee, Reverend Ambrose, Miss Emma, and my aunt. They were quiet, sitting in semidarkness. The only light in the kitchen came from the open door of the stove. No one looked around when I came in, and Reverend Ambrose and Miss Emma barely answered when I spoke their names. My aunt was completely silent.

I went to the icebox and took out the pitcher of water, and while I poured a glassful, I looked at the three of them at the table. They were quiet, not even drinking their coffee now.

"I'll be in my room," I said to my aunt.

"That's all you got to say?" she snapped at me.

"I spoke, Tante Lou."

"You know what I'm talking about."

"He was all right," I said.

"That's all?" my aunt said. "Or did you forget to go?"

"I went, and he was all right," I said.

"You got more than that to say, Mr. Man," my aunt said. "Folks been setting here hours, waiting for you."

"I see you recovered from your cold, Miss Emma. I'm glad it wasn't too—"

"Sit down," my aunt said.

I went around the table and pulled out the fourth chair.

"He was all right," I said.

My aunt looked at me. Reverend Ambrose and Miss Emma stared out into the yard.

"That's not what she want to hear," my aunt said. "How he was when you got there, how he was when you left?"

"He was all right both times," I said.

"You know what I'm talking about," my aunt said.

She looked at me the way an inquisitor must have glared at his poor victims. The only reason she didn't put me on the rack was that she didn't have one.

"We both ate some of the food, and we talked," I said.

All this time Miss Emma had been gazing into the yard. Now she looked at me—no, toward me. Her thoughts were far distant.

"He et?"

"Some," I said.

"Y'all talked?" Her mind was still far away.

"A little," I said.

Now her focus became closer, much closer. She was looking *at* me now.

"What y'all talked about?"

"Different things. I told him you didn't come to see him because you had a bad cold."

She looked at me, waiting to hear his answer. But I couldn't think of another lie, so I shifted to something else.

"Then I asked him how he was getting along. He said he was all right. The deputy had already told me he was okay. Guidry was in the office today. He said that Jefferson was getting along fine—didn't cause any trouble. He is using that comb and brush I bought for him. And he was wearing one of my shirts, the khaki one. I think he's doing okay."

Miss Emma and my aunt both studied me. Miss Emma wanted to believe what I was saying, but I could see she had doubts. My aunt still wanted to put me on the rack. And Reverend Ambrose continued to look out into the darkness.

"What else y'all talked about?" my aunt said. "You left from here 'fore one-thirty."

"I can't remember everything we talked about," I said. "We just talked."

"More than five hours, and you can't remember nothing else?"

"I was with him about an hour, then I went back of town. I have a girl back of town. I like to see her sometime."

"And maybe that's where you spent all your time?"

"If you don't think I went to the jail, you can always go up there and ask them."

"I didn't ask for none of your uppity, mister."

"I don't mean to be uppity," I told her. "I'm just telling you the truth. I spent an hour with him. I had a drumstick and a biscuit, and he had something—I can't remember exactly what it was. Then we talked. Then I left and went back of town. Exactly what I did."

"Deep in you, what you think?" Reverend Ambrose suddenly turned from looking out into the darkness. "Deep in you?"

"About what, Reverend?"

"Him? What's he thinking? What he's thinking deep in him? Deep in you, what you think?"

"Who knows what somebody else is thinking? They say one thing, they may be thinking about something else—who can tell?"

"You the teacher," my aunt said, not so kindly.

"Deep in you?" Reverend Ambrose said. "Deep in you, you think he know, he done grasped the significance of what it's all about? Deep in you?"

"The significance?"

"The gravity."

"The gravity?"

Reverend Mose Ambrose was a short, very dark man whose face and bald head were always shining. He was the plantation church's pastor. He was not educated, hadn't gone to any theological school; he had heard the voice and started preaching. He was a simple, devoted believer. He christened babies, baptized youths, visited those who were ill, counseled those who had trouble, preached, and buried the dead. All these things could be simply accomplished. But when it came to a discussion with a teacher, though he had known that teacher since his birth, then suddenly things were not so simple.

"His soul," he said.

"I don't know anything about the soul, Reverend Ambrose."

"I baptized him," Reverend Ambrose said. "He was 'leven or twelve then. But like so many others, he didn't keep the faith, either. Like yourself."

He stared at me as though I was one of the worst of sinners. Maybe I was. Backsliders were usually worse than those who had never been converted. At least that is what people like him tried to make you believe.

"Y'all talked about God?" he asked me.

"No, sir. We didn't get around to that."

"Didn't get around to God?"

"No, sir."

He looked at me and nodded his head. If we didn't talk about God, then what else on earth was important enough to talk about to someone who was about to meet God?

"I figured that's where you came in, Reverend. There's enough room for both of us, I can tell you that."

"Me, Sister Emma, Sister Lou, going up there Monday," he said. "Anything I ought to take him?"

"Food, I suppose. Maybe some clean clothes. I can't think of anything else."

"I was thinking more about the Bible," Reverend Ambrose said.

"That would be nice too," I said.

Reverend Ambrose did not have any more to say. He and my aunt continued to stare at me until I excused myself and left the table.

Now, on Sunday, as I sat at the table, trying to do my work, I could hear them singing in the church. It seemed that I had listened to this singing, and their praying, every Sunday of my life. No, I had done more than just listened; I participated until my last year at the university. There was no one thing that changed my faith. I suppose it was a combination of many things, but mostly it was just plain studying. I did not have time for anything else. Many times I would not come home on weekends, and when I did, I found that I cared less and less about the church. Of course, it pained my aunt to see this change in me, and it saddened me to see the pain I was causing her. I thought many times about leaving, as Professor Antoine had advised me to do. My mother and father also told me that if I was not happy in Louisiana, I should come to California. After visiting them the summer following my junior year at the university, I came back, which pleased my aunt. But I had been running in place ever since, unable to accept what used to be my life, unable to leave it.

I pushed away the papers and listened to the singing. Miss Eloise was singing her 'Termination song, "Were You There When They Crucified My Lord?" You could hear that high, shrill voice all over the plantation. I had been hearing it all my life, all my life. After her there would be someone else, then someone else. It would go on for three or four hours. And it was impossible to do anything but listen to it or leave.

I thought I heard a car stop before the door, but I didn't leave the table. Then I thought I heard someone come onto the porch, and when I looked up I saw her standing in the doorway. But I did not believe it was she, because she had never come here before. She wore a blue blazer and a maroon pleated skirt. A black patent-leather purse hung from her right shoulder.

"I hope you don't mind."

"Only if I'm dreaming."

She smiled and came into the room.

14

▼

"I FINISHED all my work. I wanted to see you,"
Vivian said.

I had already stood up. I moved around the table and kissed
her.

"I couldn't have wished for anything more. But why today?"

"I don't know," she said. "I just missed you. I wanted to see
you."

"Where are the children?"

"Dora," she said. "I hope I'm not keeping you from anything."

"Only from a boring afternoon."

Vivian smiled and looked around the room.

"Not much to look at," I said, apologizing for the place.

This had been my parents' room before they went to California during the war. There was a bed, a chifforobe, a washstand, a table, and a couple of chairs. All the furniture was old. On the mantelpiece were three pictures, in five-by-seven wood frames: one of Vivian and me, one of my mother, and one of my father.

A photocollage of Frederick Douglass, Abraham Lincoln, and Booker T. Washington hung over the mantel. Several pictures from calendars over the past few years were tacked to the wall. The wallpaper had brown, red, and green squares, and in places it was torn from age.

Vivian picked up the picture of my mother.

"Mom?" she said.

"Yes."

"Pretty."

"About your complexion, very fair."

She replaced the picture and took up my father's.

"Dark and handsome," she said.

"I suppose you can say that."

"I don't know those other two," she said, looking at our picture. She looked around the room. "I love it. Rustic."

"It's rustic, all right. Probably the most rustic place you will ever visit."

"Pastoral," she said.

"That too," I said. "With the singing and praying up at the church, really pastoral."

"I like it," she said.

"Try staying here about a year."

She had gone to the window, and she was looking across the vegetable garden toward the church up the quarter. I moved behind her and put my arms around her waist, and I could smell her perfume. She turned to me, and I brought my hands up to her face and held it a moment, while we looked at each other. Then I kissed her, kissed her very tenderly, and when I looked at her again, I could see in her face that she loved me as much as I loved her.

"I'm sorry I don't have anything here to drink," I said.

"Don't worry about that."

"Would you like to eat something? My aunt made a cake."

"I had a good breakfast," Vivian said.

"What about some coffee?"

"Don't bother."

"It's already made."

"Okay."

We went through my aunt's room, which was even more rustic than mine, then into the kitchen. In the kitchen was a black four-lid wood stove, a five-foot-tall white icebox, a handmade table with four wood-bottom chairs around it, a safe with screen doors for the dishes, a broom that had seen better days, an ax in the corner, and several black pots and aluminum pans, hanging from nails on the wall. Very, very rustic.

Vivian stood at the back door, looking across the yard toward the field, where some of the cane had been cut. The cane had not been hauled to the derrick yet, and it was lying across the rows. A little farther over, where another patch of cane was standing, tall and blue-green, you could see the leaves swaying softly from a breeze.

After warming the coffee, I poured each of us a cupful. I cut two slices from the chocolate cake my aunt had in the safe, then we sat down at the table, facing the yard and the field.

"It's really peaceful," Vivian said.

"Sunday is the saddest day of the week."

"Not for those who have to work in the field."

"It has always been for me."

"You ought to find something to do on Sunday. Like going to church."

I didn't answer her.

"I know you believe," she said. "You don't want to, but I know you do."

"The only thing I believe in is loving you."

We finished our cake and coffee, and I put the cups and saucers in the pan of soap water on the window shelf.

"We ought to wash them," Vivian said.

"They're okay."

"No," she said. "It's not fair to her. You wash, I'll dry."

"It's going to be like that, huh?"

"Un-hunh," she said.

There was hot water in the kettle on the stove, and I poured some into the dishpan. Vivian had already taken down another pan from the wall, and I poured the rest of the hot water into it; she added cold water from the faucet by the icebox. I washed and rinsed the dishes, and she dried them and put them into the safe. It felt good doing this with her.

"Is that enough?" I asked when we had finished. "Or do you want me to sweep out the kitchen and mop, too?"

She looked down at the floor.

"I don't think so," she said. "It looks pretty clean."

We had been playing. Now I became serious.

"How long can you stay?"

"I have some time."

"Would you like to go for a walk down the quarter?"

She nodded. "But first I must go back to your little girl's house."

I nodded toward the toilet, which was set on the ditch near the cane field.

She left the kitchen, and I went to my room and put on a warmer shirt. I also got my knife, in case we wanted a piece of sugarcane. I was standing on the porch when she came in from the back.

"Rustic enough out there for you?"

"I've been in worse. I'm a country girl, remember?"

We left the house. Up at the church, Reverend Ambrose had just started his 'Termination song, "Amazing Grace." We went down the quarter.

Most of the people who had not gone to church were indoors.

Seldom was someone sitting out on the porch, and no one worked in the gardens or chopped wood in the yard. Horses and mules were grazing in the pastures beside and behind the houses, but that was about as much movement as you saw. Above, a low ashen sky loomed over the plantation, if not over the entire state of Louisiana. A swarm of black birds flew across the road and alighted in a pecan tree in one of the backyards to our left. The entire plantation was deadly quiet, except for the singing coming from the church up the quarter behind us.

We crossed the railroad tracks and turned right. In front of us were three or four boxcars of sugarcane, waiting to be picked up by a train and taken to the mill. We could also see the weighing scales left of the full boxcars, and the derrick that lifted the cane from wagons and trailers and swung it onto the boxcars. Left of the weighing scales and the derrick was the plantation cemetery, where my ancestors had been buried for the past century. The cemetery had lots of trees in it, pecans and oaks, and it was weedy too, and since there were so few gravestones, it was pretty hard to see many graves from the road. Just before we came up to the cemetery, we turned left on a road that would take us farther into the field. This was Vivian's first time back here, and I told her that my people had worked these fields ever since slavery, and many of them were buried in the cemetery behind us. I asked her if she wanted a piece of cane, and she said yes. I jumped over the ditch and crossed a couple of rows until I found a good stalk, then I came back to where she was waiting for me. I cut off the first two joints and threw them away; they didn't look sweet enough. Then I peeled the third joint and tasted it. It was good. I cut off a round and gave it to Vivian. She chewed it and let some of the juice run down her chin, the way a small child would do. The small child would not have been able to help it, but she could. I cut off a round for myself and chewed it. It was very soft, very sweet.

We chewed cane and walked the road for at least three quarters of a mile. Just before coming up to the gate that would lead into the swamp, I noticed a pecan tree to our right. I had picked pecans under that tree many times, and I suggested we go over there and see if we could find some. The tree stood at the headland of the cane field. We searched for pecans in the grass on the headland and down between the rows of cane. We found a couple of dozen big ones, big and soft-shelled, and I cracked them by squeezing two together. I gave Vivian one half, and I kept the other. We sat under the tree, and I cracked pecans for both of us. Suddenly, we were too quiet.

"You want me here?" Vivian asked.

I was not looking at her when she said it, and I could tell by her voice that she was not looking directly at me.

"Yes," I said.

She had been gazing down at the ground. Now she raised her eyes to me.

"That's what I want too," she said.

"I love you, Vivian," I said. "I want you to know that. I love you very much."

"I hope you love me half as much as I love you."

I left her for a while, and when I came back I saw that she had moved farther down between the rows, where the cane would hide us better. She had taken off everything except her brassiere and slip. I took off everything except the heavy shirt, which I unbuttoned. Vivian raised her arms up and out to me as I lay down beside her.

I lay on my side and touched her brown nipples with my finger. Then I leaned over and kissed each tenderly, and raised up and looked at her. She was smiling at me. I went back and I passed my tongue over each and I kissed each again and rubbed my chin over them. My beard must have been rough, because I could feel her drawing away some, but when I looked at her she was smiling again. I smiled back at her.

"I think something happened," she said.

"What do you mean?"

"I have a strange feeling."

I looked at her, and I felt happy. But my face must have changed.

"What is the matter?" she asked.

"Nothing."

"But you frowned."

"I'm happy."

"But you frowned when I said it."

"Maybe I was just thinking. I don't know if I want Paul to grow up here."

"Don't spoil it," she said. "It's been too good. Don't spoil it."

"I'm sorry, sweetheart."

"And suppose it's Molly?"

"No, it's Paul."

"It could be Molly. Molly Wiggins. I don't know if I like that name. You think it's a good name—Molly Wiggins?"

"It sounds okay."

"Sounds kind of whorish to me—Molly Wiggins."

"Then let her decide. If she likes it, we'll keep it. If she doesn't, we'll call her Paulette."

"Paul and Paulette—that sounds good. Maybe I'll have twins."

"If not, we'll go till there is a Paulette."

"She may be first."

"Then we'll go till there is Paul," I said. "You ought to put on something. You might catch cold."

"Not if you hold me close. Not if you put that shirt round both of us."

I lay upon her, kissing her hair, her eyes, her nose, her mouth.

15

VIVIAN STOOD with her back to me while I brushed
off her blazer and her skirt. A few small blades of yellow grass
clung to her hair. I removed them and picked up her purse, and
I could see how clean the ground was where we had lain, and
I could see where she had dug her heels into the ground. We left
the field and started for the main road, to return to the quarter.
It had become colder, and we walked faster than we had when
we came out into the field.

"We start our Christmas program next week," Vivian said.

"It's about that time, huh?"

"You're having a program, aren't you?"

"I don't know." I hadn't given it much thought.

"You only have about a month."

"I guess I'll mention it to the children tomorrow. I'll see what they want. That stuff in Bayonne's been keeping me so busy I've just about forgotten everything else."

"When are you going to see him again?"

"I don't know. His nannan, my aunt, and their pastor are going up there tomorrow. I'll probably go Friday. I don't know."

"You have any idea?" she said, not looking at me directly.

I thought I knew what she was talking about.

"It's up to the big boss in Baton Rouge," I said.

Vivian was quiet.

We crossed the railroad tracks and entered the quarter. People were leaving church and coming out into the road.

"You think your aunt has made it home?" Vivian asked.

"She is usually the last one to leave."

"You want me to go before she gets home?"

"I want you to stay."

"You think it'll be all right?"

"She'll have to get used to it."

"I don't want to cause any trouble."

"There won't be any trouble," I said. "We went over all that last Friday."

"What happened?"

"She wanted to know what had kept me in Bayonne so long. I told her I had been with you. That's all."

"That's all."

"That's all."

"I want her to like me."

"She will when she gets to know you."

"I wish I could say the same for them in Free LaCove."

Vivian had met and married a dark-skinned boy while attending Xavier University in New Orleans. She had not told her people about the wedding, because she knew that they would be opposed to it. After she and the boy were married, she took him back to Free LaCove. Everything turned out just as she had feared. Her family had nothing to say to her husband and hardly anything to say to her. He never went back. When her first child was born, she took the baby to visit. No one held the child or gave it a present or any attention. That was three years ago, and she had not been home since, not even when the second child was born, nor when she separated from her husband. One of her sisters visited her sometimes, and occasionally a male cousin would see her in Bayonne. Her mother and aunts wrote letters; there was no other communication.

Vivian and I stood on the porch and watched my aunt, Miss Emma, Miss Eloise, and Inez come down the quarter. I saw my aunt looking at Vivian's little blue Chevrolet parked in front of the house, then looking toward the house. The women around her went on talking, but she was much more concerned with Vivian and me than with their conversation.

They stopped before the house, and I saw Miss Eloise talking to my aunt. I am sure she was asking her whether they should come in or not. My aunt said yes, because they all proceeded into the yard, walking Indian file, my aunt in front. I introduced her to Vivian as soon as she came up the steps.

"Miss," my aunt said, and gave a slight nod. She didn't look at me.

I introduced Vivian to the other women.

"Howdy do," Miss Eloise said. "How you?" Miss Emma said. "Glad to know you," Inez said.

But they were not glad to know her. They didn't feel comfortable at all. They were at my aunt's house, and they were not about to show much more enthusiasm than she had shown.

They went inside in single file. You could smell their sweet powder all over the place.

"You think I ought to go?" Vivian said.

"No. Come on inside."

We had to pass through my aunt's room to go back into the kitchen. Tante Lou and the other women had taken off their hats and coats and laid them, along with their pocketbooks, on the bed. They were in the kitchen, sitting at the table. My aunt had brought them here for coffee and cake.

"I'll have to make some more coffee," I said.

"I'll make my own coffee," my aunt said.

"I'll make it," I said.

"Not here."

"Vivian and I drank the coffee, and I'll make more. That's all there is to it."

"You go'n walk over me?" she asked.

"No, ma'am, I'm going around you," I said. "But I'm going to make the coffee."

I filled the kettle with water and set it on the stove. My aunt was watching me. Her friends, sitting at the table, were quiet.

"Grant?" Vivian said. "I think—"

"Just be quiet."

"You taking over my house?" my aunt said.

"No, ma'am," I said. "But we drank the coffee. And this is the woman I'm going to marry one day. So you might as well start getting along right now."

The women at the table did not look at us and were afraid to look at one another. My aunt was like a boulder in the road, unmovable, so I had to go around her. She could see that I was not going to change my mind. And she had three choices. She could stop me physically, she could leave the room, or she could sit down at the table with her friends. She was afraid to approach me physically, because I might leave and not come back. If she left the kitchen, then her friends would leave. If she sat at the table, only her pride would be hurt. She thought that was best.

"How was service today, Miss Eloise?" I asked.

"Oh, fine."

She said it so fast that it sounded like only one word. I grinned to myself.

"You find anything funny in that, mister?" my aunt asked, looking at me again.

"No, ma'am," I said. She stared at me long enough to let me know that it was not over between her and me, not yet. She turned to Vivian, not saying anything, just contemplating her. The other women were quiet, looking either down at the table or out the back door, but never at one another.

"I hear you from Free LaCove," my aunt said to Vivian.

"Yes, ma'am."

"I hear they don't like dark-skin people back there."

"Some of them don't," Vivian said.

"Not all of them?" my aunt questioned her.

"No, ma'am."

"How about your own folks?"

"I don't visit back there," Vivian said.

"You don't love your mama? You don't love your daddy?"

"I love both of them," Vivian said, and looked at me. "But I have to live my own life."

"You go to church?"

"I'm Catholic."

My aunt looked at Vivian and nodded her head, as if she was thinking, What else could you possibly be?

"You went to church today?"

"I went to nine o'clock mass," Vivian said.

"You going next Sunday?"

"Yes, ma'am."

"Sunday after that?"

"I hope so."

"This one," my aunt said, nodding toward me but still looking at Vivian, "he don't have a church. What y'all go'n do then?"

"We'll work it out," Vivian said.

"You go'n leave your church?"

"I hope I don't have to," Vivian said. "But if I had to, then I suppose I would."

"You'll leave your church and just become—nothing?"

"We'll work it out," Vivian said.

My aunt nodded her head. "I hope you know what you doing, young lady."

"I think that water is hot," I said.

I poured water over the fresh coffee grounds and watched the container fill up, and when the level went down, I poured in more water. Now the aroma of the coffee had taken over from the ladies' powder, or maybe it was because I was closer to the coffeepot than I was to the table.

"Get some dishes out of that safe," I said to Vivian. "Cups and saucers, and four plates for cake."

"Grant?"

"Just do what I said," I told her.

She brought the four cups and saucers to the stove on a tray, and I poured hot water into one of the cups. Vivian rinsed out all the other cups and poured the water into the dishpan on the window shelf. She set the tray of cups on the shelf and went back to the safe and began to cut slices of cake and put them on plates. By the time she had finished, enough coffee had dripped and I was pouring it into the cups. Vivian put a fork on each plate and placed cake before the women. They said thanks, but they said it quietly. Vivian came back to the window for the coffee. Everyone said thanks again.

"Thank you, ma'am," my aunt said politely.

My aunt knew how to make you feel that she was of a lower caste and you were being too kind to her. That was the picture she presented, but not nearly how she felt.

Vivian and I went out onto the porch.

"I'm glad to get out of there," Vivian said.

"She's pulled that jazz on others," I said. "It's not going to work this time, though."

"Well, I see that mine are not the only ones," Vivian said.

"It's not the same thing," I said. "Far from being the same thing."

Vivian became very quiet. Then: "Well, I better be going."

"Something I said?"

"No. It's getting late, that's all. I have to get my purse and tell them goodbye."

She went back inside, and she must have stood a good distance away from the table, because I could hear them clearly from the porch.

"I come to say I'm leaving," Vivian said. "It was good meeting you all."

There was silence awhile, then I heard my aunt saying, "You're a lady of quality. Quality ain't cheap."

"Thank you, ma'am."

"Don't give up God," my aunt said. "No matter what, don't ever do that."

"Yes, ma'am."

"You're a lady of quality," my aunt repeated.

"And a pretty young lady too," Miss Eloise said.

"That's for sure," Inez chipped in. "A pretty young lady. Good manners. Quality is what you have. Quality."

They were quiet again. Maybe they didn't have any more to say. Vivian came back outside, and we went out to the car.

"Well, what do you think of the place?" I asked her. "Still think it's pastoral?"

"It is pastoral," she said, looking around.

One of the Washington boys and a Hebert girl came from up the quarter, holding hands. They had just left church, the boy wearing a black suit, a white shirt, and a tie. The girl wore a light-blue coat over her dress. Both of them spoke to me at the same time, saying, "How you, Mr. Wiggins?" And they nodded to Vivian as they went by us, still holding hands. Good luck, I thought to myself.

Vivian was watching them too, as they continued down the quarter. "I'm glad I met your aunt and her friends," she said.

"They'll have a lot to talk about," I said.

"You think I did okay?"

"With all that quality, how could you fail?"

Vivian smiled without opening her mouth. I kissed her on the tip of her nose.

"Uh-uh," she said. "Not in public. I have too much quality for that."

16

▼

I WAS WALKING around the schoolyard with my ruler when I saw my aunt, Reverend Ambrose, and Miss Emma come back down the quarter after seeing Jefferson. The car stopped in front of Miss Emma's house, and the three of them got out and went into the yard. Reverend Ambrose looked over his shoulder toward the church, but the picket fence kept him from seeing me. After they had gone inside the house, I continued around the schoolyard, slapping my leg with the ruler. It was a quarter to three, nearly time to dismiss the children for the day.

I reentered the church through the front door. Irene Cole and another girl and a boy stood at one of the blackboards. We had discussed our Christmas program, and now they were writing down names of the students who would bring the Christmas tree as well as those who would decorate it. I went to my desk and tapped my ruler for attention.

"It's about time to go home. Any questions before we dismiss? Irene?"

"No, sir," she said, from the blackboard. "Marshall and Clarence and Aleck are getting the tree. Shirley, Odessa, and I will see that it's decorated. Mr. Joseph's got some lint cotton in his crib. And we can get some crepe paper from Miss Eloise. She said she had a lot left over from making the Mardi Gras hats."

"What about the tree, Clarence?"

"Guess we'll just go back in the pasture and get one like we did last year." He grinned.

"Do you think you might be able to find a little pine tree this time?"

"We'll try," he said, and laughed to himself.

The year before, the boys had brought in a small oak tree. They had dragged it through the mud all the way from the pasture, and by the time it got to the school, it had lost many of its leaves. The girls who were to decorate the tree had to wash it clean before putting on the lint cotton and crepe paper. It turned out to be a beautiful Christmas tree.

"One other thing before we dismiss class. I want you all to remember one person during this Christmas season. I'm sure I don't have to remind you who I'm thinking about. If there are no other questions, you may collect your things and leave. And I don't want to hear any noise out there in the quarter. Class dismissed."

After they had gone, I sat down at the table, looking over the test I had given the sixth graders in geography. The assignment was to draw a map of Louisiana and write in the names of the parishes in their appropriate places. After about five minutes, I heard footsteps entering the church, then saw that one of the boys had stopped halfway down the aisle. I knew what he was going to tell me.

"Miss Emma say on your way home, stop by."

I nodded my head, and he left, walking slowly until he got to the door, then he burst out running. I gathered up all my papers, and after closing and locking the back door, I went out through the front. Miss Emma's house was only a short distance down the quarter. They were sitting at the kitchen table drinking coffee when I came in.

"Some coffee?" Miss Emma asked me.

"No, ma'am. Thomas said you wanted to see me."

"Sit down, Grant," she said.

I could tell by the way she said it and by the silence of my aunt and Reverend Ambrose that things had not gone well at the jail. I pulled out a chair and sat down, facing Miss Emma. My aunt and Reverend Ambrose sat opposite each other.

"You didn't tell me the truth the other day, did you?" Miss Emma said.

"I don't know what you're talking about, Miss Emma."

"When you come back from seeing him."

"Sure, I told you the truth," I said.

"No." She shook her head, pressing her lips tight as she looked across the table at me. "He didn't like the food. He didn't ask about me."

"He did last Friday."

"No," she said, and shook her head again. " 'Cause I had to hit him today."

She stared at me, her lips pressed tight, and she lowered her head. Reverend Ambrose reached out and touched one of her arms as he said, "Sister Emma, Sister Emma." My aunt put her hand on the other arm and looked at me.

A couple of days later, Miss Eloise came up to the house, and from my room I could hear my aunt telling her what had happened.

Jefferson was asleep or pretended to be asleep when they got to the cell. The deputy rattled the big keys against the bars and called Jefferson's name before opening the door. After they had gone inside, the deputy locked the door and told them that he would be back within the hour. They could call if they wanted to leave earlier.

Jefferson lay on the bunk with his back to them, and there was no place for them to sit. Miss Emma managed to get a small place to sit by pushing him gently closer to the wall. She passed her hand over his head and his shoulder while she whispered his name.

"Ain't you go'n speak to me?" she said. "Ain't you go'n speak to your company?"

Finally, he turned, looking in their direction. He wasn't seeing them, my aunt told Miss Eloise. He acted as though they were not even in the room. His eyes were a total blank, my aunt said. "Just blank, blank," was how she said it.

"I brought you some food," Miss Emma told him. "I bought you a shirt too, a pretty shirt. You want to see it?"

She took a polo shirt from the paper bag and spread it out with both hands. But he showed no sign of seeing the shirt, or even of hearing Miss Emma. Reverend Ambrose went up to the bunk and said to him, "Young man, I pray for you every night, and I know the Lord is hearing my prayers. Put all your faith in Him, and He'll bring you through."

That touched something in him. He looked up at the reverend, and for a moment it seemed that he would say something, something cruel, mean, my aunt said. She said that standing back, looking at him, she could see his hate for Reverend Ambrose.

Miss Emma put the shirt back into the bag and opened the basket with the food.

"Come on, eat something for me," she said. "I brought all the best things you like."

"You brought corn?" his voice said. Not him, my aunt said, just the voice. He didn't show a thing in his face. His eyes were blank, blank, my aunt said.

"Corn?" Miss Emma asked.

He didn't answer her.

"Roast nyers?"

He looked at her, but he didn't answer. And his eyes were just blank—blank, blank, my aunt said. He could have been looking at the wall or the floor, for all the recognition he showed her.

"This ain't roast nyers season, Jefferson," Miss Emma told him. "That's in the spring. This November. Roast nyers all over now."

He didn't look at her with hate, as he had the reverend, but there was no pity either, my aunt said. He didn't show any feeling at all.

"Corn for a hog," he said.

"Corn for a hog? A hog, Jefferson? You ain't no hog, Jefferson. You ain't no hog."

"Th'ow something," he said.

"I'll never th'ow you nothing, Jefferson," Miss Emma said. "You th'ow a bone to a dog. Slop to a hog. You ain't no hog."

"That's all I'm is," he said. He turned away from her. "I didn't ask to be born."

"Jefferson?" Miss Emma said. "Jefferson?"

He wouldn't answer her. And she used all her great bulk to pull him over.

"You ain't no hog, you hear me? You ain't no hog."

"That's all I'm is," he said. "Fattening up to—"

She slapped him.

Then she fell upon him and cried, my aunt told Miss Eloise. My aunt and Reverend Ambrose went to the bunk and tried to pull her away, but she was still slumped over him when the deputy came back to let them go.

At her kitchen table now, as I sat there, Miss Emma looked at my aunt.

"What I done done, Lou?" she asked. "What I done done? What I done done my Master to deserve this?"

My aunt saw that she was going to cry, and she stood up and

put her arm around her shoulders. "Em-ma," she said. "Em-ma. The Lord is merciful."

"What I done done?" She was shaking her head and crying now. "What I done done my Master?"

"Have patience," my aunt said, patting her on the shoulder. "The Lord is merciful."

"What I done done," she cried, "to make my Master hate me so?"

"The Lord don't hate you, Sister Emma," Reverend Ambrose said, touching her on the arm. "The Lord is with you this moment. He is only testing you."

Miss Emma looked up at me. The tears were still rolling down her face.

"Go back," she said.

"Why, Miss Emma?"

" 'Cause somebody go'n do something for me 'fore I die."

"Why me?"

" 'Cause you the teacher," my aunt said.

I got up from the table.

"And where you think you going?" Tante Lou asked me.

"I don't know," I said. "But I'll go crazy if I stay here, that's for sure."

"You going back up there, Grant."

"What for?" I said. "What for, Tante Lou? He treated me the same way he treated her. He wants me to feel guilty, just as he wants her to feel guilty. Well, I'm not feeling guilty, Tante Lou. I didn't put him there. I do everything I know how to do to keep people like him from going there. He's not going to make me feel guilty."

"You going back," she said. "You ain't going to run away from this, Grant."

"Tante Lou," I said. I wanted to take her face in my hands. I wanted to hold her gently, gently, because anger and screaming were not working. Maybe gentleness would work better.

Maybe feeling my hands on her face would make her understand what I was trying to say to her. But as I moved toward her, I could see in her eyes that nothing I said was going to change anything. I left them at the table and went back home to my room.

17

BETWEEN MONDAY when I talked to Miss Emma, and Friday, when I visited Jefferson again, something had happened inside me, and I wasn't so angry anymore. Maybe it was the Christmas season and the children rehearsing their parts for the play. Or maybe it was just me. I could never stay angry long over anything. But I could never believe in anything, either, for very long.

At the jail, I had to go through the usual search. Then, while the young deputy and I walked down the corridor to the cellblock, I thought I would feel him out. Of the three of them at the jail, I figured he was the most likely to be honest with me. He was nearer my age, and he seemed better educated than the chief deputy or the sheriff. And I had heard from people in the quarter who knew his people that he had come from pretty good stock.

"How's he doing?" I asked.

"He's doing all right," the deputy said.

"Does he ever eat the food we bring him?"

"Some of it," the deputy said. "He leaves a lot of it, and we give it to the other prisoners, like she said. We've all eaten some of it. Good food, too."

"How do the other prisoners treat him?" I asked.

"They're just curious, that's all. But they don't bother him."

"Do they ever talk to you about it?"

"The execution?"

"Yes."

"Sometimes they ask me things. I tell them I don't know a thing about it. I've never seen an execution."

"Does he ever bring it up?"

"No. I'm sure he doesn't want to even think about it."

"He must think about it," I said. "He must, because I know I do. I've seen myself walking to that chair, more than once. I've woken up at night, sweating. How do you take it? That's the question."

"I suppose every man wonders about death sometimes in his life."

We came up to the landing just before the big door to the cellblock. The deputy stopped and looked at me.

"Listen," he said. "We might as well call each other by our names. You're Grant, aren't you?"

"Grant Wiggins," I said.

"Paul Bonin," he said.

We shook hands.

"Listen," he said. "I'm not going to get too close to him—okay?"

"Sure."

"I've been warned: you don't get too close to somebody going to be executed. Be decent, treat him right, but that's all. This can get messy before it's over, and I will do my duty."

"I feel the same way," I said.

We looked at each other a moment, then we continued to the cellblock.

"What's a day like?" I asked Paul.

"He eats one hot meal a day and a sandwich. Lots of beans, cabbage, potatoes, rice—you know. Sometimes the sandwich is the first meal. Ten in the morning, four in the evening. He can come out once a week and spend an hour in the dayroom. Walk, sit-ups, run—anything he wants. Most times he walks or just sits there at the table. Once a week he gets a shower. We have another prisoner give him a haircut. He's had one since he's been here. The barber can shave him, but you can see his face doesn't need shaving. That's about it."

"He talk at all to the other prisoners?" I asked.

"I never hear him."

The deputy opened the heavy steel door to the cellblock.

"Well, well, well, if it ain't Mr. Rockefeller," one of the prisoners said. He wore the green coveralls given to all the prisoners who did not have their own clothes. He also wore a red knit cap, his own. "Mr. Rockefeller always leave you chicken and biscuits," he went on. "But no bread for the cigarettes."

"Just cool it, Henry Martin," the deputy said. "You won't get chicken or biscuits either, you keep that up."

"I hope you brought some plarines," another prisoner said.

"Anything," another one said. "This jailhouse food 'nough to kill a man."

"Then don't eat it," Paul said to him.

"What? And starve to death? Uh-uh." The prisoner laughed.

We came down to the last cell, Jefferson's cell, and Paul let me inside.

"See you in a while," he said, as he locked the door.

Jefferson sat on the bunk, slumped forward a little, his big hands clasped together down between his legs. He was looking through the barred window toward the sycamore tree, where several black birds were perched on a limb.

"How's it going?" I said to him.

He nodded his head, but he didn't turn to look at me.

"I brought you some food."

"I ain't hongry."

"Well, you might get hungry later," I said, and set the large paper bag of food on the end of the bunk. "I was speaking to Paul, the deputy. He told me you always share with the other prisoners."

"If they want it, they can have it."

I looked at his back, then I went by him and stood under the window, facing him. He was still gazing upward, and I noticed his eyes, large and inflamed. Since my last visit he had gotten a very close haircut, which exposed the structure of his almost triangular head.

"Jefferson, we have to talk," I said.

He continued looking above my head toward the barred window.

"When your nannan came back from seeing you the other day, she broke down crying."

"Everybody cry," he said. "I cry."

"Is that what you want—her to come home crying every time she sees you?"

He didn't answer.

"You can keep her from crying," I said. "You can make it easier for her. You can do her that favor."

He continued to look above my head toward the barred window.

"She wants somebody to do something for her before she dies."

"That's 'fore I die," he said, lowering his eyes to look at me. He repeated it. "That's 'fore I die."

"Is it asking too much, Jefferson, to show some concern for her?"

" 'Cause I'm go'n die anyhow—that's what you trying to say?"

Now it was I who didn't answer.

"That's what you trying to say, Mr. Teacher?" he asked.

"We're all going to die, Jefferson."

"Tomorrow, Mr. Teacher, that's when you go'n die? Next week?"

"I don't know when I'm going to die, Jefferson. Maybe tomorrow, maybe next week, maybe today. That's why I try to live as well as I can every day and not hurt people. Especially people who love me, people who have done so much for me, people who have sacrificed for me. I don't want to hurt those people. I want to help those people as much as I can."

"You can talk like that; you know you go'n walk out here in a hour. I bet you wouldn't be talking like that if you knowed you was go'n stay in here."

"In here or out of here, Jefferson, what does it benefit you to hurt someone who loves you, who has done so much for you?"

"I never asked to be born."

"Neither did I," I said. "But here I am. And I'm trying to make the best of it."

"Like coming here vexing me?" he asked.

"Am I vexing you, Jefferson?"

He grunted. "Just keep on vexing me," he said. "I bet you I say something 'bout that old yellow woman you go with."

"You're speaking of Vivian?"

"Just keep on vexing me," he said.

"If you're talking about Vivian, it's Vivian who keeps me coming here."

"Keep on vexing me," he said. "See what I won't say. Just keep on vexing me."

"Go on and say anything you want to say, Jefferson."

"Keep on vexing me—bet you I'll scream," he said.

"So Guidry would come up here and tell me to get out, is that it? Is that it, Jefferson?" I had been trying my best not to become angry again. But nothing I said made a difference. He just sat there grinning at me. "Go on and scream, Jefferson. Go on and scream for Guidry, if that's what you want."

We looked at each other, and I could see in those big reddened eyes that he was not going to scream. He was full of anger—and who could blame him?—but he was no fool. He needed me, and he wanted me here, if only to insult me.

"Her old pussy ain't no good," he said.

My heart suddenly started pumping too fast. I made a fist of my right hand. If he had been standing, I would have hit him. If he had been anyplace else, I would have made him get up and I would have hit him. I would have hit any other man for saying that. But I recognized his grin for what it was—the expression of the most heartrending pain I had ever seen on anyone's face. I rubbed my fist with my left hand, and gradually I began to relax.

"That lady you spoke of, boy, cares a lot about you," I said to him. "She's waiting at that school right now for me to bring her news about you. That's a lady you spoke of, boy. That's a lady. Because it's she who keeps me coming here. Not your nannan, not my aunt. Vivian. If I didn't have Vivian, I wouldn't be in this damn hole. Because I know damn well I'm not doing any good, for you or for any of the others. Do you hear what I'm saying to you? Do you?"

I saw that grin slowly fade as he lowered his eyes toward the floor. When he looked up again, I saw tears in those big reddened eyes.

"Manners is for the living," he said. He looked at me awhile, then he swung around and knocked the bag of food off the bunk. The bag burst open on the floor, and there was fried chicken and biscuits and baked sweet potatoes all over the place. "Food for the living, too," he said.

When the deputy came back to let me out, I had picked up all the food and put it back into the torn paper bag, and I had placed the bag on the small steel shelf by the washbowl. Jefferson and I had not exchanged a word for fifteen minutes. He had lain down on the bunk facing the wall.

I heard Paul coming down the block, speaking to the prisoners, calling them by their first names, threatening this one with hard work, praising another one for being good. He looked at Jefferson as he let me out of the cell. Jefferson lay with his back toward us.

"How did it go?" he asked.

"Okay."

We went down the cellblock, and the prisoners asked me what I had brought Jefferson to eat. I didn't answer. Just before we reached the heavy metal door, Henry Martin yelled out to me, "Goodbye, Mr. Rockefeller. I'll be here when you come back."

"That's for sure," Paul said to him.

He opened the steel door, and we went out.

"Sheriff wants to see you in his office," Paul said.

"Is something the matter?"

The deputy shrugged his shoulders. "He just told me that he wanted to see you before you left."

The sheriff was talking on the telephone when Paul and I came into his office. The chief deputy was talking to the fat man whom I had seen at Pichot's house. The sheriff sat back in his chair, his cowboy boots propped on his desk. He was talking to someone at the state prison in Angola. The chief deputy and the fat man were talking about fishing at Old River. They continued their conversation for another five or ten minutes as if I weren't there. Paul stood beside me awhile, then he went into another office. I stood waiting.

The sheriff hung up the telephone and looked at me over the tips of his boots.

"Well, Professor, making any headway?" he asked.

"I don't know," I said.

"You been seeing him a month. You still don't know if you're making any headway?"

"No, sir."

The chief deputy and the fat man had quit talking, and they were looking at me too.

"You wouldn't be trying to hide something, now, would you?" the sheriff asked me.

"No, sir."

"Glad to hear that," he said. "Hear that, Frank? He ain't hiding nothing."

The fat man grunted and looked at me. Guidry drew his boots from the top of the desk and dropped his feet heavily to the floor.

"Women," he said. "Always coming up with something new. Now they want all y'all to meet in the bull pen—picniclike."

He looked at me as though I was supposed to know what he was talking about.

"Well, what do you think?" he asked me, when I didn't offer an answer.

"That's up to you, Sheriff," I said.

"Yes, I know that," he said. "But the things they come up with. They want to meet him in the dayroom or another comfortable room—'comfortable room'—where they can all sit down, 'cause they can't all sit down in that cell. You ever heard of anything like that before?"

"I don't know what you're talking about, Sheriff," I said.

"Don't you, Professor?"

"No, sir, I don't."

He regarded me awhile, and so did the chief deputy and the fat man. The deputy was looking very mean.

"You don't know they came up to my wife?" the sheriff asked me.

"I don't know a thing that you're talking about, Sheriff."

"They came up to the house and said they couldn't sit down and could she, 'please, ma'am,' speak to me about arranging a place so they can sit down—and you don't know anything about that?"

"No, sir, I don't."

"You playing with me, Professor?" the sheriff asked.

"Sheriff, I just don't know what you're talking about."

I would learn later. Miss Emma, my aunt, and Reverend Ambrose had visited the sheriff's wife a day after they had last seen Jefferson. The sheriff's wife greeted them graciously and set a precedent by having them sit in the living room, while her maid served them coffee. They talked about little things before they came to their purpose in coming there. The sheriff's wife was stunned. She nearly spilled her coffee. What was wrong with the cell? Wasn't it big enough? Yes, but they couldn't all sit down. Was it necessary that they all sit down at the same time? Couldn't they take turns? She was sure that Reverend Ambrose didn't mind standing. And maybe Jefferson could stand up too, and let Tante Lou and Miss Emma sit down.

It was then that Miss Emma reminded the sheriff's wife of all the things she had done for the family over the years. The sheriff's wife was suddenly taken with a splitting headache. She wondered where the maid had gone to, but she didn't call for her. She frowned and rubbed her temples. She told Miss Emma that she would see what she could do. "But don't count on it," she said. "The sheriff makes up his own mind in these matters."

"Just speak to him, if you don't mind," Miss Emma said. "I done done a lot for you and your family over all these years."

"Oh, Lord, do I know," the sheriff's wife said. "Do I know, do I know, do I know. I'll speak to the sheriff. Lord, I'll be glad when all this is over."

Miss Emma dropped her coffee cup on the floor and started calling on God.

"I didn't mean it that way," the sheriff's wife said. "God in heaven knows I didn't mean it that way. Lou, Reverend Ambrose—can't y'all do something? The Lord knows I didn't mean it that way."

"Women," the sheriff said to me. "Always coming up with something new." He looked at his deputy. "Well, Clark? What do you think?"

Clark's gray eyes looked like marbles in his big face.

"Let him stay where he's at."

"My sentiments exactly," the sheriff said. "But if we put him in handcuffs and leg chains?"

"I wouldn't even bother," Clark said.

"I wouldn't either," the sheriff said. "But you got these women."

"He ain't here for no picnic," Clark said. "He killed Mr. Gropé. Let him stay right there in that last cell. Till that last day."

"What you say, Frank?" the sheriff asked the fat man.

The fat man shrugged his shoulders. "I'm just standing here."

"I'll go to him, and I'll leave it up to him," the sheriff said to me. "If he wants to come in the dayroom in shackles—all right. If he wants to stay in his cell unshackled—all right. But cell or dayroom, if I notice any aggravation, I stop all visits. You see, I know you haven't done a thing yet. Boys on the block tell me you haven't done a thing. And I doubt if you ever will."

I didn't answer him. But I was thinking, Sheriff, you don't know how right you are.

"You can take her this message," the sheriff said. "He can meet her in the dayroom if he wants, but he will be shackled. Every moment of the rest of his life, he's going to know he's in jail, and he's going to be here till the end. This ain't no school, and it ain't no picnic ground. All right?"

"Yes, sir."

"Good. I'll see you later, Professor."

18

▼

AS HE HAD PROMISED, the sheriff went to Jefferson and asked him if he would like to meet his visitors in the dayroom instead of his cell. The sheriff explained that he would be shackled hand and feet there. He also told Jefferson that it was entirely up to him and that his wishes would be carried out.

"If that's what they want," Jefferson said.

"No, not what they want; what you want."

"If that's what they want," Jefferson repeated.

"Is it yes, then?"

"If that's what they want," Jefferson said. "I'm go'n die anyhow."

When Miss Emma and my aunt and Reverend Ambrose went to the courthouse, they were led to the dayroom by the young deputy, Paul. The large room contained three tables, made of steel, with benches attached on either side, also of steel. There were no other visitors in the dayroom, and Miss Emma selected the center table. Paul told them that he would be back in a few minutes. While he was gone, Miss Emma took out the food and placed it on the table. She set places for four, two on either side of the table. My aunt and Reverend Ambrose stood back, watching her. My aunt would say later that Miss Emma went about setting the table the same way she would have done at home, humming her 'Termination song to herself.

"This go'n be his place, and this go'n be my place," she said. My aunt said that Miss Emma, still humming to herself, passed her hand over the table to make sure there was no dust, no specks there—just as she would do at home. "That's your place there, Lou, and that's yours right there, Reverend Ambrose," she said. "Don't it look nice? Ain't this much better?"

My aunt and Reverend Ambrose agreed that it looked nice and that it was much better than the cell.

Then they heard the chains. And a moment later, the door at the far end of the room opened and Jefferson came in, followed by the deputy. Jefferson had not been chained before, and he took long steps that caused him to trip, my aunt said. He came to the table like somebody half blind, and he didn't sit down until Paul told him to do so. Paul told him that he had to stay in that one place until he was returned to his cell.

"He ain't go'n move," Miss Emma said. "I'm go'n see to that. I thank you kindly."

"You understand, don't you, Jefferson?" Paul said.

"I yer you," Jefferson said.

"He go'n mind," Miss Emma said. "I'm go'n see to that."

"Y'all have a good dinner," Paul said, and left.

"He come from good stock," Miss Emma said. "Y'all sit down. Well, Jefferson, how you feeling?"

He did not answer her. He sat with bowed head, his cuffed hands down between his knees under the table.

My aunt and Reverend Ambrose sat down. Miss Emma dished up the food. Mustard greens with pieces of pork fat mixed in it. There was stewed beef meat, rice, and biscuits. A little cake for dessert, my aunt said.

"You go'n eat for me, Jefferson?" Miss Emma asked him.

He kept his head bowed, his shackled hands under the table, and he did not answer her.

"You'll eat if I feed you?" she asked.

When he did not answer her, she dished up a small piece of meat and some mustard greens on the spoon and held it up to his mouth. He would not open his mouth. Miss Emma looked at my aunt, and my aunt, who had been trying to eat, could see all the hurt in her face.

When I came up there a couple of days later, the chief deputy told me I could meet Jefferson in his cell or in the dayroom. I told him it didn't matter to me where we met. The chief deputy told me it didn't matter to him either, but he told Paul to take me to the dayroom.

I sat at the center table, just as Miss Emma and my aunt and Reverend Ambrose had two days before. And I heard the chains out along the cellblock before I saw anyone. Then they came in, Jefferson in front, shackled, walking with short steps, his head bowed and his shoulders stooped. They came up to the table, and Paul told him to sit down. He sat without looking at me, his shoulders hanging low and closer together than they should be.

"I'll be back," Paul said.

"Can we walk?" I asked him.

"He had his exercise," Paul said. "I'll have to ask Clark."

"No, that's all right," I said. "Maybe next time."

Paul left.

"How's it going?" I said.

"Aw right," Jefferson said, without raising his head.

"You want to eat something?"

"I ain't hungry," he said.

"Yes you are," I said. "I know I am."

There was store-bought bread, fried pork chops, and baked sweet potatoes. I put some of it in front of him and some in front of me. I started eating.

"Come on, eat something," I said.

He raised his head slowly and studied me awhile. He had lost some weight. What had been a round, smooth face when he first came here was beginning to show some bone structure. His eyes were still bloodshot. I had seen them many times in my sleep the past month.

"What you want?" he asked me.

I was eating. I shrugged my shoulders.

"Just want you to eat something, that's all."

"What you want?" he asked again. His expression hadn't changed, and there was no change of inflection in his voice. His reddened eyes accused me of wanting something without saying it.

"Us to talk," I said.

" 'Bout what?"

"I don't know," I said. "Anything you want to talk about. What do you want to talk about?"

"That chair," he said. He watched me now, because he knew he had caught me off guard.

I looked at him a moment, then I started eating again. That chair was the last thing that I wanted to talk about.

"We're starting our Christmas program," I said. But I could see that he was thinking about other things. "You remember those Christmas programs when you were in school?"

"It's Christmas?" he asked. But he was not thinking about Christmas; he was thinking about something else. And he knew that I knew he was thinking about something else.

"No, Christmas is still a few weeks off," I said. "But we're getting ready."

"That's when He was born, or that's when He died?" he asked.

"Who?" I said.

He looked at me, knowing that I knew who he was talking about.

"Born," I said.

"That's right," he said. "Easter when they nailed Him to the cross. And He never said a mumbling word."

I had not finished eating, but I knew I couldn't eat any more. I put the rest of the pork chop and the slice of light bread on the napkin before me.

"Jefferson, do you know what 'moral' means?" I asked him.

He looked at me, knowing that I knew what he was thinking about.

"Obligation?" I said. "Do you know what 'obligation' means?"

He didn't answer. But he kept looking at me.

"No matter how bad off we are," I said, "we still owe something. You owe something, Jefferson. Not to me. Surely not to that sheriff out there. But to your godmother. You must show her some understanding, some kind of love."

"That's for youmans," he said. "I ain't no youman."

"Then why do you speak, Jefferson?" I said. "Human beings are the only creatures on earth who can talk. Why do you talk? And wear clothes? Why do you wear clothes?"

"You trying to get me wool-gathered," he said.

"I'm not trying to confuse you, Jefferson. She loves you, and I want you to give her something. Something that she can be proud of."

"Hogs don't give nothing. Hogs don't leave nothing," he said.

"Jefferson, do you like coming out here, or you prefer staying in the cell?"

"Anything y'all want," he said. "Don't matter to me."

"It matters to her, Jefferson. Out here she can sit down."

He grunted. "I'm the one go'n have to sit down."

"You can be kinder to her, Jefferson. Every time she comes up here, she comes back to the quarter looking worse and worse."

"She ought to stay home," he said.

"All she'd do is worry more if she didn't see you."

"Hogs don't worry. Hogs just know," he said.

"Hogs don't know anything, Jefferson," I said. "Only human beings know. Only human beings worry."

"This hog know. Fattening up for Christmas. Kill him at Christmastime," he said.

"Nobody is going to die at Christmas," I said.

"How you know? They told you?"

"Nobody told me anything," I said. "I just know. Nothing is going to happen at Christmas."

"I be glad when it's over," he said. "Old hog get him some rest then."

"Do you want me to leave, Jefferson?"

"Leave when you want. Old hog don't care."

He lowered his head. The chains jangled under the table. I wanted to leave, but it was too early: the sheriff would have had his proof that I hadn't reached Jefferson, that I was giving up.

"They found a pine tree this year," I said. "A nice little pine tree."

His head was bowed. He didn't answer. His hair had begun to grow back, but you could still see the big bones of his skull.

A half hour later, Paul came in to return him to his cell. Jefferson walked in short steps, his head bowed, his arms hanging low, his shoulders too close together. After locking him in, Paul came back to the dayroom, and he and I walked down to the main floor together.

"What do you think?" he asked.

"I don't know. But that's what she wants."

Paul nodded. He understood. He had come from good stock.

I went back of town to the Rainbow and had a couple of beers. When I figured Vivian would be out of class, I drove over to the school. One of the teachers was directing the children onto the bus, and Vivian and another teacher stood by the flagpole, talking. Vivian saw me and came over and got into the car.

"Hi," she said, and kissed me.

"A drink or a sandwich?" I said.

"A drink's not too bad," she said.

I pulled away from behind the bus where the teacher was still commanding the children, and we went back to the Rainbow. The place was quiet and dark, and we sat at a table far over in the corner. The teachers who were already there knew that we wanted to be alone. The waitress hadn't come in yet, so Claiborne brought us our drinks. After he left, Vivian looked across the table at me.

"I don't think we ought to go to Baton Rouge tonight," I said.

Vivian drank and set her glass back down and looked at me, waiting for me to go on. We had talked about going to Baton Rouge that night, but she knew I had seen him today, and we had been noticing that after my visits with him, things did not always go well for us in bed.

"How's the program going?" I asked her.

"All right," she said, waiting.

"Mine's about the same," I said. "The children found a nice little pine tree this year. Before, it was oak or anything else they could find. But this year, a little pine tree; not very tall, but nice. Nice and round."

Vivian nodded. She was looking at me closely.

"I love you more and more," I said. "If you'd just say the word, God knows I'd drop everything."

"And hate each other for the rest of our lives, Grant? No," she said.

"I could never hate you—ever."

"You could, and you would," she said.

"No," I said.

"Yes, Grant, you would hate me for letting you make this decision. Or I would hate you for doing it."

"I'm not doing any good up there, Vivian," I said. "Nothing is changing."

"Something is," she said.

19

IT WAS COLD and it rained for the two weeks preceding our Christmas program. It rained too much for the people to go out into the field to cut cane, and the field and the roads were too muddy for the cane to be brought to the derrick for loading and then shipment to the mill for grinding. People stayed at home around the fireplace or near the stove in the kitchen. You could see gray-blue smoke rising from the big chimneys in the fronts of the houses and from the smaller chimneys in the backs. And because the wind always came into the quarter from the river this time of year, you could see the smoke drifting from the quarter back across the field toward the cemetery and the swamp. The only time you were likely to see someone out in the yard was to cut more wood to throw onto the fireplace or put into the kitchen stove. The rest of the time, the quarter was deserted, the doors and windows shut tight against the cold wind and the rain.

There was still a light drizzle on the night of the program, but it did not keep the people away. I had told the students that this program should be dedicated to Jefferson, and they had taken the message home, and many people who had never attended a Christmas or graduation program came to the church that night. The program began at seven o'clock, but people were there much earlier. Because of the rain, they could not drive cars in the quarter, so they either walked or came by wagon. Reverend Ambrose, who lived up the river and not on the plantation, parked his car along the highway and walked to the church. As usual, he was dressed in a dark suit, white shirt, and dark tie, but tonight he also wore a yellow slicker. Most of the other people wore their "going-to-town" clothes. Not their everyday working clothes, and not their Sunday best either. Going-to-town clothes were old clothes, but without any visible patches. The shirts and the dresses may have been faded, but they were clean and they were neat.

No one lingered outside, as they would have had the weather been better. After scraping off their shoes on the bottom step, they kicked the mud on the ground and came inside the church. The womenfolks who had brought food set their pots or pans or bowls on the tables that we had placed against the blackboards in the back. Mrs. Sarah James, who had arrived at six-thirty, sat guarding the food until after the program, when everyone would eat. The other women took vacant seats as close to the heater as they could get. The men and the older boys stood in the back, talking, until the womenfolks told them to sit down.

I was behind the curtain with the students who had been chosen to participate in the Christmas play. The curtain was made up of four bedsheets, suspended from a wire that extended from one side of the church to the other. Three of the sheets were very white; the fourth was a light gray. This one belonged to Miss Rita Lawrence, and as long back as I could remember, she had insisted on contributing something to the Christmas program, and every time it was a sheet, probably the same one, and it was never as white as the others. The audience always knew which sheet was Miss Rita's, and they thought it was embarrassing to have it hanging up there with all the others, but no one had the courage to speak to Miss Rita about it, and each year it was one of the four that made up the curtain.

Irene Cole and Odessa Freeman were assisting me in preparing the students behind the curtain. The two shepherds wore brown crokersacks over their dress clothes, and each of them carried a tall bamboo cane curved at the top and tied with black thread. The three wise men wore crepe-paper robes. The robes were red, green, and yellow. Irene and Odessa continued to remind the wise men to be careful not to tear their robes by moving around so much. Mary, the mother of Jesus, wore a wrinkled blue denim dress to show that she was a poor woman. Joseph, her husband, had on overalls and carried a hammer in the loop of his pants. Baby Jesus was a white alabaster doll dressed in a long white gown. The girls in the choir wore white dresses, the boys white shirts.

Every so often I would part the curtain to see how many people had come in. Miss Rita Lawrence and her big grandson, Bok, were two of the first people there and sat up front, with Bok taking up almost a third of the bench. Twice Bok had been sent to the mental institution at Jackson, but the doctors there knew he was not dangerous and felt they could do no more for him than Miss Rita probably could do for him at home, and after keeping him a week or two they sent him back to her. Bok had one peculiarity other than being unable to look after himself, and that was his love for marbles. He carried them with him all the time. He sat there now, playing with the marbles in the right pocket of his overalls. Miss Rita occasionally had to touch him on the hand to keep them quiet.

On the bench with Bok and Miss Rita sat Julia Lavonia, who

had two children in the program, the boy as one of the shepherds, and the girl as Mary, mother of Jesus. James, her husband, was not there. A short, big-headed mulatto with curly
black hair and gray eyes, he had told me once that he had better
things to do than go to a coon gathering. But Julia was there, and
I knew that she had brought pecan and coconut pralines, just as
she did every year. The Freemans had come in too. Joe Freeman
sat far in the back, but his wife, Harriet, and her mother, Aunt
Agnes, and several of the children were up front, directly behind
Miss Rita, Bok, and Julia Lavonia. The Coles, Irene's people, sat
behind them—Norman and his wife, Sarah, Sarah's mother,
Lelia Wells, Sarah's sister, Esther, and Esther's boyfriend,
Henry, and two or three children. Sarah usually brought crack-
ling and baked sweet potatoes to the Christmas program.

On the other side of the aisle, in the front row, and still
wearing their overcoats because they were far from the heater,
sat my aunt and Miss Emma, Miss Eloise Bouie and Inez.
Behind them were Farrell Jarreau and his little wife, Ofelia.
Ofelia was a delicate mulatto woman whose sisters came to the
plantation every Sunday morning to take her to the Catholic
church in Bayonne. She would return late in the evening, and we
would hardly see her again until the next Sunday, when she
would climb into the back of the car to go to mass. I supposed
it was her husband, Farrell, who got her out tonight, because she
had never come before. Behind them sat most of the Martin
family—about ten of them—most, but not all. The father, Her-
bert, was not there, and neither was the idiot boy, Jesse, or the
pregnant daughter, Vera, or the old grandmother. But Viola, the
mother, was there, along with eight or nine of her children. Two
others were in the choir, behind the curtain. The Williamses
were there—four of them; three Ruffins—mother, son, and
daughter—were there. The Griffins, Harry and Lena, with their
two grown-up unmarried daughters, Alberda and Louberda,
were there. So the church was nearly full, and it was only a
quarter to seven. The bad weather had not kept them away but

probably had brought them out tonight. Since they could not work in the field or in their gardens, they had no reason to stay at home, claiming to be tired.

At seven o'clock I parted the curtains and stepped out to face the audience. I told them how happy the children and I were to see them all here tonight and that I knew they would enjoy the program because their children had worked so hard the past weeks to make it a success. I invited Reverend Ambrose, who sat in one of the side pews, to lead us in prayer. He stood and asked all to stand and bow their heads. The Lord's Prayer was first. Then he thanked God for letting us see a brand-new day and for allowing us to gather together in His house in such inclement weather. (The minister was a small man and seemed timid, but he did possess a strong, demanding voice when he prayed.) He asked God to go with all the sick and afflicted, both at home and in the hospitals across this land. He asked God to visit the jail cells all over the land and especially in Bayonne and to go with the guilty and the innocent. He asked God to go with all those here tonight who did not know Him in the pardon of their sins and thought they did not need Him. No matter how educated a man was (he meant me, though he didn't call my name), he, too, was locked in a cold, dark cell of ignorance if he did not know God in the pardon of his sins. He closed by beseeching God to look down upon this humble little church and bless this gathering.

The people responded with "Amen" and sat back down. My aunt said "Amen" louder than anyone, and she was looking directly at me.

I went behind the curtain and, taking one of the middle sheets while a student did the same on the other side, pulled the curtain back to reveal the stage. The choir of a dozen boys and girls moved down below the altar to sing "Silent Night." Irene Cole directed them. I stood behind the gathered curtain on the right so that I could watch both the choir and the audience.

The children had worked hard, and they sang beautifully—

and this, too, was due to the bad weather. At any other time they would have had to go home to work in the field or around the house. But since the weather had been so inclement—to use one of Reverend Ambrose's words—they had had more time for practice. The audience appreciated the singing. Even those who did not respond with "Amen, Amen" gave the choir their closest attention. So did Bok. Once he raised his hand to point, a sign to show how affected he was by the singing, but Miss Rita took the hand gently and brought it to his knee. She kept her hand on his, not pressing it, but comforting him.

After "Silent Night," the choir sang "O Little Town of Bethlehem," and my eyes left the audience, and I looked at the little pine tree stuck in the tub of dirt, decorated with strips of red and green crepe paper and bits of lint cotton and streamers of tinsel and a little white cardboard star on its highest branch. And under the tree and propped against the tub was one lone gift, wrapped in red paper and tied with a green ribbon and with a red and green bow. The children had contributed nickels, dimes, quarters—money they had made from picking pecans— and Irene, Odessa, and Odeal James had gone to Baton Rouge and bought a wool sweater and a pair of wool socks.

The people sitting up front could see the package, and they knew who it was for, and at times I could see their eyes shifting from the choir toward the tree, and I could see the change in their expressions.

But "Jingle Bells," a gayer and livelier song than the previous two, brought everyone's attention back to the choir, and I could catch in people's faces relief from their thoughts.

Odessa Freeman's " 'Twas the Night before Christmas" followed, and it was more than a simple recitation; it was a dramatic performance. In her long white dress with long sleeves, and with her black hair, recently straightened and shining, combed back and tied with a white silk ribbon, and her body swaying, and her arms spread out one moment, then closed so that the palms of her hands came together, and her voice rising to fill the church, then falling to a whisper that you could barely hear—Odessa not only made you see the room where the stockings were hung, but enabled you to hear the reindeer on the roof and hear Santa before you saw him come down the chimney to fill the stockings. You heard him call the name of each reindeer after ascending the chimney, and you actually watched the reindeer going to the next house in the quarter. It was so real that Bok felt it too and pointed again, and Miss Rita nodded that she understood his feeling, and she drew back the hand and placed it on his knee and kept her own hand on his to comfort him.

Following the poem came an essay, "The Little Pine Tree," written and read by Albert H. Martin III. He told of all the other Christmas trees over the years—of oak, of cypress, of strange bushes that could not be named. He told of how the trees had been cut in the pasture and dragged back to the quarter and how the girls had washed the leaves to make the tree presentable. Then he came to the little pine tree: not a great tree—it was not tall, not blessed with great limbs—but it was pine, and it was the most beautiful of all the Christmas trees. The little pine tree even took on a character of its own, it was so happy to be here. While he spoke, Albert Martin III gestured toward the tree, and everybody looked at the tree and at the single gift underneath it.

"Hark! the Herald Angels Sing" came next, and led into the nativity scene. As the song ended, two shepherds in their crokersack robes came onstage behind the choir. The shepherds were attending their flock, when suddenly a light appeared on the back wall under the pictures of Christ and Reverend Ambrose. The light came from a flashlight held by a student from stage right.

Shepherd One: (Pointing) A star in the east.

Shepherd Two: And so bright.

Shepherd One: What does it mean?

Shepherd Two: Wish I knowed.

(Shepherd One looked at Shepherd Two as if he were about

to correct his grammar, but changed his mind. No one in the audience seemed to have noticed.)

Three wise men enter from stage right, dressed in red, green, and yellow robes of crepe paper. (Several people in the audience snickered and made comments.)

Shepherd One: Wise men. They can tell us.

Shepherd Two: Tell us, O wise men. What yon star mean?

Wise Man One: It shines down on Bethlehem.

Wise Man Two: Little town of Bethlehem.

Wise Man Three: We must go to Bethlehem.

They all look at the star. (The star moved a little, as if the person holding the flashlight was getting tired.)

Shepherd One: But what it mean?

Wise Man One: In time you will know.

Shepherd Two: How we go'n know?

Wise Man One: He'll let us know.

Shepherd One: God on high?

Wise Man One: Works in mysterious way.

(The light moved again, as if the person was changing hands or giving the flashlight to someone else to hold.)

Wise Man Two: Wonders to perform.

Shepherd Two: But we ain't nothing but poor little old shepherds.

Wise Man One: The lowest is highest in His eyes.

Wise Man Two: Let us be off.

Wise Man Three: To yon Bethlehem.

The wise men leave stage right.

Shepherd One: Brightest star I ever seen.

Shepherd Two: Got to mean something.

(The star dipped down and came back up. Shepherd One looked at the person holding the light, and looked back at me to be sure I had seen it too.)

Shepherd One: Let us kneel down. Nothing will bother the flock tonight.

The shepherds kneel as the curtain closes. The curtain opens immediately afterward. We see Mary sitting on a bench holding baby Jesus. Joseph stands beside her, looking down upon the baby. A hammer hangs from Joseph's overall loop. Offstage right, people are heard approaching.

First Speaker: The star points yon.

Second Speaker: We close now.

Third Speaker: Yon. Yon. The stable.

The three wise men enter from stage right and immediately kneel down before Mary and baby Jesus.

Wise Man One: Surely, He come.

Wise Man Two: (Nodding) Him, all right.

Wise Man Three: Our Savior.

All Three: We bring Thee gifts, O Lord. (Each places a penny on the bench beside Mary.)

Mary: (Surprised) My little baby? Savior?

Wise Man One: (Nodding) Your little baby.

Mary: (Happy) My little baby. (She holds Him up to Joseph.) Look, Joseph. My little baby. Savior.

Joseph nods but does not speak.

Mary, rocking baby Jesus in her arms, begins to sing "Joy to the World, the Lord is come." The wise men stand and join her, and so does Joseph and the shepherds and the choir and all the others, including the boy who held the flashlight. As the song ends, they all bow to the audience.

While the children remained onstage, I asked Reverend Ambrose if he had any last remarks. Again he thanked God for allowing so many people to come out tonight. Again he reminded us that we were not all saved from sin. Even with book learning, we were still fools if we did not have God in our hearts. Again he asked God to go with those locked up in prison cells. He thanked God for all his blessings. And the congregation responded with "Amen, Amen, Amen."

I thanked the minister and told the congregation that that was our program for this year, and I reminded them that there were refreshments in the back.

The children waited onstage to hear what I thought of the program. I told them that it was fine, just fine. The children left the stage to get in line for food.

"Do you want me to bring you something, Mr. Wiggins?" Irene asked me.

"No, thanks," I said.

"Something the matter, Mr. Wiggins?"

"No. Why?" I said.

"You don't look too happy."

"I'm okay," I said. "Go on and get something to eat."

Irene left to get in line, but she looked back at me over her shoulder.

She was right; I was not happy. I had heard the same carols all my life, seen the same little play, with the same mistakes in grammar. The minister had offered the same prayer as always, Christmas or Sunday. The same people wore the same old clothes and sat in the same places. Next year it would be the same, and the year after that, the same again. Vivian said things were changing. But where were they changing?

I looked back at the people around the tables, talking, eating, drinking their coffee and lemonade. But I was not with them. I stood alone.

I saw one of the little Hebert girls coming up the aisle toward me, balancing a napkin of food on both her hands. She had to pass by the tree before reaching the pulpit. She watched the food all the time to be sure she did not drop anything.

"Miss Lou say bring you this."

"Thanks, Gloria."

I sat on a chair inside the pulpit, eating fried chicken and bread. The people were still laughing and talking. Just outside the pulpit was the little pine Christmas tree with its green and red strips of crepe paper for lights, its bits of lint cotton for snow, and the narrow strings of tinsel for icicles. And there was the lone gift against the tub of dirt.

20

IT WAS LATE FEBRUARY, and we were just over a month into the spring semester. I sat at the table, going over fourth-grade arithmetic papers while the children were out at recess. The older children could be heard playing ragball behind the church. In front, a group of smaller boys were shooting marbles, and several girls were jumping rope beside the church. I could hear the rope hitting the ground and the rhythmic handclapping and singing. The marble game was barely audible, but the ragball players behind the church were loud and clear, and it took all my concentration to go on with my work. The children had been outside about ten minutes, when I felt that one of them had come back inside and was standing down the aisle in front of me. I finished correcting the paper before looking up.

Farrell Jarreau stood in front of the table with his hat in his hand.

"Mr. Farrell?" I said, standing quickly.

He looked very small and very sad. He had come to tell me something, but he didn't know how to say it.

"Didn't mean to barge in," he said.

"I was just sitting here," I said, trying to put him at ease.

He looked at me and batted his eyes a few times.

"Is something the matter, Mr. Farrell?"

"They want you up there," he said.

He wanted me to read more into what he had said than he had told me.

"At the front?" I asked him.

He nodded. He wanted me to read more into his nod. I waited for him to go on.

"That boy." He fidgeted with his hat. He didn't want to say any more.

I waited.

"They done set the date," he said, but not wanting to say it. "They want you and Mose up there. They want y'all to tell her."

"When?"

"Right now, I reckon."

"I still have another hour of class."

"I just take they message, Professor."

He lowered his eyes and fidgeted with his hat again.

"Thank you, Mr. Farrell."

He nodded and started up the aisle, stoop-shouldered and very small. I saw him put on his hat as he went down the steps into the yard. When he came out into the road, he looked up the quarter toward the big house, but instead of going back to work, he turned left and went home.

I had followed him to the door, and now I went outside to tell the children that recess was over. They formed a double line, boys in one line and girls in the other, according to grades and sizes. After they had come in and sat down, I gave them assignments and told them I had to go up to the big house and that I was leaving Irene in charge. If anybody caused any trouble, I would deal with that tomorrow. I asked Irene to walk with me to the door, and I told her to dismiss the children at three o'clock. I didn't tell her why I had to go to the house.

The sky was overcast, and there was a chill in the air. Grinding was over, and the people had begun to chop up the ground for new planting. Flocks of blackbirds followed the tractors, searching in the fresh, uncovered earth for insects and worms. The plum tree in the Coles' front yard and the cherry tree in the Freemans' side yard were covered with blossoms, white and lavender. The pecan trees were bare, gray and leafless, but the live oaks and magnolias were full of leaves. The road was fairly dry, but the ditches on either side still held water from the heavy rain we had had during the past couple of months.

When I came up to Henri Pichot's house, I saw Reverend Ambrose's black Ford parked under the tree in the backyard. Inez opened the kitchen door when I knocked. The preacher sat at the table, drinking coffee. Inez asked me if I wanted a cup of coffee, but I said no. She left the kitchen. Reverend Ambrose asked me about my aunt. He had seen her at church only a few days before, but he didn't know what else to talk to me about. I told him she was all right. He wanted to know about school, and I said that everything was going pretty well there too. We were quiet then, because he could not think of anything else to say to me, and I had nothing to say to him. Inez came back into the kitchen and told us that Henri Pichot had called the sheriff and that the sheriff would be here in fifteen to twenty minutes.

"I hope this is not one of those days," I said. "I thought he was already here."

"You sure I can't get you a cup of coffee?" Inez offered again.

"No, thanks," I said. "I have a lot of work to do at school. I hope I don't have to hang around here all day." ⸘

"I'm sure he's on his way," Inez said.

Reverend Ambrose, who sat very close to the table, raised his coffee cup to his mouth, then returned it to the saucer quietly.

As promised, the sheriff was knocking on the front door about fifteen minutes later. His knock was not a request for entry; it was an announcement that he was already coming in. Inez sighed deeply, thanking God, and went to the front of the house. I heard the sheriff asking her if we were there, and a moment later she came back into the kitchen.

"They want y'all in the front," she said.

This was the first time I had been in any part of Pichot's house other than the kitchen, and I was sure that it was the first time for the minister as well. I waited for him to move first, but he was waiting on me. I made a respectful gesture for him to precede me, but he would not move, was afraid to move, until Inez took the lead.

Henri Pichot and the sheriff stood by the fireplace, talking. Pichot wore a brown and tan plaid jacket, a tan vest, an open-collar shirt, and dark trousers. Sheriff Guidry wore a gray suit, a string tie, and black cowboy boots. He held his cowboy hat against his leg. He and Pichot looked at us as we came into the room. I had never seen Pichot look so worried.

"Have a seat," he said. "The sheriff has something to say."

All the furniture in the room was old. Faded overstuffed chairs; an old overstuffed love seat; an overstuffed couch; and a rattan rocker with a pillow. The lamp tables were old, and the lamps and lamp shades looked just as old. Reverend Ambrose and I sat on the edge of the couch.

The sheriff sat in one of the chairs and held on to his hat, so I figured that what he had to say was not going to take very long. Henri Pichot stood at the fireplace, his back against the mantel. Behind him, a couple of smoldering logs sent a thin stream of gray smoke and an occasional spark up the chimney.

"The warrant came down from the governor today." Guidry spoke hesitantly. "It happens second Friday after Easter."

Inez came into the room with two cups of coffee on a silver tray. Pichot added sugar and milk to one cup and removed it from the tray. The sheriff rested his hat on one knee as he took the other cup from the tray. He added sugar, stirring slowly.

"I want things to go on as they have. Don't cause trouble for him." The sheriff looked at me. "When I left him he was calm, he seemed to understand. I want to keep it that way. Any questions?"

Reverend Ambrose and I exchanged glances, but neither of us had a question now.

"What about her?" Guidry asked. "The wife said she might need a doctor."

"That's mighty kindly," Reverend Ambrose said. "My thanks to Miss Edna."

"I'll send Dr. Gillory when I get back to town," the sheriff said. "Any other questions? I want us to have an understanding."

"Why that date?" I asked.

Guidry drank from his cup and looked over the rim at me. He did not like me; I was one of the smart ones. He and Pichot exchanged glances. I could tell that they had been talking about it before Reverend Ambrose and I came into the room. Pichot left the explanation up to the sheriff.

"Easter," he said. He did not want to go on, but he felt he should. After all, a man was going to be put to death. "It had to be before or after Easter. It couldn't happen during Lent."

I would learn later from the young deputy that the governor had originally signed an execution order to be carried out two weeks before Ash Wednesday. But one of his aides pointed out that another execution was scheduled during that time, and because of our state's heavily Catholic population, it might not go well to have two executions just before the beginning of Lent.

"Can we still visit him like we've been doing?" I asked.

"Sure," the sheriff said. "But just remember, keep it down. I don't want you aggravating him. He's got just over a month. April eighth."

"April eighth," I said to no one. "April eighth."

"Friday, April eighth, between noon and three," the sheriff said.

"Between noon and three," I said to no one.

"Well, if there ain't no more questions, I'll have to get on back to town," Guidry said.

He finished his coffee and set the cup and saucer on a lamp table.

"You won't forget the doctor, Sheriff?" Reverend Ambrose asked.

"You think she'll need him?"

"She ain't been too well lately," the reverend said.

"I'll call him from here," Guidry said. "Can he drive down the quarter?"

"It's passable," Pichot said. "I went down there yesterday."

The sheriff went to the telephone table and made his call to Bayonne. I could hear only part of what he was saying, because I could not get that date and time out of my mind. How do people come up with a date and a time to take life from another man? Who made them God?

"Audrey, let me speak to Sid," Guidry was saying over the telephone.

Twelve white men say a black man must die, and another white man sets the date and time without consulting one black person. Justice?

"The old woman," the sheriff was saying to the doctor. "I think she is the one who attended the trial. Worked for the family."

"His nannan," Reverend Ambrose said weakly.

The sheriff did not hear the minister. "Yes, it's passable, Sid. You won't get your brown and white shoes dirty."

They sentence you to death because you were at the wrong place at the wrong time, with no proof that you had anything at all to do with the crime other than being there when it happened. Yet six months later they come and unlock your cage and tell you, We, us, white folks all, have decided it's time for you to die, because this is the convenient date and time.

"Oh, she's all right, and how is Lucy?" the sheriff asked the doctor about his wife.

And on Friday too. Always on Friday. Same time as He died, between twelve and three. But they can't take this one's life too soon after the recognition of His death, because it might upset the sensitive few. It can happen less than two weeks later, though, because even the sensitive few will have forgotten about their Savior's death by then.

"Give Lucy my love," Guidry said. "I owe you one."

The sheriff hung up the telephone and turned to us.

"He's on his way. And I have to head on back myself. No other questions?"

We had no more questions.

"Thank you all for coming," Pichot said.

But he was not thanking us for gracing his home with our presence so much as he was telling us that it was time to leave. Reverend Ambrose and I got up from the couch and went back into the kitchen. Inez looked at us, crying. ⟵

"We must all show courage for Sister Emma's sake," Reverend Ambrose said to her.

Inez raised the end of her apron and wiped her eyes.

"You drove?" Reverend Ambrose asked me.

"I walked."

"Well, you can ride back down the quarter with me," he said.

"I'm not going back down there right now," I said. "I'm not going back down there and tell her he's going to die April eighth. Not me."

"You'd have the strength if you had God," Reverend Ambrose said.

"That's where you come in, Reverend," I said. "I'm going for a walk, a long walk in the opposite direction. Excuse me."

I went across the backyard out to the road, and I turned left and walked over to the highway and down to the river. The river still ran high from all the rain we had had in the past couple of months and from the water that drained into it from the bayous and fields. I walked in the ankle-high grass a safe distance from where the water flowed upon the bank, until I found a good place to stop. I could see the houses and trees on the other bank, and the cars moving on the road behind them. I tried wiping that away. I wanted to see nothing but miles and miles of clear, blue water, then an island where I could be alone. Or Vivian and me, just the two of us, and absolutely no one else. No one else.

But the river remained the same, high and muddy, and I started walking again. When I could go no farther without getting my feet wet, I went up the bank and walked alongside the road. I must have gone three or four miles before turning back. I figured that by now the minister and my aunt had seen Miss Emma, and the doctor had probably visited her, and other women in the quarter had gone to look after her too. It was near dark when I reached the quarter, and I went back to the church to get my satchel. Irene had collected all the papers and stacked them neatly on the table and had left me a note saying that the children had been orderly. I stuffed the note and the papers inside my satchel and left the church.

21

▼

TWO CARS WERE PARKED in front of Miss Emma's
house, and as I got closer I saw that one was Reverend Ambrose's. The porch light was on, and though I didn't feel like
going into the house, I thought I owed Miss Emma that respect.
The door was shut against the cold, but someone opened it
immediately when I knocked. The room was crowded and warm
from a nice fire in the fireplace. People spoke quietly, but still
it was noisy. Inez was there, and I asked her about Miss Emma.
She nodded toward the bed.

Miss Emma lay under a quilt, her head resting on two pillows.
The mosquito bar hung on the bed behind her. I asked her how
she felt. She did not answer; only a slight movement at the

corners of her mouth showed that she had heard me. Her eyes were looking at something that was not in the room. I left the bed and went into the kitchen, where most of the talking was going on. My aunt was in charge back there. As Miss Emma's best friend, she was taking over now that Miss Emma had taken to her bed. She was at the stove, making coffee. You could smell that Luzanne coffee all over the kitchen.

Reverend Ambrose was sitting at the table, talking to a couple of people who did not live in the quarter. He gave me a long, hard look to let me know what he thought of me, but I already knew what he thought of me, and I turned away from him. Irene, who was helping my aunt in the kitchen, asked me if I wanted a cup of coffee. I told her no, and I thanked her for taking over the class for me that afternoon. She told me she liked the practice; I knew that she wanted to be a teacher. My aunt heard us talking and turned from the stove to look at me. I could see in her face that she and Reverend Ambrose had had a conversation about me, and he had probably said some things that I would not care to hear. She told me that my food was on the back of the stove at home, but I would have to warm it if I wanted to eat. She had nothing else to say to me, and started talking to someone else. After I had been there ten minutes, I left the house.

At home, I lit a fire to warm the food—cabbage with salt pork and Irish potatoes. I didn't have to warm up the corn bread. I made a fire in my aunt's room so it would be warm when she came home, and I went around to my side of the house and lit a fire there too. By now the food was warm, and I went back into the kitchen to eat, sitting near the stove, with the plate balanced on my left hand. I had just finished eating and was washing the plate in the pan of soap water when I heard someone come up on the front porch. Vivian was at the door. We stood there looking at each other a moment, then she came in and took off her coat and galoshes. We went to sit at the fire in my room. I

told her the only thing I could offer her was a cup of coffee. We
went into the kitchen and warmed the coffee and returned to my
room to sit before the fire.

"After I heard about it, I knew I had to see you," she said.

"I was coming to you tonight."

"I didn't know that."

"I'm glad you came."

We finished our coffee, and I took the empty cups to the
kitchen and washed them. When I came back to the room, I
asked Vivian to lie on the bed beside me. We lay on our sides
for a while, then we lay on our backs, looking up at the ceiling.
The room's only light came from the fireplace.

"When are you going back?" Vivian asked me.

"I don't know," I said. "I'll have to talk to Miss Emma."

"Have you seen her?"

"She's in bed."

Vivian was quiet a moment.

"Is that her house up there where the cars are?"

"Yes."

"I wanted to stop in, but I didn't know if I should."

"You can go by before you leave."

"You think I ought to?" she asked.

"I want you to," I said.

"You think this is a good time?"

"I think so."

"I don't want to cause any trouble."

"You won't."

"I want them to like me," she said.

"They will. They'll have to."

"I don't want it that way."

"I'm going to live my own life, Vivian, and I hope you're part
of it. If they like it, it's all right; if they don't, it's the same."

Vivian was quiet. We were holding hands, lying very close
together with all our clothes on.

After fifteen or twenty minutes, we got up and got our coats;

Vivian put on her galoshes. Her car was parked behind mine in front of the house. I said that we could come back and get her car later. I told her to walk in my tracks so her galoshes would not get muddy. We could hear the people inside the house as we came onto the porch. There were more people at the house now, and we had to push our way through to reach the bed.

"I brought someone to see you, Miss Emma," I said.

Vivian moved closer to the bed, and Miss Emma's face showed that she remembered her. Vivian leaned over and whispered something to Miss Emma, and as she stood back, Miss Emma's eyes followed her. I could see in her eyes that she was pleased with what Vivian had said.

I introduced Vivian to others in the room, then we went into the kitchen. Tante Lou was at the stove, pouring hot water over the coffee grounds while talking to Mrs. Sarah James. Mrs. Sarah greeted me, and my aunt turned around and saw Vivian standing there.

"Miss Louise," Vivian said.

"Miss," Tante Lou said, very polite. She really knew how to be polite to people when she felt they were interfering with something that belonged to her. She would not look at me.

Irene Cole came into the kitchen, and she gave Vivian the same look—polite but cold. I introduced Vivian to her. Vivian nodded and smiled. Irene nodded but did not smile.

"I can get you a cup of coffee?" she asked Vivian.

"Yes, thank you," Vivian said. I knew Vivian didn't want the coffee, but it would have seemed impolite to refuse it.

With her cup of coffee, Vivian and I went into the front room again. Inez told me that Miss Emma wanted to speak to me before I left. I went back to the bed. Miss Emma nodded for me to sit down. The people who stood near the bed moved away so that Miss Emma and I could speak in privacy. Miss Emma looked up at me, and I was hoping that she would not start crying again. I felt very uncomfortable just sitting there.

"I don't know when I can go back up there," she said. She

was speaking slowly and just above a whisper. She was not trying
to keep others from hearing her, she had cried so much that she
could not speak any louder. "It's in your hands," she said. "You
and Reverend Mose. I just hope—I just hope—I just hope y'all
work together."

I looked away from her for a moment, but when I faced her
again, I saw that those eyes had not changed. I told her that I
would try, and I stood up and looked around for Vivian. She was
standing with one of my students by the door to the kitchen.
Vivian was nodding and smiling.

"That's your girlfriend, Mr. Wiggins?" the boy asked when I
came over.

"Yes," I said. "You're not trying to steal her, are you?"

"Sir?" The boy seemed surprised. "No, sir. She too old for
me."

Vivian laughed.

"You're about ready?" I asked her.

She took her empty coffee cup into the kitchen, and when she
returned to the front room, she went to the bed to let Miss
Emma know she was leaving. I saw Miss Emma watching her as
she came back to me.

"I need a stiff drink," I said, when we were outside. "You
don't have anything in your car, do you?"

"Nothing," Vivian said.

"What time is it?" I asked.

"Seven-thirty, quarter to eight," Vivian said, without looking
at her little wristwatch.

"It's still early. I'll follow you back to town."

"There's nothing closer?"

"Not unless I went to that back room at the corner store. You
know I can't do that."

It was dark after leaving the yard, and we walked single file
and close to the ditch until we reached the cars. I opened the
door, and Vivian got inside and rolled down the window.

"I'll see you at the Rainbow," I said, and kissed her.

I showed her a good place to turn around, then I got into my car and followed her red lights out of the quarter.

Twenty minutes later, we were sitting at a table at the Rainbow Club in Bayonne. I asked for a brandy setup, and Shirley brought us a half pint of Christian Brothers, a small pitcher of water, a bowl of ice, and four glasses. We drank the brandy straight up from two glasses, then we followed it with ice water from the other glasses.

"I think Irene is in love with you," Vivian said suddenly, as though she had been holding this in for a while.

"Just as my aunt is," I said.

"The other way," Vivian said.

"I can name about a dozen younger than Irene, and about that many old as my aunt, who are in love with me," I said. "But I love only one woman."

"Don't you think she loves you?" Vivian asked, seriously.

"Sure," I said.

"I mean it," she said. "I'm not playing."

"I mean it too," I said. I had taken a good shot of the brandy, and I was beginning to feel much better. "Irene loves me. My aunt loves me. The rest of them love me, too, and don't want an outsider taking me away from them. They want me for their own. Isn't that how it is everywhere?"

"I don't know anything about everywhere," Vivian said.

"Of course you do," I said. "It's the same old story. People want to keep a local boy for themselves, because they have so little."

"I'm not talking about the people," Vivian said. "I'm talking about Irene, with those big brown cow eyes."

"Big brown cow eyes?" I said.

"You know what I'm talking about," Vivian said.

"Don't tell me you're jealous of that child."

"Well?"

"Well, what?"

"Is she in love with you?"

"Well, I'll be damned," I said. I had taken another shot of the brandy.

"Well?"

"You still don't understand, do you?"

"I understand young gals—very well," Vivian said. "Do you?"

"I understand young gals, and old ladies too," I said. "And by the way, what did you say to Miss Emma to make her look at you the way she did?"

"I told her I was praying for both of them," Vivian said.

"That's the best thing you could have said."

"Get back to Irene," Vivian said. "She's the one we're talking about."

"Irene and my aunt want from me what Miss Emma wants from Jefferson," I said. "I don't know if Miss Emma ever had anybody in her past that she could be proud of. Possibly—maybe not. But she wants that now, and she wants it from him. Irene and my aunt want it from me. Miss Emma knows that the state of Louisiana is about to take his life, but before that happens she wants something to remember him by. Irene and my aunt both know that one day I will leave them, but they are not about to let me go without a fight. It's the same thing, the very same thing. Miss Emma needs a memory. Do you know what she told me when I sat on the bed? That Reverend Ambrose and I should get along, and together—together—we should try to reach Jefferson. Why not only Reverend Ambrose? Why not only the soul? No, she wants memories, memories of him standing like a man. Oh, she will meet him soon, and she knows that. But she wants memories, if only for a day, an hour, here on earth. Do you understand?"

"No," Vivian said. She wasn't drinking anymore.

"Let me explain it to you, let me see if I can explain it to you," I said. The brandy was really working well now. "We black men have failed to protect our women since the time of slavery. We stay here in the South and are broken, or we run away and leave them alone to look after the children and themselves. So each time a male child is born, they hope he will be the one to change this vicious circle—which he never does. Because even though he wants to change it, and maybe even tries to change it, it is too heavy a burden because of all the others who have run away and left their burdens behind. So he, too, must run away if he is to hold on to his sanity and have a life of his own. I can see by your face you don't agree, so I'll try again. What she wants is for him, Jefferson, and me to change everything that has been going on for three hundred years. She wants it to happen so in case she ever gets out of her bed again, she can go to that little church there in the quarter and say proudly, 'You see, I told you—I told you he was a man.' And if she dies an hour after that, all right; but what she wants to hear first is that he did not crawl to that white man, that he stood at that last moment and walked. Because if he does not, she knows that she will never get another chance to see a black man stand for her.

"And for my aunt and Irene it is the same. Who else does my aunt have? She has never been married. She raised my mother because my mother's mother, who was her sister, gave my mother to her when she was only a baby, to follow a man whom the South had run away. Just as my own mother and my own father left me with her, for greener pastures. And for Irene and for others there in the quarter, it's the same. They look at their fathers, their grandfathers, their uncles, their brothers—all broken. They see me—and I, who grew up on that same plantation, can teach reading, writing, and arithmetic. I can give them something that neither a husband, a father, nor a grandfather ever did, so they want to hold on as long as they can. Not realizing that their holding on will break me too. That in order for me to be what they think I am, what they want me to be, I must run as the others have done in the past." I drank. "Now do you see? Do you see?"

"Will that circle ever be broken?"

I drank some ice water to chase down the brandy. "It's up to Jefferson, my love."

22

WHEN I CAME INTO the office, Paul looked me straight in the face. He knew it was unnecessary to search me and the food, but he knew he had to do it. He also knew that he should not even think about not doing it. It was as much his duty as wearing the uniform and carrying the cell keys. But you could see in his eyes that he was wondering why. Even when he was searching me and not looking in my face, I could tell by the light touches on my pockets that he didn't want to do it. And with the food it was the same. The chief deputy sat behind the desk, watching everything. To him, this was how things were supposed to be and how they would be.

Paul and I left the office and walked down the narrow, dark corridor.

"Where would you like to meet him?" he asked.

"In his cell. I don't mind."

"You want me close by?"

"No, I don't think so."

"It can be different now," Paul said.

"I'll be okay," I said. "How is he?"

"He's taking it pretty good."

"Any changes?"

"I haven't noticed any."

We came up to the steel door to the cellblock.

"You sure you want to be alone?" Paul asked again. "You're the first visitor since that news."

"I'm sure I'll be all right."

"If you say so."

He opened the steel door. For the first time, the prisoners did not call to me or stick their hands through the bars as I passed. Some spoke quietly, others only nodded, but all were watching. Paul and I continued down the block to the last cell. Jefferson was lying on his back, staring up at the ceiling. Paul looked at me again. I nodded to him to indicate that I was not afraid and that I wanted to be alone with Jefferson. The deputy opened the cell door and let me in, then he locked it and left.

"How are you, Jefferson?"

"I'm all right."

"I brought you some food," I said.

His body took up the bunk, so I set the bag of food on the floor near his head. I went to the wall and stood under the window.

"You need anything, Jefferson?"

He shook his head.

"You want to talk about anything?"

He shook his head again. Then he just lay there staring up at the ceiling while I stood watching him.

"What day it is?" he asked, without looking at me.

"It's Friday, Jefferson," I said.

"Friday," he said to himself. "Friday."

He was quiet for a moment, then he slowly let his feet slide to the floor as he sat up on the bunk.

"Look like it's pretty out there," he said, gazing up at the window.

"Yes, it's a nice day," I said. "No clouds anywhere. Just blue."

"You think it's go'n be like that that day?" he asked.

I didn't answer him. He was looking out the window when he said it. Now he turned to me.

"I hope it's the kind of day you want, Jefferson," I said.

"The kind of day I want?" he said. "The kind of day I want? I never got nothing I wanted in my whole life. Now I'm go'n get a whole day?"

I didn't know what to say. He looked at me awhile, then he turned to the window again.

"Do you like fruit, Jefferson?" I asked him. "I can pick up some fruit—and some pecans. Ice cream? Funny books? Things like that."

"I want me a whole gallona ice cream," he said, still looking out the window. I saw a slight smile come on his face, and it was not a bitter smile. Not bitter at all. "A whole gallona vanilla ice cream. Eat it with a pot spoon. My last supper. A whole gallona ice cream." He looked at me again. "Ain't never had enough ice cream. Never had more than a nickel cone. Used to run out in the quarter and hand the ice cream man my nickel, and he give me a little scoop on a cone. But now I'm go'n get me a whole gallon. That's what I want—a whole gallon. Eat it with a pot spoon."

"I can bring you some ice cream anytime, Jefferson," I said.

"I'm go'n wait," he said. "I'm go'n wait. I want a whole gallon. Eat it with a pot spoon. Every bit of it—with a pot spoon."

He smiled. He smiled now because he had something pleasant to look forward to, though it would be on that last day. And he would save it until the very last moment.

"You want to hear about the news from the quarter?" I asked him. "Stella had her baby."

He looked at me, not as he had done in the past, in pain, with hate. He looked at me with an inner calmness now. Was it the ice cream?

"He favor Gable?" he asked.

"With little babies, they don't favor anybody too much," I said.

"Old Gable," he said, and smiled to himself. "Got hisself a baby, got hisself a baby." Then I saw the face change. He was no longer smiling but staring at the wall. "We was suppose to go hunting that day."

He had forgotten about the ice cream now. He was remembering the day he was supposed to go into the swamp with Gable but instead had ended up with Brother and Bear at the liquor store.

"Inez is still giving her fairs up the quarter," I said, trying to get him back. "But no music. No dancing. She calls that sinning. If you want your music at a fair, you have to go down to Willie Aaron's house. Willie still has that stack of old low-down blues—Tampa Red, Mercy Dee—you know, all of them."

He was not listening to me now. He seemed to be thinking about hunting with Gable.

"I just thought of something," I told him. "Let me bring you a little radio. You can have music all the time. You can listen to *Randy's Record Shop* late at night."

"Randy still on?" he asked, looking at the wall, not at me.

"Yes, he's still on," I said. "I was listening to him just the other night. I have to play the radio low so Tante Lou can't hear it. These old people, you know—all music except church music is sinning music. So I play it so low I can hardly hear it myself."

I laughed to make him laugh. But he did not.

"Do you want me to bring you a little radio next time I come?" I asked him.

He nodded. "Yeah."

"Edwin's has these little Philcos. Not too big," I said, and I boxed my hands to show him the approximate size of the radio. "Would you like one of those?"

He nodded.

"I wish I had the money on me," I said. "I'd go and get it right now."

"Don't bother," he said. He said it as though he didn't believe I really wanted to get it for him.

"I'll get it tomorrow," I said. "I'll have them bring it to you so you'll have music over the weekend."

He didn't have anything more to say. He sat there, not looking out the window now but looking down at the floor as if he had forgotten about the radio, about the ice cream, about Gable—about everything.

I wanted to leave then to go home for the money to buy the radio, but I was afraid that the sheriff and his deputies might misinterpret my reason for leaving so early. I was sure they were paying closer attention to everything now, and they would not have understood my reason for leaving earlier than I usually did. So I just stood there until the deputy came to let me out. Paul wanted to know how everything had gone between Jefferson and me, and I told him it was better than ever. He looked at me as if he felt I was making this all up, but I could see in his face that he wanted to believe it. I told him that I had promised Jefferson a radio and that I would go home and get the money to buy one. I would get it from Edwin's department store and then leave it here for one of them to take to Jefferson so that he would have music over the weekend. Paul thought it was a good idea, and he promised to give the radio to Jefferson himself.

I didn't go home. I thought I would borrow the money from Vivian, and I went back of town to the Rainbow Club, to wait until she got out of class. The bar was in semidarkness as usual, with the usual two or three old men, talking more than drinking, and Claiborne behind the bar, talking with them. I ordered a beer and told Claiborne about the radio. He didn't charge me for the beer, and he went back down the bar and spoke to the old men, then he came back with a couple of dollar bills and some change. He took five dollars out of an old leather wallet that had once been light brown but had turned almost black over the many years that it had gone in and out of Claiborne's back pocket.

"Thanks," I said. "I'll get it back to you sometime this week-end."

The muscle in his left jaw moved a little to show that he had smiled. Then he jerked his head toward the wall, a sign that I should go around to the other side and see what I could get in there. So after finishing the beer, I went through the side door into the café. It was much more brightly lit than the bar, warmer, and you could smell the food from the kitchen. A man and a woman ate at one of the tables, another man sat eating alone at the counter, and Thelma was behind the counter, near the cash register.

"Well, well, look what the cat dragged in," she said.

I had been at the Rainbow quite a few times lately, but I had not eaten in the café.

I told Thelma about the radio, and I told her that Claiborne had donated something. She listened patiently, and I could see her face changing from patience to sadness to anger. Her mouth tightened as she looked around the room at her three customers, then back at me again. The anger had left.

"You hungry?" she asked. It was stern, but loving too.

"No. I ate before I came," I told her.

She didn't believe me. "I got some smothered steaks there," she said. "Shrimps. Chicken."

"I'm not hungry."

"You want to get that radio now?"

"I would like to get it this afternoon."

"How much they cost?"

"About twenty dollars."

"Eat something. I'll make up the rest," she said.

She went back into the kitchen and dished up some rice and beefsteak and sweet peas, and she added a little lettuce-and-tomato salad and couple of slices of light bread.

"How much more you need?" she asked, after she had set the food down before me.

"About ten bucks," I said. "But listen, Thelma, I can borrow some of that money from Vivian."

"Vivian got them children," she said. "I can let you have it."

"I'll bring it back tomorrow."

"I ain't in no hurry."

I ate the food hungrily because I had not had dinner, and I sopped up the gravy with the light bread. Thelma watched me all the time. When I was finished, she put a wrinkled ten-dollar bill on the counter by my plate.

"Here."

It was the kind of "here" your mother or your big sister or your great-aunt or your grandmother would have said. It was the kind of "here" that let you know this was hard-earned money but, also, that you needed it more than she did, and the kind of "here" that said she wished you had it and didn't have to borrow it from her, but since you did not have it, and she did, then "here" it was, with a kind of love. It was the kind of "here" that asked the question, When will all this end? When will a man not have to struggle to have money to get what he needs "here"? When will a man be able to live without having to kill another man "here"?

I took the money without looking at her. I didn't say thanks. I knew she didn't want to hear it.

I went out to my car and drove back uptown. Edwin's was not the best store in town, but it was the place where most people bought what they needed. Those with money went either to Morgan's department store or to Baton Rouge and New Orleans. As you came into the store, you saw clothes for women on the left and clothes for men on the right, all set out neatly.

There were no other customers, and just one saleswoman, who did not show much interest in me. I went to the back of the store, passing the furniture department, with its chairs, couches, beds, chifforobes, dressers, then the refrigerators and iceboxes, gas and wood-burning stoves, washing machines. Then there was the garden and yard equipment—hoes, rakes, shovels, ax handles, mowing machines, yoyo blades, cane knives. And at the very end of the store were the radios and kitchen appliances, on shelves against the wall. I saw the little radio that I had in mind, and I took it down from the shelf to look at more closely and feel its weight. Then I set it back on the shelf and turned on the knob, and after warming up for a few seconds it started playing. I moved the lighted dial to get another station. I could find only three, two in Baton Rouge and one in New Orleans. But that was normal for this time of day. At night you were able to tune in others. You could get one as far west as Del Rio, Texas, and another as far east as Nashville. I was still listening to one of the Baton Rouge stations when the saleswoman came up behind me.

"You go'n buy that?"

I looked around at the short, stout, powdered-faced white woman.

"Yes, ma'am."

Her face changed, but only a little.

"How much is it?" I asked.

"Twenty dollars, plus tax."

"Do you have one in a box?"

"That one's brand-new," she said. Her face was getting hard again.

"It's a present," I said. "I would like one in a box."

"I can put this one in a box," she said.

"No, ma'am, I want a brand-new one," I said. "If you have one."

"You can have this one for a dollar less," she said.

"I prefer a brand-new one, please, ma'am," I said.

She snapped the radio off and turned away. She was gone about fifteen minutes. I knew it couldn't possibly take her that long to find another radio, but because I had refused to take the used one, and because she felt quite sure there was no place in Bayonne where I could find another one, she knew I had little choice but to wait until she got back.

"Brand-new one," she said behind me. "Seal ain't even broke."

"Does it have batteries?" I asked her.

"It's ready to play," she said. "You want it?"

"Yes, ma'am," I said.

She started up the aisle toward the cash register, but just about then another white woman came into the store. The clerk set the radio beside the cash register and went to see what the white woman wanted. The other woman was not buying anything; she only wanted to talk. So they stood there about ten minutes before the clerk came back to wait on me. After ringing up the bill, she asked me if I needed a bag. But she asked it in a way that I knew she didn't want to give me one. No, thanks, I told her, and after paying, I tucked the little radio under my arm and left.

The courthouse was to the right and across the street from the store. I walked between the parked cars and passed the statue of the Confederate soldier and the state, national, and Confederate flags. Paul and Sheriff Guidry were in the office. Paul saw the package under my arm, and I could see that he was happy that I had remembered. The sheriff looked up at me from his desk.

"Well, Professor, is that the radio?"

"Yes, sir. I hope you don't mind."

"No, I don't mind this time," he said. "But from now on, you ask permission before you bring anything else in here."

"I spoke to the deputy."

"The deputy can't give you permission to bring things in here. I do," he said.

I was quiet.

"Leave it," the sheriff said. "I'll see that he gets it. Batries, I hope."

"Yes, sir, batries," I said. I had almost said "batteries."

"How did it go today?" he asked.

"All right," I said.

The sheriff nodded.

"I'll see he gets it."

"Thank you, sir."

I looked at Paul. He nodded and smiled. He probably would have said something encouraging if the sheriff had not been there.

I went to my car and drove back to the Rainbow, hoping that Vivian would be there and that we would have a drink and just sit there in the semidarkness alone together.

23

▼

MISS EMMA FELT well enough on Monday to accompany my aunt and Reverend Ambrose to visit Jefferson. After the usual search, Paul led them to the dayroom, then went to the cell for Jefferson. Jefferson asked if he could take the radio. The deputy said no. Jefferson said he wouldn't go.

I would hear later that Jefferson had not turned the radio off since Paul brought it to him on Friday evening. The other prisoners could hear the radio at all times of the day and night. No one else had a radio, and the prisoners wished he would play it louder, but no one would dare say anything to him. The prisoners nearest his cell could faintly hear the music he played, but the ones farther away could only hear static, though he searched, day and night, for stronger stations.

"You want me to bring them here?" Paul asked Jefferson.

Jefferson went on listening to the radio without answering him.

The deputy returned to the dayroom and told Miss Emma what had happened. She had already set the table, and she and my aunt and Reverend Ambrose had taken their places, leaving a space for Jefferson. The food—beef stew and Irish potatoes—was still in the pot and covered. A tablespoon and a paper napkin lay beside each tin pan, on a white tablecloth.

"Radio?" Miss Emma asked Paul.

"Grant bought him one."

"When?"

"Last Friday."

"That mean he ain't coming?"

"That's what he said," the deputy told her.

Miss Emma sat staring at the space where Jefferson was supposed to sit, then she looked up at Paul again.

"Can we go to him?" she asked.

"Sure," he said. "But it's going to be uncomfortable, y'all trying to eat out of them pans standing up."

"We don't mind," Miss Emma said, and pushed herself up from the table.

My aunt helped her collect everything, then the three of them followed the deputy back to the cell. Jefferson lay on his bunk, listening to music on the radio.

Forty-five minutes later, when Paul returned to the cell, he found the radio turned off and Jefferson lying on his side, facing the wall, his back to the people. The deputy opened the door to let them out, and Jefferson turned from the wall and snapped on the radio. Paul told Miss Emma that the sheriff wanted to see her.

The sheriff was sitting behind his desk. There were two empty chairs, but he did not ask anyone to sit down.

"He give you any trouble back there?" the sheriff asked Miss Emma.

"No, sir."

"I said from the start I didn't want any trouble," the sheriff said. "If that radio is causing any trouble, I'll get it out of there."

"It ain't causing no trouble," Miss Emma said.

"He didn't come to the dayroom."

"We went to him. We managed."

"Standing up?"

"Yes, sir. We didn't mind."

"You minded before," the sheriff said. "That's why you went and worried my wife."

"Yes, sir," Miss Emma said.

"Listen," the sheriff said, pointing a finger across the desk. "He hasn't got much time. I don't want any trouble. Y'all have to work together—with that teacher."

"We go'n work together," Miss Emma said. "I'll talk to Grant when I get back."

"What about you, Reverend?" the sheriff asked.

"My duty to stand by Sis' Emma," Reverend Ambrose said.

"And what about Jefferson?" the sheriff asked. "What about his soul?"

According to Paul, who told me this later, Reverend Ambrose lowered his eyes and did not answer.

"All right," the sheriff said. "Y'all work it out your way. Any problems, and I'll take that radio, or stop the visits."

Reverend Ambrose came back to the quarter between two-thirty and three o'clock, and when I dismissed school one of the boys came back to tell me that my aunt wanted to see me at Miss Emma's house before I went home. All three of them were sitting around the kitchen table when I came in. They had already finished their coffee. The cups were still on the table, but empty.

"You know what you done done?" my aunt asked me. I could tell by her face and her voice that she was mad.

"What did I do?" I asked.

"Why?"

"Why what, Tante Lou?"

"That radio!" she said. "That radio!"

"What's wrong with the radio?"

"What's wrong with it?" Reverend Ambrose cut in. "What's wrong with it? That's all he do, listen to that radio, that's what's wrong with it."

"And what's wrong with that?" I asked.

"He didn't have time to come sit down with us today, that's what's wrong with that," the minister said. "He ain't got time for nothing else, that's what's wrong with that."

"Jefferson needs something in that cell," I said.

"Yes, he do," the minister said. "You hit the nail on the head, mister. Yes, he do. But not that box."

"And what do you suggest, Reverend Ambrose?" I asked.

"God," the minister said. "He ain't got but five more Fridays and a half. He needs God in that cell, and not that sin box."

"What sin box?" I said.

"What you call that kind of music he listen to?" the minister asked. "Us standing in there trying to talk to him, and him listening to that thing till she got to reach over and turn it off—what you call it?"

"I call it company, Reverend Ambrose," I said.

"And I call it sin company," he said.

"And I don't care what you call it!" I said to him.

"Grant!" my aunt said. I could see that she was becoming more and more angry with me. Now she got up from her chair. "You don't talk like that!" she said. "Never!"

"Louise," Miss Emma called to her. "Louise?"

"I didn't raise you that way," my aunt said, coming toward me.

"Louise, please. Lord—don't!" Miss Emma pushed up from her chair.

My aunt stopped a step or two away from me, though it was clear she wanted to slap me.

"We have to get something straight around here," I said.

"And right now. I don't know a thing about God or sin. What I do know is—"

"My Lord," the minister said, looking at me as if I were the devil himself. "Listen to the teacher of our children."

"Last Friday," I continued, "was the first time, the very first time, that Jefferson looked at me without hate, without accusing me of putting him in that cell. Last Friday was the first time he ever asked me a question or answered me without accusing me for his condition. I don't know if you all know what I'm talking about. It seems you don't. But I found a way to reach him for the first time. Now, he needs that radio, and he wants it. He wants something of his own before he dies. He wants a gallon of ice cream for his last supper—did he tell you that? Did he tell you he never had enough ice cream? Did he tell you that he never had a radio of his own before? Did he tell you any of this? He wants those things before he dies. He has only a month to live. And all I'm trying to do is make it as comfortable as I can for him."

"And after that radio and that ice cream, how 'bout his soul, mister?" my aunt asked me.

"I don't know a thing about the soul," I said.

"Yes you do," she said. She tightened her mouth. She wanted to cry. And she wanted to slap me. Not only for this moment, but for all those years that I had refused to go to her church. "Yes you do," she said, shaking her head. " 'Cause I raised you better."

"And you sent me to him, Tante Lou," I said. "And I'm only trying to reach him the best way I can."

"Turning him 'gainst God?"

"Tante Lou, that radio has nothing to do with turning Jefferson against God," I said. "That radio is there to help him not think about death. He's locked up in that cage like an animal—and what else can he think about but that last day and that last hour? That radio makes it less painful. Now, if you all want that radio out of there, you just go on and take it from him. But I won't go back up there anymore."

"We got to have it your way or else, that's it?" Reverend Ambrose cut in.

"No," I said. "You can have it your way. You can take it from him. But you won't reach him if you do. The only thing that keeps him from thinking he is not a hog is that radio. Take that radio away, and let's see what you can do for the soul of a hog."

"Then I'm the one that's not needed," the minister said.

"No," Miss Emma said. "You have to go, Reverend Ambrose. I'll make him see."

"You saw today how it was," the minister said. "He can't hear me through that wall of sin."

"I'll make him see," Miss Emma said. "He needs you. Maybe he don't know it yet, but he needs you. Maybe you don't know it yet either, Grant."

"All I know, Miss Emma, is that last Friday was the first time I reached him," I said. "It was the first time he didn't call himself a hog."

"And that whole gallona ice cream?" the minister said. "You sure you reached him?"

I didn't know how to answer that.

"Well, Mr. Teacher?" Reverend Ambrose said. "I'm waiting for your answer."

My aunt and Miss Emma were also waiting.

I went back to see Jefferson again on Wednesday. On Tuesday, I had asked the children at the school to bring large pecans and roasted peanuts for me to take to him. Some brought pecans in paper bags, some brought them in little flour and rice sacks, others brought them in their pockets. There were about twenty-five pounds of pecans, about half that many pounds of roasted peanuts. I took a few pounds of each and left the rest to be distributed among the children after school. In Bayonne I bought a half-dozen apples, some candy, and two or three comic books.

You did not hear the music until you got near the cell. He was lying on his bunk, the little radio on the floor at his head. Paul let me in and left.

"How's it going, partner?" I said. "The children sent you some pecans and peanuts. I bought you some apples and a couple candy bars. Some funny books."

He let his feet slide to the floor as he sat up on the bunk. I stood there awhile, then I sat down at the foot of the bunk and handed him the bag. He took it without saying anything and set it on the floor. The radio was still playing.

"Doing all right?" I asked him.

He sat there staring at the wall in front of him, his big hands clasped together. He nodded his head.

"How's the radio?" I asked him.

"All right."

"Did you get Randy over the weekend?"

"Yeah, I caught him."

"I listened to him a little bit myself," I said. "You didn't have any trouble getting the station, did you?"

"No, I got him all right," he said.

We were quiet. He stared at the concrete wall. The radio was playing western music on a station out of Baton Rouge.

"You want to ask me anything?"

He shook his head. I waited a moment, until I thought it was a good time to speak.

"I saw your nannan the other day after she came back from seeing you, Jefferson. She said you didn't have dinner with them in the dayroom. They had to come here, and they couldn't sit down."

He didn't say anything.

"When they come back, can you meet them in there, Jefferson? She needs that."

"All right."

"You'll do it for me, for her?" I asked.

"All right."

"She would love that, Jefferson. And Reverend Ambrose—will you let him talk to you?"

"All right."

I didn't know anything else to talk about, and he had nothing to say, so we just sat there quietly awhile.

"Jefferson," I said finally, "I want to be your friend. I want you to ask me questions. I want you to say anything that comes to your mind—anything you want to say to me. I don't care what it is—say it. I'll keep it to myself if you want, I'll talk about it to other people if you want. Will you do that for me?"

He nodded his head. He was staring at the wall.

"I just thought of something," I said. "Sometimes at night—sometimes when you're thinking about something and may not be able to remember it when I come back—I was just thinking maybe I could bring you a little notebook and a pencil. You could write your thoughts down, and we could talk about it when I came back. Or maybe you could talk to Reverend Ambrose about it when he came to visit you. Would you like that?"

"All right."

"You want me to bring it?"

"If you want."

"And you would write down your thoughts? Anything you want to talk about?"

He nodded his head. But he was still looking at the wall.

"Do you believe I'm your friend, Jefferson?" I asked him. "Do you believe I care about you?"

He didn't answer.

"Jefferson?"

But he was not listening.

I looked around the cell—at the seatless brown-stained commode, the washbowl whose faucet never stopped dripping, the little metal shelf over the bowl, which held his pan, tin cup, and spoon. Through the barred window I could see the branches of the sycamore tree stirring from a soft breeze. There was still a chill in the air, and Jefferson wore one of my heavy wool shirts.

On the floor, the little radio had been playing one western song after another.

"You like that country stuff, huh?"

"It don't matter."

"Me, I go for Randy," I said. "I like those low-down blues."

I heard someone opening the big steel door at the other end of the cellblock. And as he came down the aisle, I could hear Paul speaking to the prisoners.

"Well, I guess I'll be taking off," I said. "Anything you want me to tell your nannan?"

I had stood. Now he looked up at me. There was no hate in his face—but Lord, there was pain. I could see that he wanted to say something, but it was hard for him to do. I stood over him, waiting.

"Tell—tell the chirren thank you for the pe-pecans," he stammered.

I caught myself grinning like a fool. I wanted to throw my arms around him and hug him. I wanted to hug the first person I came to. I felt like someone who had just found religion. I felt like crying with joy. I really did.

I held out my hand. He raised his. A big hand, but with no grip. Cool, dead weight. I squeezed his hand with both of mine. I must have had that grin still on my face when Paul opened the door to let me out.

"Everything's okay?" he asked.

"Yes," I said.

24

MISS EMMA THOUGHT we should all visit Jefferson together as often as we could. I wasn't crazy about the idea of being at the courthouse at the same time as the minister, but one look from my aunt, and I decided that I would go along, at least once. Leaving Irene Cole and Odessa Freeman in charge of classes, I drove to Bayonne with a bag of pecans and peanuts. I remembered my promise to Jefferson, so I dropped by the drugstore for a notebook and a pencil. It was a little after two when I got to the courthouse. The minister, Miss Emma, and my aunt were waiting for me outside. They stood by the minister's car, near the statue of the Confederate soldier and the three flags. The flags hung limp beneath the overcast sky. The minister and my aunt looked at me, and both seemed angry, as if I had kept them waiting deliberately. I had not, of course. If I had not stopped for the notebook and pencil, I probably would have arrived there before they did, but I did not explain this to them. Miss Emma did not feel the same as they did, and that was all that mattered. Both she and my aunt carried food baskets covered with dish towels. As I approached them, Miss Emma pushed herself away from the car and started heavily toward the entrance to the courthouse. My aunt and the minister walked behind her, and I followed.

Paul was not there, and the chief deputy, after searching the food and us, led us out of the office, into the corridor. He walked several paces ahead of us, as if we were not with him. When we came to the rest room marked WHITE MEN, he went inside. We waited for him along the wall. Five minutes later, he came out with another white man. They stood there talking another minute or two before he continued along the corridor. We went up the steps and into the dayroom, and, without a word, he opened the door and left us.

Miss Emma and my aunt spread out a tablecloth on the table, then they placed a pan, a spoon, and a paper napkin in five places. After they had set up everything, they and the minister sat down, but I remained standing.

The first thing you heard were the chains around his ankles, then Jefferson entered the room through the rear door, followed by the deputy. Jefferson wore the same brown wool shirt he'd had on a couple of days before. He had on a pair of faded denims and brogans with no laces. He was dragging his feet to keep the shoes on.

"Here he is," the deputy said. "See y'all at three."

"Paul's not here today?" I asked.

"Mr. Paul's got other duties," the deputy said. He looked at me as if to remind me that I was supposed to say Mister before a white man's name. He stood there eyeing me until he felt that I understood.

"I brought you some good old gumbo," Miss Emma said to Jefferson.

"How's it going, partner?" I said, as I took my seat beside him.

"All right," he said.

"The radio still playing?"

He nodded his head.

"Good," I said.

Miss Emma put rice in each pan, then she poured gumbo over the rice until the pan was nearly full. Besides shrimps, she had put smoked sausage and chicken in the gumbo, and she had seasoned it well with green onions, filé, and black pepper. Gumbo was something you could always eat, even if you were not hungry. I started in. But I was the only one. And I soon realized why.

"May we bow our heads," the minister said, after I had put down my spoon.

Jefferson's head had been bowed from the moment he sat down. I lowered my eyes.

"Our Father who art in Heaven," Reverend Ambrose began. He went through the Lord's Prayer, but that was only for warming up. Then he really got down to praying. He asked God to come down to Bayonne, into the courthouse, into the jail; walk along the cellblock, go into each cell, touch each heart; come into this room and touch the hearts of those here who did not know Him in the pardon of their sins. As he prayed, the minister would slump closer and closer to the table. Then he would jerk his head up and gaze at the ceiling. Miss Emma and my aunt responded with "Amen, Amen, Amen." But Jefferson was quiet, and so was I. Whether or not he was listening, I don't know; but all I was thinking about was the gumbo getting cold.

Finally, Reverend Ambrose brought his prayer-sermon to an end, begging God to bless the gift on the table, which was there to nourish our bodies so that we might do His bidding. Everyone responded with "Amen," except Jefferson.

I started eating. The gumbo was warm but not hot.

"Ain't you go'n eat, Jefferson?" Miss Emma said.

"Ain't hongry."

Miss Emma was not eating either. But the minister and my aunt and I were. I broke off a piece of bread from one of the loaves that Miss Emma had baked. I didn't look at her; I didn't want to see her face.

"The children sent you some more pecans and peanuts," I said to Jefferson. "Did you eat the others I brought you?"

"Some," he said.

"The peanuts too?"

"Few," he said, his head down.

"I brought you that notebook and that pencil," I said. "Do you remember what we talked about?"

He nodded shortly.

"Have you been thinking of questions to ask me?"

He nodded again.

"Do you want to ask me now?"

He didn't say anything. I finished my pan of gumbo.

"There's more there, Grant," Miss Emma said.

"No, ma'am. That was good," I said, glancing at her. I didn't want to look at her too long. I knew what I would find in her face, and I didn't want to see it.

"You want to walk?" I said to Jefferson.

He moved on the bench without answering. You could hear the chains around his ankles as he swung his legs over the bench, then he braced his cuffed hands against the table to push himself up. We started walking around the room. Miss Emma watched us. My aunt and the minister went on eating, but they did not seem to be enjoying their food.

"Jefferson, I want us to be friends," I said. "Not only you and me, but I want you to be friends with your nannan. I want you to be more than a godson to her. A godson obeys, but a friend— well, a friend would do anything to please a friend." We were passing by the table, so I lowered my voice. Jefferson shuffled along beside me, his cuffed hands hanging below his waist, his shoulders too close together, his head down. "A friend does a lot of little things," I went on. "It would mean so much to her if you would eat some of the gumbo." I stopped when we came to the corner of the room. He stopped too, his head still down. "Look at me, Jefferson, please," I said. He raised his head slowly. I smiled at him. "Will you be her friend? Will you eat some of the gumbo? Just a little bit? One spoonful?" He made a slight nod. I smiled at him again.

"Jefferson," I said. We had started walking. "Do you know what a hero is, Jefferson? A hero is someone who does something for other people. He does something that other men don't and can't do. He is different from other men. He is above other men. No matter who those other men are, the hero, no matter who he is, is above them." I lowered my voice again until we had passed the table. "I could never be a hero. I teach, but I don't like teaching. I teach because it is the only thing that an educated black man can do in the South today. I don't like it; I hate it. I don't even like living here. I want to run away. I want to live for myself and for my woman and for nobody else.

"That is not a hero. A hero does for others. He would do anything for people he loves, because he knows it would make their lives better. I am not that kind of person, but I want you to be. You could give something to her, to me, to those children in the quarter. You could give them something that I never could. They expect it from me, but not from you. The white people out there are saying that you don't have it—that you're a hog, not a man. But I know they are wrong. You have the potentials. We all have, no matter who we are.

"Those out there are no better than we are, Jefferson. They are worse. That's why they are always looking for a scapegoat, someone else to blame. I want you to show them the difference between what they think you are and what you can be. To them, you're nothing but another nigger—no dignity, no heart, no love for your people. You can prove them wrong. You can do more than I can ever do. I have always done what they wanted me to do, teach reading, writing, and arithmetic. Nothing else—nothing about dignity, nothing about identity, nothing about loving and caring. They never thought we were capable of learning these things. 'Teach those niggers how to print their names and how to figure on their fingers.' And I went along, but hating myself all the time for doing so."

We were coming up to the table again, and the ones at the table were quiet and trying to hear what we were saying. I did not start talking again until we had passed them.

"Do you know what a myth is, Jefferson?" I asked him. "A myth is an old lie that people believe in. White people believe that they're better than anyone else on earth—and that's a myth. The last thing they ever want is to see a black man stand, and think, and show that common humanity that is in us all. It would destroy their myth. They would no longer have justification for having made us slaves and keeping us in the condition we are in. As long as none of us stand, they're safe. They're safe with me. They're safe with Reverend Ambrose. I don't want them to feel safe with you anymore.

"I want you to chip away at that myth by standing. I want you—yes, you—to call them liars. I want you to show them that you are as much a man—more a man than they can ever be. That jury? You call them men? That judge? Is he a man? The governor is no better. They play by the rules their forefathers created hundreds of years ago. Their forefathers said that we're only three-fifths human—and they believe it to this day. Sheriff Guidry does too. He calls me Professor, but he doesn't mean it. He calls Reverend Ambrose Reverend, but he doesn't respect him. When I showed him the notebook and pencil I brought you, he grinned. Do you know why? He believes it was just a waste of time and money. What can a hog do with a pencil and paper?"

We stopped. His head was down.

"Look at me, Jefferson, please," I said.

He raised his head. He had been crying. He raised his cuffed hands and wiped one eye, then the other.

"I need you," I told him. "I need you much more than you could ever need me. I need to know what to do with my life. I want to run away, but go where and do what? I'm needed here and I know it, but I feel that all I'm doing here is choking myself. I need someone to tell me what to do. I need you to tell me, to show me. I'm no hero; I can just give something small. That's all I have to offer. It is the only way that we can chip away at that myth. You—you can be bigger than anyone you have ever met.

"Please listen to me, because I would not lie to you now. I speak from my heart. You have the chance of being bigger than anyone who has ever lived on that plantation or come from this little town. You can do it if you try. You have seen how Mr. Farrell makes a slingshot handle. He starts with just a little piece of rough wood—any little piece of scrap wood—then he starts cutting. Cutting and cutting and cutting, then shaving. Shaves it down clean and smooth till it's not what it was before, but something new and pretty. You know what I'm talking about, because you have seen him do it. You had one that he made from a piece of scrap wood. Yes, yes—I saw you with it. And it came from a piece of old wood that he found in the yard somewhere. And that's all we are, Jefferson, all of us on this earth, a piece of drifting wood, until we—each one of us, indi-vidually—decide to become something else. I am still that piece of drifting wood, and those out there are no better. But you can be better. Because we need you to be and want you to be. Me, your godmother, the children, and all the rest of them in the quarter. Do you understand what I'm saying to you, Jefferson? Do you?"

He looked at me in great pain. He may not have understood, but something was touched, something deep down in him—because he was still crying.

I cry, not from reaching any conclusion by reasoning, but because, lowly as I am, I am still part of the whole. Is that what he was thinking as he looked at me crying?

"Come on," I said. "Let's have some gumbo."

And we went back to the table.

25

REVEREND AMBROSE, my aunt, and Miss Emma returned to the quarter, and I went back of town to the Rainbow Club. The place was in semidarkness as usual, with three old men at the bar, doing more talking than drinking, and only two other people in the place, a couple of mulatto bricklayers, sitting at a table. I had come here to tell Vivian that everything had gone well—Jefferson and I were communicating, and he and his nannan were also talking. I was feeling very good, and I wanted to tell it to her before I told it to anyone else. How he and I had gone back to the table, and how we had eaten the gumbo though it was cold, and how his nannan was so proud. I wanted to tell her that. I did not wish to tell her about the envy I had seen in the minister's face. No, I would not say that, that the minister felt I was controlling Jefferson's life, and that he, the minister, thought that since Jefferson had only a short time left to live, it should be he in control, and not I. No, I didn't want to say that to her. I only wanted to talk about things that made me feel good. The look on his nannan's face, the look on my aunt's face, the way Jefferson raised the spoonful of gumbo and rice to his mouth with both hands, and dipped the spoon again, and raised it to his mouth, because I had asked him to do it—that's what I wanted to talk about. About how he picked up the bag of pecans and peanuts and the bag with the tablet and pencil when the deputy came to the table to take him back to his cell. And though he did not walk as straight as I wished he would, the fact that he was carrying the notepad and the pencil made up for it. I wanted to talk about that to Vivian. Not about the minister, his envy, the way he looked when Jefferson and I had come back to the table. Sure, he was happy to see that Sister Emma was happy, but it was not he who had made her so, and he did not like that. Sin (or the sinner) had done this, not he. I wanted, too, to talk about how Jefferson's nannan looked at him as he ate the gumbo she had cooked especially for him, and about how he said goodbye when he had to go—that was what I wanted to talk about.

It was near three-thirty when I got to the Rainbow Club, and I had thought that by now Vivian would be there with some of her teaching friends. Since she was not, I thought I would have a drink or two till she showed up.

I could hear the mulatto bricklayers talking over in the corner. I was in a very good mood—at least I thought I was—and at first I wasn't paying much attention to what they were saying. I could hear them well enough, but I had no idea that they were speaking for my benefit. I had ordered a bourbon and water from Claiborne, and I was sipping it slowly and thinking about Vivian and about Jefferson. Things had not been going too well for Vivian and me in bed, and I knew it was because of Jefferson, my worrying about him. Between him and school, I was drained of my energy. Vivian knew that too, and she was ready to accept it. Much more than I was. She knew how it had been before, and she knew how it would be again—and she told me not to worry about it. But that was not enough for me. I did worry. I didn't think anything in the world was worth us not being able to make it well in bed. Nothing. And that was one of the reasons I had come back here to see her, to tell her that I had finally reached him and that I would be more relaxed now, and that it was going to be all right between her and me from now on.

The two brick-colored bricklayers were still talking over in the corner, and for a long time I didn't pay their conversation any close attention. I heard the word "nigger" a few times, and I heard the words "should have been done long ago," but I never made the connection. After I finished my first drink, I nodded for Claiborne to come down the bar. And now Claiborne heard them too. Maybe they wanted him to hear. Maybe they wanted him to hear so he would say something to me. Maybe. But all Claiborne did was serve me another drink, glance at them a couple of times, and go back to where the three old men were doing much more talking than drinking.

I went on sipping from my second drink, and thinking about Vivian and Jefferson. I was wondering what Vivian had worn today and how her hair was combed and how she would look when she came into the place. I was thinking about that. And about Jefferson and what he would write on the notepad—questions or comments? I was wondering what his handwriting would look like, and whether I would have the nerve to question him about anything I did not understand. These are the things I was thinking while the two bricklayers went on talking over in the corner. Down the bar, I saw Claiborne glancing their way again. He could not hear them now, but he had heard them when he was serving me, and he knew I could be listening.

There was a tall one and there was a short, fat one. The tall one was doing most of the talking, and I could tell he was angry. Maybe it was over his job. I had seen both of them before, without being friendly, and I knew that like so many of the mulattos in this part of the state, they did bricklaying or carpentry, and possibly some housepainting. All this by contract. And all this to keep from working in the field side by side with the niggers. Since emancipation, almost a hundred years ago, they would do any kind of work they could find to keep from working side by side in the field with the niggers. They controlled most of the bricklaying business in this part of the state. Even took that kind of work from the white boys, because they would do it so much cheaper than the white boys would. Anything not to work alongside the niggers. With school it was the same. Many of them would drop out of school, would get a trade—bricklayer or carpenter—rather than sit in class side by side with the niggers. Their sisters went to high school and college, but they would not. Rather take a trade than to sit next to the niggers. And these two who were talking now were of that way of thinking. Dumb as hell, but prejudiced as hell. They had no other place to go to do their drinking—they would not dare go to any of the white clubs—so they would come here and bring their prejudiced attitude with them. They would keep it down when there were several blacks in the place, but with only me and the three old men standing at the bar today, they felt pretty safe.

"Should have burned him months ago," one said. I figured it was the tall one, because out of the corner of my eye I had seen that he was doing most of the talking. "That kind of sonofabitch make it hard on everybody," he went on. "I'd pull the switch myself, they ask me."

I knew now what they were talking about and who they were talking about, but I told myself to keep it cool. Let them talk. They were probably out of work, and it was just plain frustration that made them go on like that. Just cool it, I told myself. You just cool it now.

But when I looked down the bar, I could see that Claiborne was listening to them too. And even the old men had looked back once or twice. So now we were all hearing them, but I could hear them better, because I was closer to their table.

And the Old Forester was not doing anything to keep me from listening. It was helping me listen. That's the way it is with booze, it gives and takes. It keeps you from doing what you're supposed to do well in bed, and other times it makes you listen to things you should not listen to. Like now.

Let them talk, I said again to myself. If you can't stand here and take it, then get into your car and leave. Go somewhere else and get a drink. He's got only a few more weeks, and you have to do all you can for him, for all the others. You came here in a good mood because this was one of the best days you have had with him, and you can't let this kind of trash destroy that good feeling. So don't. All right?

I finished the drink and sucked on an ice cube as I rolled the glass around in the palms of my hands. I raised the glass for the last drop, before setting it on the bar. I turned around slowly and looked at them, the tall one with a cowboy hat, and the short fat one with a baseball cap turned backward on his head. All I was going to do was lean back against the bar a moment, then I was going to walk out. They knew I was looking at them, and they were quiet a moment. Then the tall one said something, and the fat one snickered, and I thought I had heard enough. I went up to their table.

"Shut up."

"What?" the tall one said.

"You heard me," I said. "Shut up."

He grinned at me. "You don't mean that."

"You shut up, or get up," I said. "I mean that."

He looked at his buddy, then back at me. And the hatred in those light-brown eyes was thick enough to cut with a cane knife.

He grinned. "Fine with me, partner."

He braced himself against the table to stand up. But he was getting up with too much confidence, and I hit him before he had a chance to protect himself, and down he went over the back of that chair. Just as I expected, old fat boy jumped up too, and I caught him in the face with the side of my fist, and I saw him fall back and throw his hand up to his mouth. I got my back to the wall so I could keep both of them in front of me.

I don't know whether Claiborne came over the bar, under the bar, or around the bar, but he was there now, and he had grabbed the fat one and he was hollering for me and the other one to cut it out.

"Not in here," he was hollering. "Not in here, goddammit."

The tall one was up, and he was trying to move in on me, and when I saw that Claiborne had grabbed fat boy, I moved away from the wall with my guard up. Claiborne was wrestling with the fat one, but hollering at us. The tall one kept coming in on me. Then he swung, and I moved, and he went into the wall. His back was to me, but I didn't hit him. Not that I'm a gentleman fighter; I didn't hit him because he was between the wall and the table, and if I had moved in close enough to hit him, I would not have had room to move around. He came off that wall, and he swung at me again—not with fist first, but with both arms at once, just as Frankenstein had done it in the movies. He missed. But I could feel the force of his swing, even his body heat, and I knew that if nobody stopped this thing, I was in for a fight. He was taller and heavier and stronger than I, and he had three or four generations of bricklaying genes in him, while I had only cane cutting in mine.

Out of the corner of my eye I could still see Claiborne wrestling with the fat one, while continuing to holler at me and the tall one to stop. But since the tall one was not paying any attention to him, I wasn't about to drop my guard. He swung at me again, and I went under his arm and struck him in the side with all I had, but it seemed as if I had hit a wall. I told myself, Partner, you got your work cut out for you. He doesn't know how to fight, but he's strong as a mule. He came back, and this time he landed. Not his fist; his arm. And I thought it was chickenshit of him to hit me with an arm and not a fist, as a man

should hit a man, but I was thinking this from the floor. I don't
know what was going on in his mind, but he was standing over
me as though he was waiting for me to get up before hitting me
again. I kicked him in the shin, he fell back, and I got to my feet.
He was right on me again, and he swung. I went under it and
intentionally caught him below the belt. He buckled over, grab-
bing at his nuts with both hands. I moved in, and he started
swinging with the one arm to ward me off. I hit him twice, hard.
He kept swinging with one arm, the other hand holding on to
his nuts. His face showed pain, but he would not stop, he would
not go down. Those three or four generations of bricklaying
genes, his hatred of the black/white blood in him, and his plain
frustration with life would not let him go down.

Thelma Claiborne and several others were in the barroom
now, and Thelma had a broom. I felt the broom on my back,
then I saw it flash in front of me as she swung it at the bricklayer.
Then it was hitting something else—maybe the other bricklayer,
maybe her husband—because I heard Claiborne saying, "Goddammit, go find Vivian. Put that goddamn thing down, woman,
and do like I say."

I could hear all this, but I wasn't about to turn my head,
because the tall bricklayer was still on his feet. He was insane
now, like a wounded animal in pain, and nothing could stop
him. I kept moving back, maneuvering, so that I could land a
good punch when he came in. I felt something heavy and soft
behind me, and as I glanced around at Thelma, with that
damned broom, the bricklayer hit me solidly on the arm, and
down I went. I had never felt so much pain before, and I knew
that there was no way I was going to get up, that I was going to
die there. I was on my knees, and I was sure that the next feeling
(my last) would be a shoe under my chin or in my side. I was
waiting for it to happen, the way a condemned man must wait
that last hundredth of a second for the guillotine to fall. But it
never did, because Thelma, with her broom, got between us. He
was too much of a gentleman to knock her out of the way, or

maybe he realized that such a thing would bar him from the place forever. Whatever it was, it gave me time to get to my feet.

"Boxing is over," I said, and I grabbed a chair and threw it at him. He grabbed it and threw it back at me. I grabbed another one.

Above all the noise those chairs were making, I could hear Claiborne: "Go find that woman . . . schoolhouse . . . children play in yard . . ."

He was saying all this between sounds of something hitting the wall, something like flesh and bone and a baseball cap turned backward. I was hearing this, I wasn't really seeing it. Because the tall bricklayer still had a chair, and so did I—and Thelma had a broom, and it was hitting me on the head, the bricklayer on the shoulder, me in the side, the bricklayer in the chest.

Claiborne and the fat boy fell down on the floor and scrambled back up, and I heard Claiborne: "Gusta, Gilley, y'all can't yer neither? Gusta, crank your old ass up and go find that woman. Gilley, find my gun. Won't listen to reason, they'll listen to lead."

This was said between the thumping of flesh and bone and a baseball cap turned backward, blows followed by groans. And Claiborne saying, "No, you ain't got enough yet."

While the tall bricklayer and I kept trying to find an opening with those chairs so we could kill each other, I heard a solid, mean, crunching sound and a deep groan, followed by something heavy falling from the ceiling or pushed violently forward to the floor. I heard Claiborne screaming for the tall bricklayer and me to stop, and I heard Thelma plead, "Don't do it!"

That was the last thing I heard. After that it was dark. Completely dark. One moment, as I remember it, the bricklayer and I were circling each other with chairs. The next moment, absolute darkness. The darkness came at the exact moment as a blow to the side of my head.

I could hear a voice before I knew who was talking or where I was. Then I began to think I knew the voice, but I was not absolutely sure. Then I began to think I knew where I was—but I was not sure about that either. Then I began definitely to identify the voice—though still not sure where I was. Then I was able to see and feel, and I knew the voice. Because she was down on the floor with me and holding my head in her lap.

"He's all right," Vivian said.

"Get him out of here," Claiborne said.

"Are you all right?" Vivian asked.

"Hi, honey," I said.

"Are you all right?" Vivian asked.

"I'm okay."

"Can you stand up?"

I tried to nod my head.

"Get him out of here," Claiborne said.

"You all right, honey?" Vivian said.

"I'm all right."

"Get him out of here," Claiborne said. "I don't give a shit if he's all right or not. 'Fore you know it, the law'll be here. Get him out of here."

"Can you stand up, honey?" Vivian asked again.

"I can stand up."

"Come on. Stand up for me, honey," Vivian said.

"I can stand up," I said. "Damn it, I can stand up."

"He can stand up," Vivian said. "See? He's standing up now. Come on, honey."

26

"WHAT HAPPENED?"

"Claiborne knocked you out."

"Why did Claiborne knock me out?"

"You wouldn't stop fighting."

"Did he knock him out too?"

"No."

"Well, why didn't he knock him out?"

"He quit. Claiborne told him he would shoot his head off if he didn't, and he quit. You wouldn't."

"I didn't hear Claiborne say anything like that to me."

"That's what he told me. Said he knocked Griffin out first. You were the next one closest to him. He hollered at you to stop—kept hollering at you—and you went on swinging that chair. So he just came up behind you and knocked you out."

"With that gun?"

"That's all he had in his hand when I got there. Poor Mr. Gusta running up and down the street, calling my name. Come stop you. Come stop you."

"I'm sorry, honey."

"No, you're not sorry."

"I just couldn't help it."

"Yes, you could."

"I couldn't."

"You could have walked out of there."

"Can Jefferson walk out of where he is?"

We were sitting on her bed. There were matching lamps with matching shades on either side of the bed. The shades were pink, with little white tassels. A chifforobe was in the room, and there were a soft chair and a dresser. I could see us, me and her, in the mirror above the dresser. I had a wet towel on the top of my head, and my left hand was holding the towel in place. I didn't look too good, and I felt even worse.

Vivian sighed. "Well, I guess that's that," she said.

"That's what, honey?"

"You'll have to stay here tonight."

"What for?"

"Because you're in no condition to go home."

"I'm all right," I said. "I'll be all right in a minute."

"I'm calling Dora. Let her keep the children."

"Don't do that, honey. Please."

"She's kept them before."

"Honey, I don't want you in any trouble."

"Well, you should have thought about that at the Rainbow Club," she said.

"They were talking about Jefferson, honey. What would you have done?"

"I would have walked out of there."

"No, you would not. You would have said something."

"Maybe that's what you should have done instead of swinging that chair."

"Vivian, what about your marriage? What about the school?"

"All they can do is fire me. Maybe he'll take the children. But you weren't thinking about that," she said.

"I'm going to leave. I don't want you in any trouble."

"I'm already in trouble. Mr. Gusta running up and down the street calling my name. Come quick. Come quick. And me leading you by the hand out of a barroom fight. What do you call that?"

"I don't want you in any deeper trouble."

I tried to stand up, but my head felt as if it would burst open, and I sat down on the bed again.

"I'll leave in a few minutes," I said. "If I can't drive, I'll call somebody to take me home."

"You're not going anywhere," she said. "I'm calling Dora to keep the children. I have some red beans and rice back there. Couple of fried pork chops."

"I'm not hungry," I said.

"Well, I am."

"Don't be mad, honey."

"I'm not mad. Just disgusted."

"I had to do it, honey. I had to. I just couldn't take it anymore."

"That's how you all get yourselves killed."

"I didn't start it."

"Maybe you didn't. But you were ready."

"It's been all that other stuff. The jail, the preacher—all of that."

She got up from the bed.

"I'm going to warm the food," she said. "I'll be in the kitchen."

"Don't be mad, honey. Please."

She didn't answer. She went into the living room, and I heard her on the telephone, speaking to Dora. Then I heard her hang up the telephone and go into the kitchen.

I sat on the bed with my head bowed and my left hand holding the towel in place. I didn't dare look in the mirror again. I glanced over my shoulder toward the window on the other side of the bed, and I could see through the curtain that it was nearly dark outside.

I got up from the bed and went through the living room and back into the kitchen. I could smell the red beans warming on the stove. I couldn't smell the rice—you don't smell rice unless it's burning—and I didn't smell the pork chops either. Vivian was at the sink, making a salad. I went up to her and put my right arm around her waist while my left hand held the towel on my head.

"What are you doing, honey?"

She knew I could see what she was doing, so she didn't answer me.

"Still mad, huh?"

"I'm not mad."

"You still love me?"

She didn't answer.

I kissed her on the jaw. She went on making the salad.

"Do you want to know what happened today, honey?"

"I already know what happened today," she said.

"At the jail, I mean."

She went on with her salad. Now she was slicing up a cucumber to add to the lettuce and tomato.

"It went well today, honey. It went very well. He and I walked around the room, while I talked to him. Then we ate. His nannan was so proud. I brought him the pencil and notepad I told you about. It went good today, honey. Aren't you proud?"

She put the sliced cucumber into the bowl with the cut-up tomato and the lettuce, then she added oil and vinegar. She took the salad to the table. She dished up the rice and spread red beans over the rice and placed a pork chop on each plate. She brought the two plates to the table and sat down. I sat opposite her.

"You want me to ask the blessing, honey?"

She didn't answer. I bowed my head and made the sign of the cross and asked God to bless the food. I looked up at her and started eating. She was not eating.

"Still mad, huh?"

"I'm just thinking," she said.

I ate and looked at her.

"I heard from him," she said. "He won't give me a divorce unless he can see his children every weekend."

My head started throbbing again. "When did you hear from him?"

"Yesterday. I was going to tell you today when I saw you."

"He's still in Texas?"

"Yes."

"And I suppose he has heard about us?"

"I suppose so."

"And that's to keep us from going away?"

"I suppose so."

"The sonofabitch," I said. "All of a sudden he needs to see his children every weekend?"

I put down my fork. I didn't feel like eating anymore.

"I'm going to leave," I said.

"You don't have to."

"I don't want to give him any more fuel to work with."

"Suit yourself."

"Don't you think that's best?"

"It doesn't matter," she said. "We get hurt no matter what happens."

She picked at her food, but she didn't eat. I sat there looking at her.

"I need you, honey," I told her. "I need you to stand with me.

He's got only a few more weeks. I need you now more than ever."

She didn't answer. She held the fork in her hand, but she did not bring it up to her mouth.

"Well, I better go," I said.

She didn't look at me.

"Honey, suppose someone said something about you—would you want me to just walk away?"

Again, nothing from her.

"Honey, you have anything in here to drink?" I asked her.

"Bottle in that cabinet," she said.

"Honey, you going to fix me a drink?"

She didn't move. I got up from the table and got the bottle of Old Forester out of the cabinet. It was three quarters full.

"You want one, honey?"

"No."

I poured myself a double, then I added some water from the pitcher in the refrigerator.

"Still mad, huh?" I said, after I sat down.

"Never was mad. Just disgusted."

"About the same thing," I said. "I'll finish my drink and leave."

"That's up to you."

"I love you, honey, and I need you. But I'm only human."

"One day I'll bring flowers to the graveyard," she said.

"That's not you talking, honey."

"No?" she said, looking up at me. She had been holding it in a long time, and now she was going to let it out. I saw it coming as soon as I spoke. "What *is* me?" she said. "Tell me, what *is* me?"

"Honey—"

"No, tell me," she said. "Who am I? Who are you? Who are we? Tell me."

"All I know is I love you," I said.

"That's not enough," she said. "What is love?"

"Honey—"

"What is it?" she asked. "That bed? That's love?"

"Honey—please."

"No. Give me some answers. Give me some answers—today. Today I want answers."

"Honey, I love you."

"That's no answer. I don't know what you mean by love. That bed? The cane field? What is love? Tell me what love is."

I didn't know what to say. Nothing I would say was going to change anything.

"I'll leave," I said.

"Sure, that's the easy way out—leave."

"Well, what do you want? What the hell do you want from me? What the hell do you all want from me?"

"I don't know what the others want. I just want something I don't have."

"I've done my best," I said.

"No, you have not," she said. "In bed for a few moments is not enough."

"Is that all I've ever given you? Is that all?"

"What else? Any consideration?"

I got up from the table. I jerked the towel from my head and slammed it down on my plate.

"You can have your goddamn red beans and rice and towel and everything else. Damn this shit."

I went to the front door and jerked it open, and there was the screen. And through the screen I could see outside into the darkness, and I didn't want to go out there. There was nothing outside this house that I cared for. Not school, not home, not my aunt, not the quarter, not anything else in the world.

I don't know how long I stood there looking out into the darkness—a couple of minutes, I suppose—then I went back into the kitchen. I knelt down and buried my face in her lap.

27

▼

AFTER CHURCH, the minister came back to the house with my aunt, Miss Eloise, Miss Emma, and Inez for coffee and cake. I lay across the bed in my room, looking out the window at the stack of bean poles in the garden. As far back as I could remember, my aunt would pull up the rows of poles at the end of each season and stack them in that same corner of the garden, until a new crop of beans was ready to be poled. Beyond the poles, on the other side of the road, I could see the tops of the pecan trees in Farrell Jarreau's backyard. The trees had begun to bud again. The buds looked black from this distance. I could see above the trees how heavy, low, and gray the sky was. I had intended to go for a drive, but I was afraid it might rain while I was gone, making the road too muddy for me to drive back down the quarter. Anyway, I had work to do. But as usual, I ended up doing only a little, because of the singing and praying up at the church. After Tante Lou and her company had been at the house awhile, she came into my room.

"You 'sleep?" she asked.

"I'm awake."

"Reverend Ambrose like to talk to you."

"What about?"

I lay on my back, gazing up at the ceiling, my hands clasped behind my head so that my arms stuck out, forming a cross.

"I done told you that's bad luck," my aunt said.

Without shifting my eyes from the ceiling, I unclasped my hands from behind my head and clasped them on my chest. Tante Lou stood there looking at me.

"He can come in?"

"Sure. He can come in."

"You go'n put on your shoes and tuck in that shirt?" she asked.

"I'll put on my shoes and tuck in my shirt," I said.

She stood there watching me awhile, then she left the room. I sat up on the bed and passed my hands over my face. When the minister came into the room, I had tucked in my shirt and put on my shoes, and I was standing at the window looking out at the garden. My aunt had prepared a half-dozen rows about thirty feet long for spring planting. She would start her planting the week after Easter if the ground was dry enough.

The minister stood behind me, and I turned from the window to look at him.

"Care to sit down, Reverend?"

There were only two chairs in the room, the one at my desk and a rocker by the fireplace.

"You go'n sit down?" he asked me.

"I don't mind standing."

He looked at my desk.

"I see you been working."

"I tried to. Afraid I didn't get too much done."

He sat down in the chair and looked up at me.

"They learning anything?"

"I do my best, Reverend."

He nodded his bald head. "I do the same. My best."

My back to the window, I waited to hear what he wanted to talk to me about. He looked down at his hands and rubbed them together. For a man his size, he had really big hands. He rubbed them again before raising his eyes to me.

"There ain't much time."

"Jefferson?"

"Yes."

"Three weeks."

"Not quite."

"Minus couple days," I said.

He nodded his head, a small, tired little man. He had preached a long sermon today, and it showed in his face.

"He ain't saved."

"I can't help you there, Reverend."

"That's where you wrong. He listen to you."

I turned my back on him and looked out on the garden.

"You ever think of anybody else but yourself?"

I didn't answer him.

"I ask you, 'You ever think of anybody but yourself?' "

"I have my work to do, Reverend, you have yours," I said, without looking around at him. "Mine is reading, writing, and arithmetic, yours is saving souls."

"He don't need no more reading, writing, and 'rithmetic."

"That's where you come in, Reverend."

I stared beyond the garden toward the budding pecan trees in Farrell Jarreau's backyard. The sky was so low the trees seemed nearly to touch it.

"When you going back?" Reverend Ambrose asked behind me.

"I don't know. One day next week, I suppose."

"And what you go'n talk about?"

"I don't know, Reverend."

"I'm going back with Sis' Emma tomorrow. I'm go'n talk about God."

"I'm sure he needs to hear that, Reverend."

"You sure you sure?"

"Maybe not. Maybe I'm not sure about anything."

"I know I'm sure," he said. "Yes, I know I'm sure."

I looked out at the newly turned rows of earth, and I wished I could just lie down between the rows and not hear and not be a part of any of this.

"This is a mean world. But there is a better one. I wish to prepare him for that better world. But I need your help."

"I don't believe in that other world, Reverend."

"Don't believe in God?"

"I believe in God, Reverend," I said, looking beyond the rows of turned-up earth, toward the budding pecan trees across the road. "I believe in God. Every day of my life I believe in God."

"Just not that other world?"

I didn't answer him.

"And how could they go on? You ever thought about that?"

I looked at the buds on the trees, and I did not answer him.

"Well?" he said to my back.

I turned from the window and looked at him where he sat at my desk. School papers, notebooks, textbooks, and pencils were spread out on the table behind him.

"She told me to help him walk to that chair like a man—not like a hog—and I'm doing the best I can, Reverend. The rest is up to you."

He got up from the chair and came toward me. He peered at me intently, his face showing pain and confusion. He stopped at arm's distance from me, and I could smell in his clothes the sweat from his preaching.

"You think you educated?"

"I went to college."

"But what did you learn?"

"To teach reading, writing, and arithmetic, Reverend."

"What did you learn about your own people? What did you learn about her—her 'round there?" he said, gesturing toward the other room and trying to keep his voice down.

I didn't answer him.

"No, you not educated, boy," he said, shaking his head. "You far from being educated. You learned your reading, writing, and 'rithmetic, but you don't know nothing. You don't even know yourself. Well?"

"You're doing the talking, Reverend."

"And educated, boy," he said, thumping his chest. "I'm the one that's educated. I know people like you look down on people like me, but"—he touched his chest again—"I'm the one that's educated."

He stared at me as if he could not make up his mind whether to hit me or scream.

"Grief, oh, grief." He muffled his cry. "When will you cease? Oh, when?" He drew a deep breath, then he began to speak faster. "When they had nothing else but grief, where was the release? None, none till He rose. And He said there's relief from grief across yon river, and she believed, and there was relief from grief. Do you know what I'm trying to say to you, boy?"

"I hear you talking, Reverend."

"You hear me talking. But are you listening? No, you ain't listening."

His eyes examined me, from the top of my head to my chest, and I could see the rage in his face, see his mouth trembling. He was doing all he could to control his voice so that the others, back in the kitchen, would not hear him.

"I won't let you send that boy's soul to hell," he said. "I'll fight you with all the strength I have left in this body, and I'll win."

"You don't have to fight me, Reverend," I told him. "You can have him all to yourself. I don't even have to go back up there, if that's all you want."

"You going back," he said, nodding his bald head, and still trying hard to control his voice. "You owe her much as I owe her. And long as I can stand on my feet, I owe her and all the others every ounce of my being. And you do too."

"I don't owe anybody anything, Reverend," I said, and turned toward the window.

I felt his hand gripping my shoulder and pulling me around to face him.

"Don't you turn your back on me, boy."

"My name is Grant," I said.

"When you act educated, I'll call you Grant. I'll even call you Mr. Grant, when you act like a man." His hand still grasped my shoulder, and I needed all my willpower to keep from knocking it off. He could see what I was thinking, and he slowly released his grip and brought his hand to his side. "You think you the only one ever felt this way?" he asked. "You think I never felt this way? You think she never felt this way? Every last one of them back there one time in they life wanted to give up. She want to give up now. You know that? You got any idea how sick she is? Soon after he go, she's going too. I won't give her another year. I want her to believe he'll be up there waiting for her. And you can help me do it. And you the only one."

"How?"

"Tell him to fall down on his knees 'fore he walk to that chair. Tell him to fall down on his knees 'fore her. You the only one he'll listen to. He won't listen to me."

"No," I said. "I won't tell him to kneel. I'll tell him to listen to you—but I won't tell him to kneel. I will try to help him stand."

"You think a man can't kneel and stand?"

"It hasn't helped me."

The minister drew back from me. His head was shining; so

was his face. I could see his mouth working as though he wanted
to say something but didn't know how to say it.

"You're just lost," he said. "That's all. You're just lost."

"Yes, sir, I'm lost. Like most men, I'm lost."

"Not all men," he said. "Me, I'm found."

"Then you're one of the lucky ones, Reverend."

"And I won't let you lose his soul in hell."

"I want him in heaven as much as you do, Reverend."

"A place you can't believe in?"

"No, I don't believe in it, Reverend."

"And how can you tell him to believe in it?"

"I'll never tell him not to believe in it."

"And suppose he ask you if it's there, then what? Suppose he
write on that tablet you give him, is it there? Then what?"

"I'll tell him I don't know."

"You the teacher."

"Yes. But I was taught to teach reading, writing, and arithmetic. Not the gospel. I'd tell him I heard it was there, but I don't
know."

"And suppose he ask you if you believe in heaven? Then
what?"

"I hope he doesn't, Reverend."

"Suppose he do?"

"I hope he doesn't."

"You couldn't say yes?"

"No, Reverend, I couldn't say yes. I couldn't lie to him at this
moment. I will never tell him another lie, no matter what."

"Not for her sake?"

"No, sir."

The minister nodded his bald head and grunted to himself.
His dark-brown eyes in that tired, weary face continued to stare
back at me.

"You think you educated, but you not. You think you the
only person ever had to lie? You think I never had to lie?"

"I don't know, Reverend."

"Yes, you know. You know, all right. That's why you look down on me, because you know I lie. At wakes, at funerals, at weddings—yes, I lie. I lie at wakes and funerals to relieve pain. 'Cause reading, writing, and 'rithmetic is not enough. You think that's all they sent you to school for? They sent you to school to relieve pain, to relieve hurt—and if you have to lie to do it, then you lie. You lie and you lie and you lie. When you tell yourself you feeling good when you sick, you lying. When you tell other people you feeling well when you feeling sick, you lying. You tell them that 'cause they have pain too, and you don't want to add yours—and you lie. She been lying every day of her life, your aunt in there. That's how you got through that university— cheating herself here, cheating herself there, but always telling you she's all right. I've seen her hands bleed from picking cotton. I've seen the blisters from the hoe and the cane knife. At that church, crying on her knees. You ever looked at the scabs on her knees, boy? Course you never. 'Cause she never wanted you to see it. And that's the difference between me and you, boy; that make me the educated one, and you the gump. I know my people. I know what they gone through. I know they done cheated themself, lied to themself—hoping that one they all love and trust can come back and help relieve the pain."

28

I WENT INTO THE CELL with a paper bag full of baked sweet potatoes. The deputy locked the heavy door behind me.

"How's it going, partner?"

Jefferson nodded.

"How do you feel?"

"I'm all right."

"I brought you a little something."

Jefferson was sitting on the bunk, with his hands clasped together. I put the bag beside him on the bunk and sat down. I could hear the radio, on the floor against the wall, playing a sad cowboy song. I saw the notebook and the pencil on the floor, next to the radio. This was my first visit since I'd given him the notebook and pencil, and I could see that the lead on the pencil was worn down to the wood. I could also see that he had used the eraser a lot. We were quiet awhile.

"Hungry?" I asked.

"Maybe later."

"I see you've been writing."

He didn't answer.

"Personal, or can I look at it?"

"It ain't nothing."

"Do you mind?" I asked.

"If you want."

I got the notebook and came back to the bunk. The fellow on the radio was saying what a beautiful day it was in Baton Rouge.

Jefferson had filled three quarters of the first page. The letters were large and awkward, the way someone would write who could barely see. He had written across the lines instead of above them. He had used the eraser so much that in some places the paper was worn through. Nothing was capitalized, and there were no punctuation marks. The letters were thin at the beginning, but became broader as the lead was worn down. As closely as I could figure, he had written: *I dreampt it again last night. They was taking me somewhere. I wasn't crying. I wasn't begging. I was just going, going with them. Then I woke up. I couldn't go back to sleep. I didn't want go back to sleep. I didn't want dream no more.* There was a lot of erasing, then he wrote: *If I ain't nothing but a hog, how come they just don't knock me in the head like a hog? Starb me like a hog?* More erasing, then: *Man walk on two foots; hogs on four hoofs.*

The last couple of words were barely visible, because the lead had been worn down all the way to the wood. I read it over a second time before closing the notebook. I didn't know what to say to him. He was staring at the wall, his hands clasped together.

"Do you want me to bring you a pencil sharpener?" I asked after a while. "The little ones you hold in your hand?"

"If you can find one."

"I'm sure I can," I said. "You know, Paul would have sharpened this pencil for you. He wouldn't mind."

Jefferson had unclasped his hands, and now he was scraping the ends of his left fingernails with the index finger of the right hand. His fingernails were hard and purplish.

"When's Easter?" he asked.

"Tomorrow is Good Friday."

"That's when He rose?"

"No. He rose on Easter."

"That's when He died," Jefferson said to himself. "Never said a mumbling word. That's right. Not a word."

"Did you talk to Reverend Ambrose when he came to visit you?" I asked Jefferson.

"Some."

"You ought to talk to him. It's good for your nannan. She wants you to talk to him."

"He told me to pray."

"Do you?"

"No."

"It would be good for your nannan."

He looked at me. His eyes were large and sad and reddened.

"You think I'm going to heaven?" he asked.

"I don't know."

"You think Mr. Gropé went to heaven? You think Brother and Bear went to heaven?"

"I don't know."

"Then what I'm go'n pray for?"

"For your nannan."

"Nannan don't need me to help her get to heaven. She'll make it if it's up there."

"She wants you there with her, where there's no pain and no sorrow."

He grinned at me, a brief cynical grin.

"You pray, Mr. Wiggins?"

"No, Jefferson, I don't."

He grunted.

"But then I'm lost, Jefferson," I said, looking at him closely. "At this moment I don't believe in anything. Like your nannan does, like Reverend Ambrose does, and like I want you to believe. I want you to believe so that one day maybe I will."

"In heaven, Mr. Wiggins?"

"If it helps others down here on earth, Jefferson."

"Reverend Ambrose say I have to give up what's down here. Say there ain't nothing down here on this earth for me no more."

"He meant possessions, Jefferson. Cars, money, clothes—things like that."

"You ever seen me with a car, Mr. Wiggins?"

"No."

"With more than a dollar in my pocket?"

"No."

"More than two pair shoes, Mr. Wiggins? One for Sunday, one for working in?"

"No, Jefferson."

"Then what on earth I got to give up, Mr. Wiggins?"

"You've never had any possessions to give up, Jefferson. But there is something greater than possessions—and that is love. I know you love her and would do anything for her. Didn't you eat the gumbo when you weren't hungry, just to please her? That's all we're asking for now, Jefferson—do something to please her."

"What about me, Mr. Wiggins? What people done done to please me?"

"Hasn't she done many things to please you, Jefferson? Cooked for you, washed for you, taken care of you when you were sick? She is sick now, Jefferson, and she is asking for only one thing in this world. Walk like a man. Meet her up there."

"Y'all asking a lot, Mr. Wiggins, from a poor old nigger who never had nothing."

"She would do it for you."

"She go to that chair for me, Mr. Wiggins? You? Anybody?"

He waited for me to answer him. I wouldn't.

"No, Mr. Wiggins, I got to go myself. Just me, Mr. Wiggins. Reverend Ambrose say God'd be there if I axe Him. You think He be there if I axe Him, Mr. Wiggins?"

"That's what they say, Jefferson."

"You believe in God, Mr. Wiggins?"

"Yes, Jefferson, I believe in God."

"How?"

"I think it's God that makes people care for people, Jefferson. I think it's God makes children play and people sing. I believe it's God that brings loved ones together. I believe it's God that makes trees bud and food grow out of the earth."

"Who make people kill people, Mr. Wiggins?"

"They killed His Son, Jefferson."

"And He never said a mumbling word."

"That's what they say."

"That's how I want to go, Mr. Wiggins. Not a mumbling word."

Another cowboy song was playing on the radio, but it was quiet and not disturbing. I could hear inmates down the cell-block calling to one another. Jefferson sat forward on the bunk, his big hands clasped together again. I still had the notebook. I started to open it, but changed my mind.

"You need anything, Jefferson?"

"No, I don't need nothing, Mr. Wiggins. Reverend Ambrose say I don't need nothing down here no more."

"I'll get you that sharpener," I said.

"I ain't got nothing more to say, Mr. Wiggins."

"I'm sure you have."

"I hope the time just hurry up and get here. Cut out all this waiting."

"I wish I knew what to do, Jefferson."

"I'm the one got to do everything, Mr. Wiggins. I'm the one."

He got up from the bunk and went to the window and looked up at the buds on the higher branches of the sycamore tree. Through the branches of the tree I could see the sky, blue and lovely and clear. "You Are My Sunshine" was playing on the radio. Jefferson turned his back to the window and looked at me. "Me, Mr. Wiggins. Me. Me to take the cross. Your cross, nannan's cross, my own cross. Me, Mr. Wiggins. This old stumbling nigger. Y'all axe a lot, Mr. Wiggins." He went to the cell door and grasped it with both hands. He started to jerk on the door, but changed his mind and turned back to look at me. "Who ever car'd my cross, Mr. Wiggins? My mama? My daddy? They dropped me when I wasn't nothing. Still don't know where they at this minute. I went in the field when I was six, driving that old water cart. I done pulled that cotton sack, I done cut cane, load cane, swung that ax, chop ditch banks, since I was six." He was standing over me now. "Yes, I'm youman, Mr. Wiggins. But nobody didn't know that 'fore now. Cuss for nothing. Beat for nothing. Work for nothing. Grinned to get by. Everybody thought that's how it was s'pose to be. You too, Mr. Wiggins. You never thought I was nothing else. I didn't neither. Thought I was doing what the Lord had put me on this earth to do." He went to the window and turned to look at me. "Now all y'all want me to be better than ever'body else. How, Mr. Wiggins? You tell me."

"I don't know, Jefferson."

"What I got left, Mr. Wiggins—two weeks?"

"I think it's something like that—if nothing happens."

"Nothing go'n happen, Mr. Wiggins. And it ain't 'something like that.' That's all I got on this here earth. I got to face that, Mr. Wiggins. It's all right for y'all to say 'something like that.' For me, it's 'that'—'that,' that's all. And like Reverend Ambrose say, then I'll have to give up this old earth. But ain't that where I'm going, Mr. Wiggins, back in the earth?"

My head down, I didn't answer him.

"You can look at me, Mr. Wiggins; I don't mind."

I raised my head, and I saw him standing there under the window, big and tall, and not stooped as he had been in chains.

"I'm go'n do my best, Mr. Wiggins. That's all I can promise. My best."

"You're more a man than I am, Jefferson."

" 'Cause I'm go'n die soon? That make me a man, Mr. Wiggins?"

"My eyes were closed before this moment, Jefferson. My eyes have been closed all my life. Yes, we all need you. Every last one of us."

He studied me awhile, then he turned his back and looked up at the window.

"So pretty out there," he said. "So pretty. I ain't never seen it so pretty." I looked at him standing there big and tall, his broad back toward me. "What it go'n be like, Mr. Wiggins?"

I thought I knew what he was talking about, but I didn't answer him. He turned around to face me.

"What it go'n feel like, Mr. Wiggins?"

I shook my head. I felt my eyes burning.

"I hope it ain't long."

"It's not long, Jefferson," I said.

"How you know, Mr. Wiggins?"

"I read it."

I was not looking at him. I was looking at the wall. It had been in the newspaper. The first jolt, if everything is right, immediately knocked a person unconscious.

He came back and sat down on the bunk.

"I'm all right, Mr. Wiggins."

I nodded without looking at him.

"Care for a 'tato, Mr. Wiggins?" he said, opening the paper bag.

"Sure," I said.

29

JEFFERSON'S DIARY

mr wigin you say rite somethin but i dont kno what to rite an
you say i must be thinkin bout things i aint telin nobody an i
order put it on paper but i dont kno what to put on paper cause
i aint never rote nothin but homework i aint never rote a leter
in all my life cause nanan use to get other chiren to rite her leter
an read her leter for her not me so i cant think of too much to
say but maybe nex time

its evenin an i done eat my rice an beans an i done had my cup
of milk an the sun comin in the windo cause i can see it splashin
on the flo and I can yer ned an them talkin an thats bout all for
now

          *   *   *

i coudn sleep las nite cause i kept dremin it and i dont want dreem it cause im jus walkin to somwher but i dont kno wher its at an fore i get to the door i wake up an i want to rite in the tablet las nite but you aint got no lite in yer but the moon so im ritin this monin soon is sunup but now i done fogot what i want to say

nanan brot me some easter egg an i et one an nanan et one an reven ambros he et one an reven ambros ax me if i know why the lord die an he say he die for me so i can meet him in heven an all he want me to do is say i want be up ther wit him an the angels an say if i mean it wit all my heart an sol ill go to heven an nanan start cryin again an mis lou got to hug her an nanan say all i need to do an make her life wors livin is ax the lord forgiv me in the pardn of my sin an her an reven ambros was on they knee an mis lou was still in the cher huggin her an i was glad when paul come an got me

i dont kno what day it is but las nite i coudn sleep an i cud yer ned down the way snoin an i laid ther and thot bout samson sayin if the lord love me how com he let my wife die an leave me an them chiren an how come he dont come here an take way people like them matin brothers on the st charl river stead of messin wit po ol foks who aint never done nothin but try an do all they kno how to serv him

it look like the lord just work for wite folks cause ever sens i wasn nothin but a litle boy i been on my on haulin water to the fiel on that ol water cart wit all them dime bukets an that dipper jus hittin an old dorthy just trottin and trottin an me up their hittin her wit that rope an all them dime bukets an that dipper jus hittin an hittin gainst that bal of water so i can git the peple they food an they water on time an the peple see me an drop they hoe an com and git they buket cause they kno they string or they mark on the top an boo sittin under a bloodweed wit his wite

beans an rice and goin wher he at wher he at this yer very minit
an how com he dont giv a man a little breeze if he so merciful
an mis rachel wit her rice an grens sayin keep it up jus keep it
up an see if a clap of litenin dont come ther an nok the fool out
you an boo sayin let him i dont care cause a ded niger is beter
of an a live one any weekday an saddy im gittin drunk an say it
agin an saddy standin in the midle the road hollin up in the air
sayin com on an git me com on an git me see if i care an fallin
down in the dich an rollin out in the road an holin up the botle
so the lord coud see it an rollin back in the dich an rollin back
in the road an drinkin and holin the botle up so the lord coud
see it an sayin i kno you dont love nobody but wite folks cause
you they god not mine an com on an tho you litenin if you want
cause no niger aint got no god an the church goin people closin
they doors an windos to keep from herin boo blasfemin the lord
but me an the rest of the chiren in the quarter like boo cause he
always boght us candy an cake

i jus cant sleep no mo cause evertime i shet my eyes i see that
door an fore i git ther i wake up an i dont go back to sleep cause
i dont want walk to that door no mo cause i dont know what
back o ther if its wher they gon put that cher or if it spose to
mean def or the grave or heven i dont know i wonder if boo went
to heven cause i know he didn git religin firs

mr wigin you say you like what i got here but you say you stil
cant giv me a a jus a b cause you say i aint gone deep in me yet
an you kno i can if i try hard an when i ax you what you mean
deep in me you say jus say whats on my mind so one day you
can be save an you can save the chiren and i say i don't kno what
you mean an you say i do kno what you mean an you look so tied
sometime mr wigin i just feel like tellin you i like you but i dont
kno how to say this cause i aint never say it to nobody before an
nobody aint never say it to me

*   *   *

i kno i care for nanan but i dont kno if love is care cause cuttin wood and haulin water and things like that i dont know if thats love or jus work to do an you say thats love but you say you kno i got mo an jus that to say an when i lay ther at nite and cant sleep i try an think what you mean i got mo cause i aint done this much thinkin and this much writin in all my life befor

its munday an i aint got but just a few days lef an i hope i see my nanan jus one mo time cause mis lou and reven ambros say she aint fairin too good an coudn make it wit them this time but the lord kno mr wigin i hope i can see her one mo time on this earth fore i go is that love mr wigin when you want see sombody bad bad mr wigin thank you for sayin im doin b + work an you know the a aint too far

the shef an mr picho and mr mogan come in the cell today an mr picho ax me how im doin an i tell him im doin all rite an he say yes he can see im all rite an he ax me if he can do somthin for me an i tell him nosir im all rite and he ax if i want a brand new pencil wit a penny erase on it an i tol him i wud take the pencil but i dont need the erase cause you tol me to jus put down anything come in my hed an if it aint rite jus scratch over it an go on an he say yes he can see that an he ax me if i want him to shopen my pencil an i say yesir an he shopen the pencil on a teeny perl hanle nife an i look at the nife an i seen mr picho look up at shef guiry an mr mogan an the shef look back at him but mr mogan never stop lookin at me like he was tryin to figer me an mr picho ax me if i want the litle nife an i tell him yesir i didn mind an he unhook the litle gole chan from his belt lope an han me the nife an the chan an he say it was all mine an i say just for a few days an you can hav it back an i helt the litle nife in my han an the chan in my other han an jus look at it an i yer mr picho say well an i yer mr mogan say it aint fridy yet an mr picho say you want double that bet you want add that troter an mr mogan say it still aint fridy yet

*   *   *

ole clark been comin roun too tryin to act like a youman but i
can see in his face he aint no good an i dont even look at him
when he ax me if im doin all rite and can he git me somthin no
i jus go on ritin in my tablet an i dont care if he do see it after
im dead and gone

paul trying to be hod when he aint like he dont want get too
close to me no mo an all the time he is the only one rond yer kno
how to talk like a youman to people i kno you paul an i kno ole
clark an i kno you too shef guiry and you mr picho and mr
mogan an all the rest of yall i jus never say non of this befor but
i know yall ever las one of yall

lord have merce sweet jesus mr wigin where all them peple come
from when you ax me if some chiren can com up here an speak
to me i didn kno you was meanin all them chiren in yo clas an
jus sitin ther on the flo all quite in they clean close lookin at me
an i coud see som was scard o me but mos was brave an spoke
an my litle cosin estel even com up an kiss me on the jaw an i
coudn hol it back no mo

then after the chiren here com the ole folks an look like everbody
from the quarter was here mis julia an joe an mis haret an ant
agnes an mr noman an mis sara an mis lilia an mr harry an mis
lena an god kno who all an mr ofal an mis felia wit her beeds an
jus prayin an all the peple sayin how good i look an lord hav
merce sweet jesus mr wigin how you got bok yer in that suit that
suit look like it half bok siz cause i member mis rita got him that
suit way back ten leben yers back an bok babbin ther like he kno
me an mis rita sayin he want say he glad to see me an he want
give me one of hiss aggis an me jus lookin at bok shakin my hed
an shakin my hed an i cant stop sayin ole bok ole bok ole bok
you want giv me one o you aggis but ole bok woudn turn it loose

til mis rita had to tell him let go bok few times an still bok woudn turn loose till mis rita pri it out his han and han it to me an bok start babbin ther til mis rita had to reach out her han fo me to giv it back to her an she giv it back to bok an bok put it back in his pocket an start rattlin it wit all the others in ther an mis rita say she was sho he want to giv me somthin thats why he want to com an i tol her it was all rite i didn't need nothin but she say bok woudn res tonite if he didn giv me somethin an she tol him to giv me a diffen one if he didn want give me the aggi an ole bok lookin way over yonder kep rattlin the marbles in his pocket an jus kep on lookin way over yonder rattlin the marbles til he fond the litles one he had in his pocket an han me that

this was the firs time i cry when they lok that door bahind me the very firs time an i jus set on my bunk cryin but not let them see or yer me cause i didn want them think rong but i was cryin cause of bok an the marble he giv me and cause o the peple com to see me cause they hadn never done nothin lik that for me befor

i dont want sleep at nite no mo jus catnap in the day while they got lite and they got noise cause i dont want drem bout that door ever time i shet my eyes

when they brot me in the room an i seen nanan at the table i seen how ole she look an how tied she look an i tol her i love her an i tol her i was strong an she jus look ole and tied an pull me to her an kiss me an it was the firs time she never done that an it felt good an i let her hol me long is she want cause you say it was good for her an i tol her i was strong an she didn need to come back no mo cause i was strong an she just set ther wit her eyes mos shet like she want to go to sleep lookin at me all the time til reven and mis lou have to hep her up an take her back home

*   *   *

mr wigin when i see you girlfren an yall together i see how pretty
she is an im sorry how i talk that day when i was mad at you an
say them nasty thing bout her cause she so pretty an smil so
pretty when she look at peple an you can see she aint putin on
airs an its jus kwaly in her an she talk so nice to peple an all the
time i want look at her but scare to cause she so pretty an im so
ugly an she got on a pretty dress with pretty flowers an my close
dont smell good and i aint took a baf sens sady but i still want
look at her an she say she think im lookin good an strong an
when she put her han on my sholder i start tremblin an she lean
close an kiss me and i feel hot an i coud smell her poder cent an
i feel good an scare an hot cause thats the firs lady that pretty
ever tech me an nobody that pretty never kiss me an when yall
left i come to the door an i look at her long long is i coud and
coud smell her poder cent and still feel her mof on my face

im sory i cry mr wigin im sory i cry when you say you aint comin
back tomoro im strong an reven ambros gon be yer wit me an
mr harry comin to an reson i cry cause you been so good to me
mr wigin an nobody aint never been that good to me an make
me think im sombody

shef guiry ax me what i want for my super an i tol him i want
nanan to cook me som okra an rice an som pok chop an a
conbred an som claba an he say he gon see what he can do an
say what i want for desert an i tol him jus a little ice crme in a
cup an a moon pie

they took me an let me stan under the shoer wit a new bar a sope
an they giv me a big wite clen tower an brot me back an i put
on some clen close an set down cause my food was yer an i et
it ever bit an it was the bes meal i kno my nanan ever cook

sun goin down an i kno this the las one im gon ever see but im
gon see one mo sunrise cause i aint gon sleep tonite

*   *   *

im gon sleep a long time after tomoro

shef guiry come by after i et an ax me how im doin an i say im doin all right an he ax me he say i aint never pik up yo tablet an look in it an he ax me what all i been ritin an i tol him jus things an he say aint he done tret me rite an i tol him yesir an he say aint his deptis done tret me fair an i tol him yesir an he say aint he done let peple vist me anytime an i say yesir an he say didn he let the chiren an all the peple from the quarter com an visit me jus two days ago an i say yesir an he say is you gon put that in yo tablet an i say yesir an he say good put that down in yo tablet i tret you good all the time you been yer an he say he had to go hom cause he hadn et his super yet but for me to call a depty if i need somthin an he ax me if i want the lite to stay on all nite in case i want rite som mo an i tol him yesir an he say all rite i coud have all the lite i want

my lite on but they aint no mo lite on in the place an the place is quite quite but nobody sleepin

they got a moon out ther an i can see the leves on the tree but i aint gon see no mo leves after tomoro

i dont know if they got a heven cause samson say they cant be an boo say they aint non fo no niger but reven ambros say they is one for all men an bok dont kno

i been shakin an shakin but im gon stay strong

i aint had no bisnes goin ther wit brother an bear cause they aint no good an im gon be meetin them soon

its quite quite an i can yer my teefs hitin an i can yer my hart

*   *   *

when i was a litle boy i was a waterboy an rode the cart but now i got to be a man an set in a cher

dont kno if you can red this mr wigin my han shakin and i can yer my hart

i can yer randy but i aint listnin no mo cause he for the livin an not for me

its late an i dont know what time it is but i kno its late an i jus went to the tolet an i jus wash my face

day breakin

sun comin up

the bird in the tre soun like a blu bird

sky blu blu mr wigin

good by mr wigin tell them im strong tell them im a man good by mr wigin im gon ax paul if he can bring you this

sincely jefferson

30

SIDNEY deROGERS was on his way to George Jarreau's house to mow the lawn when the truck went by him. He didn't pay any close attention to the black truck with the gray tarpaulin cover, but he would tell the people later at the Rainbow Club that he did feel a cold chill when the truck went by. The truck turned left on the main street two blocks up ahead of Sidney, but he thought it was just another truck delivering something at one of the department stores. Around eleven o'clock, George Jarreau's wife, Lucy, came out into the yard where Sidney was raking up the grass and leaves and told him that she wanted him to go uptown to Edwin's department store and get her a large spool of white thread. Sidney drove the six blocks in Lucy's car, and as he was approaching the store he saw a crowd of people standing on the sidewalk, facing the court-house. Parked beside the courthouse was the same truck that Sidney had seen at eight o'clock that morning. The tarpaulin had been rolled back, and two men sat at the tail end of the truck, talking and smoking cigarettes. Sidney parked a little distance beyond the department store and walked back. He saw many people he knew, both white and colored, but no one paid him any attention; they were too concerned with the truck parked beside the courthouse. When Sidney came into the store, he found all the clerks up at the front, trying to see what was going on in the truck. He stood back waiting, but no one paid him any attention. Finally, he told one of the women that Miss Lucy had sent him up there for a spool of coarse white thread. Without looking around, the woman told him to go and find it himself. When he came back to pay her, she told him to have Lucy send the money some other time.

My aunt did not sleep at the house the night before. Like many of the other older people in the quarter, she spent the night with Miss Emma. Some of the others took shifts, but my aunt stayed there the whole night. Reverend Ambrose was there until mid-night, then he went home to get some sleep because the sheriff had told him he wanted all witnesses at the courthouse no later, absolutely no later, than eleven-thirty the next morning.

Vivian and I sat in a corner of the Rainbow Club that night. There were more than a dozen people in the place, but it was quieter than I had ever seen it. Vivian held on to her one drink all the time she was there, and when she left, she still had not finished it. She had gone to church after her class that afternoon, and she told me she would go again the next morning. She told me that from noon until she "heard," she would have her students on their knees beside their desks. She left the Rainbow Club at nine. After walking her to the car and kissing her good night, I went back inside and stood at the bar. Claiborne wiped glasses and did not talk to anybody. He served you when you raised your glass for another drink or your bottle for another beer, then he went back to wiping glasses. Thelma had closed up the café just after nine and gone home. Claiborne said he was going to close up at eleven tonight. I told him I wanted a half pint to take with me. Claiborne wrapped it in a brown paper bag and I paid him, but we didn't look directly at each other. At ten-thirty I left, but I still didn't want to go home, and I drove to a bar in Port Allen. I ran into a guy there who knew me and wanted to talk about it, but I didn't want to talk about it, and after I had a drink I started back for the quarter. I got back there about midnight. The place was pitch black, except for the light on Miss Emma's porch. A couple of cars I didn't recognize were parked in front of the house. I supposed they were family or friends who had come to be with her tonight. I didn't stop. There was nothing more to say. I went on home. I took the bottle out of the paper bag and drank about half of it. I had bought the liquor to make me sleep, but God knows now I didn't want to sleep. I didn't want to dream—not tonight.

The minister did not sleep at all that night, and at daybreak he got up and knelt beside his bed to say his prayers, then he went to the kitchen to warm water for his bath. His wife, Mrs. Becky, came into the kitchen to fix him a bowl of cush-cush for his breakfast. When the minister finished his bath, he sat down at the table to eat. He had a cup of coffee before he ate his food. He ate very slowly as he sat at the table thinking about what he had to do today. After he finished his breakfast, he went into the bedroom to get his Bible, then he came back into the kitchen and sat down at the table again. He had chosen the Twenty-third Psalm to read at the jail; he made that choice soon after the sheriff had given him permission to be one of the witnesses. Now he was reading his Bible and praying that God would give him the strength that he knew he needed. He had never witnessed anything like this before, and he knew he needed God

every moment that he would be there. He knew that Harry
Williams was going to be there too, and he told himself he would
stand or sit as close to Harry as he could. He also reminded
himself that he would meet LaCox soon after it was over. LaCox
was the colored mortician of Bayonne, and he would have the
coffin ready.

At six-thirty, the sheriff sat down at the table in his dining room
to eat his breakfast. His breakfast was two homemade biscuit
sandwiches. The biscuits had been split open; one contained a
pork sausage patty and the other contained figs. Lillian, their
colored maid, had preserved figs the past summer. The sheriff
also drank a glass of milk and a cup of strong coffee. Usually the
sheriff ate his breakfast at eight o'clock and arrived at the jail at
nine, but he wanted to get there no later than seven-thirty today
because that chair was supposed to arrive by eight. The sheriff's
wife sat across the table from him, drinking coffee; it was too
early in the morning for her to eat anything. As the sheriff ate,
he talked to his wife, but he avoided looking her directly in the
face most of the time. He told her that he wished this day had
never gotten here, but now that it had, he had to do what he had
to do. This was the first time he was in charge of an execution,
and he was praying that everything would go well. He told his
wife that he had asked the teacher if he wanted to be there, but
the teacher had shaken his head. He understood, he had said to
the teacher. The reverend had asked to be there, and he had
asked the reverend if one other person from the quarter would
like to be there too. The reverend said he would ask, and the
next day the reverend came in and told him that Harry Williams
had said yes. The sheriff knew Harry Williams and knew he was
no troublemaker. The sheriff ate his food and looked beyond his
wife as he mentioned the names of other witnesses. He had also
hired two more deputies to be there today, just in case he
needed them. Two people from Mr. Gropé's family were going
to be there—and he thanked God that the family had let him

handle this in a civilized way. He told his wife without looking directly at her that it would take place in the storeroom on the bottom floor in the back of the courthouse. He said everything had been cleared out of the room so there would be space for the chair and the witnesses.

Melvina Jack was sweeping off the sidewalk at Edwin's department store when the truck went by her. She had finished and was knocking the dust out of the broom when she saw the truck turn down the alley beside the courthouse. Juanita deJean, one of the white clerks in the store, came outside and asked Melvina if she had any idea what was inside that truck. Melvina did not, and Juanita told her that she would know before this day was over. An automobile drove up and parked in front of the courthouse in a space marked OFFICIAL. The sheriff's car was already parked in his personal parking space. Two men got out of the official car and went inside the courthouse. The older, heavier man wore a cowboy hat, and both men wore suits. Melvina and Juanita continued to watch the truck parked beside the courthouse. Then suddenly Melvina's heart started pumping extra fast, and Juanita heard her say, "No, no." "Yes, yes," she heard Juanita say. While they stood there watching the truck, Sheriff Guidry came out of the courthouse with the two men, and the three of them went around the side to the truck. Sheriff Guidry said something to the driver, and the truck moved toward the rear of the courthouse, up against a window. Two men got out of the cab of the truck and climbed up onto the bed and began rolling back the tarpaulin cover. Then Melvina saw it, a high-backed wooden chair with leather straps, and it took all her strength, she said later, to remain on her feet. The two men, one on either side, moved the chair to the tailgate of the truck, and two other men, who had come out the back door of the courthouse, stood on the ground with their arms extended as the chair was eased down to them. When the men on the ground had the chair secured in their hands, the two men in the truck

jumped down to the ground, and the four of them took the chair
through the door into the courthouse. There was something else
in the truck—a machine-looking thing, Melvina said. Juanita
told her that nothing would happen until twelve o'clock, and
that she could go home at eleven-thirty if she wanted to. Melvina
thanked her, but still she could not take her eyes off the truck.
She heard Juanita saying that she wished something like this
could be done somewhere else. What about those poor children
up at the school? She just hoped they would not hear that thing.
Melvina knew she was speaking of the white children at the
white school, but she had no idea what it was that could be
heard as far away as the school was from the courthouse.

During the month that he was in jail, Fee Jinkins's duty was to
clean the sheriff's office and the white men's and white ladies'
rest rooms. He started every morning between six and six-thirty
and finished around eight or a little after. He was just getting
ready to put away the mop and bucket when he saw them
bringing that chair in through the back door. Four people were
carrying it, two strangers and the two special deputies, Oscar
and Claude Guerin. The sheriff walked in front, and a man
wearing a cowboy hat followed the chair. The man with the
cowboy hat kept saying be careful, be careful; he didn't want
that chair bumping into anything. The sheriff opened the door
to the old storeroom, and the two strangers took it inside, then
everyone followed. They did not shut the door, and Fee could
hear them talking in there, though from where he was in the hall
he could not see them. He could hear the sheriff asking where
the chair should be set, and the man in the cowboy hat was
saying he wanted it against the wall not far from the window,
because those wires from the generator on the truck had to come
through the window. Other people who had come to work were
also in the corridor. A woman was saying that she had seen it,
and it looked just gruesome. A man said it did look gruesome,
and that's why they called it Gruesome Gerty. The man told the

woman that whoever sat in Gruesome Gerty's lap when she was hot never sat down again. The woman replied, "That *is* gruesome." Fee heard the man with the cowboy hat tell someone to go out to the truck and bring in the instruments. A white man standing behind Fee asked him if he had seen it. Fee said he surely had, and it looked mean. The white man told Fee he had better watch himself, or maybe they would have to bring Gerty back for him to sit in her lap. Another man laughed nervously. A woman in the hall told the man shame on him, he ought to stop that, just shame on him. Fee could hear the man with the cowboy hat talking to another man through the window. He was asking the man did everything reach okay, and the man out on the truck said yes, everything did. Out in the corridor, more people were coming in for work. They all wanted to know if the first ones there had seen it. Some of them who had not seen it said they had. Someone said if you had not seen it, you would most definitely hear it. And a woman said she wished she had played sick and stayed home today. A man told her that anyone who wanted to leave was free to stay away between twelve and three. The woman said she was not going to be anywhere around here. Someone asked was it always between twelve and three, and another man said yes, it always was. And someone else said the Lord died between twelve and three on a Friday. A woman said yes, and so did two thieves, one on either side of Him. Fee heard the woman saying that she definitely was not going to be here during that time. She said she felt sick already.

Clay Lemon, who worked at Weber's Café and Bar and Bait Shop and who ran errands for Felix Weber, had just gotten out of the car to go into the bank when he first heard the noise. The sound was coming from the direction of the courthouse, a block and a half away. Clay said later that he did not know what it was, nor did he know exactly where it was coming from. A white man and a white woman walking ahead of him were just about to go into the bank when the woman stopped suddenly and looked back. She said, "Oh, God, don't tell me that they have started—" and the man said, "Come on, dear, come on; don't listen to that." The man held the door open for the woman, but she would not go inside, and Clay would not dare go through the door until the white people did. The man told the woman that nothing was going to happen until after twelve o'clock, and they would be long gone by then. He said that they were just warming up the thing, testing those instruments to make sure everything was in working order. The woman said, "But my God, the whole town can hear that thing." The man said, "Come on, come on, dear," and put his arm around her. They went inside, and Clay followed. The woman asked the clerk behind the counter if she had heard it. The clerk asked, "Heard what?" The woman told about the noise that was coming from the courthouse. The clerk said that being inside, they heard very little from that far away. The woman shook her head and said, "It was just horrible. Just too horrible." The clerk told the woman that her little boy had asked her last night what was going to happen at the jail today, and she said that the sheriff just had to put an old bad nigger away, and she didn't want him to worry about anything. The clerk said that she checked on her little boy just before she went to bed last night, and he was sound asleep. And today when he left for school with his little book sack, there was not a solitary word; he had forgotten all about it. The clerk said all this while serving the white man and white woman. Then Clay stepped up to the counter—but he had forgotten why he was there. The clerk, who was very thin, with blond hair and gray-blue eyes, looked at him and said, "Well, well, I don't have all day—didn't you bring it?" But Clay didn't know what she was talking about. "Didn't Felix send you here to get the money, you dumbbell?" she asked him. He must have given her the sack with the note and the check, because the next thing he knew, he had the weight of quarters, nickels, dimes, and pennies in the sack and he was outside again in the bright sunlight, and he could still hear the noise from the generator a block and a half away.

Paul was in the office when the sheriff and the executioner came in, followed by the two special deputies, Claude and Oscar Guerin. The sheriff sat behind his desk and motioned for the executioner, whose name was Henry Vincent, to have a seat. Vincent took off his cowboy hat and hung it on the rack beside the sheriff's cowboy hat. Paul noticed that the hair on top of Vincent's head was not as gray as the sideburns were. The sheriff asked Vincent if he wanted some coffee, and Vincent said yes. The sheriff told Oscar to go down the hall and get that pot of coffee and bring back some cups. Vincent asked the sheriff if the prisoner had been shaved. The sheriff said no. Vincent asked the sheriff if he didn't think it was about time. The sheriff looked at Paul standing by the window. He told Paul where the things were; he should get Murphy out of the cell and have him do it. Vincent instructed Paul to make sure Murphy did it right, shaved him close. He pointed to areas on the leg and wrist. He said electrodes had to be attached there as well as to the head, and all that had to be shaved very clean. The sheriff told the executioner that the prisoner had hardly any hair on his body other than on his head. Vincent told Paul that Murphy must shave the prisoner everywhere he told him to; electricity sometimes found hair that the naked eye would never see. He said that this was an execution, not torture, that he had seen enough of that for a lifetime. Paul asked the sheriff if someone else couldn't do this. The sheriff told him that Clark would not be there until later, and that he had to do it. Paul nodded for Claude Guerin to come with him, and they went into the next room. He could hear Vincent asking the sheriff if he thought Paul was all right, and the sheriff saying that he was, but this was his first time. Vincent told the sheriff that all they needed was for one of their own men to come apart. The sheriff assured him that Paul was okay, but that this was his first time, that's all. Vincent told the sheriff he hoped he knew his men. Paul and Claude left through another door, Claude carrying a washbasin, clippers, scissors, and a safety razor. People came out of their offices to ask Paul if it was time yet. The special deputy told them that it was only hair-cutting time. A man standing at one of the office doors said oh, yes, he had heard that they got a haircut first. Someone else said what an experience, what an experience, you didn't get to witness this every day. Paul and Claude went up to the cellblock, and unlocked Murphy's cell and told him he had a job for him to do. Murphy looked at the things in Claude's hands and asked why him. Because the sheriff said so, Paul told him. Murphy came out, and the three of them went down to the last cell. Jefferson had been lying on his back, but he sat up and looked at them when they came in. He didn't seem frightened; he appeared tired. Paul could see how red his eyes were and knew that he had not slept at all. Paul asked him how he felt, and he said he was all right. He wore a blue denim shirt and denim trousers. His laceless shoes were halfway under the bunk. The radio and the notebook were on the floor beside the wall. The radio was silent. A bird sang in the sycamore tree outside the window. Paul told Jefferson that he had to have his hair shaved. He sent Murphy to get warm water and a piece of soap from the shower room. While Murphy was gone, Paul and the other deputy stood near the unlocked cell door. Jefferson sat on the bunk, leaning forward and staring down at the floor. The two deputies watched him, but no one said anything. The bird continued its chirping in the tree outside the window. Jefferson turned to look at the deputy standing beside Paul and asked him how was Miss Bernice. Claude didn't know whether he should answer, until Paul nodded, and Claude told him that his wife was okay. And little Roy? Jefferson wanted to know. Claude looked at Paul, and Paul nodded again. Little Roy was all right, too; he was at school. Jefferson looked down at the floor. Murphy came back with a washbasin of warm water and a piece of white soap. He set the basin of water on the floor at the foot of the bunk and took the clippers from Claude Guerin. Claude tried not to meet Jefferson's eyes when Jefferson looked up at him. The two deputies stood back by the door and watched as the layers of hair fell to the floor. When Murphy had finished with the clippers, he dipped his hand into the basin of warm water and started rubbing Jefferson's head with the piece of white soap. Claude handed him the safety razor. When the head was shaved, black and shining, Paul instructed Murphy to take the scissors and cut Jefferson's trouser legs and shirt sleeves. He stood over Murphy and pointed out the areas around the ankles and wrists where he wanted him to shave. All this time, Jefferson obeyed as if he were in a trance, as if he felt nothing. When Murphy was finished, he stood back and examined his work, but Jefferson was looking down at the floor. Paul asked him if he needed anything, and when he did not answer, the deputy motioned for Claude and Murphy to leave. He followed and locked the cell door. As he was about to walk away, Jefferson raised his head and looked at him. He told Paul that he wanted him to bring me the notebook and that he wanted Paul to have the radio. Paul told him he couldn't take the radio, but he would give it to the other inmates, for use in the dayroom, if Jefferson didn't mind. Jefferson asked Paul if he wanted the marble that Bok had given him, and Paul told him he would accept the marble. He told Paul to be sure that Mr. Henri got the pocket knife and the little gold chain. Paul said he would see to that. Jefferson continued to look at Paul, a long, deep look, and the deputy felt that there was something else he wanted to say. Murphy and the other deputy were still waiting. "Well," Paul said, and started to walk away. "Paul?" Jefferson said quietly. And his eyes were speaking, even more than his mouth. The deputy looked back at him. Murphy and Claude did too. "You go'n be there, Paul?" Jefferson asked, his eyes asked. Paul nodded. "Yes, Jefferson. I'll be there."

31

▼

AFTER THE STUDENTS had recited their Bible verses, and before classes began, I told them that there would be no recess period for them today, and that I would let them go home for dinner at eleven o'clock, because I wanted them all back at school no later than a quarter to twelve. I told them that at exactly twelve o'clock they would all get down on their knees and remain on their knees until I heard from the courthouse, whether that took an hour, an hour and a half, or three hours.

Louis Washington, Jr., stuck up a grimy little hand.

"S'pose somebody got to be excused?"

"Then he'll make up that time on his knees after three o'clock," I told him. "For every minute that you don't spend on your knees between twelve o'clock and until I hear from that courthouse, you will spend twice that time on your knees after three. Any other questions?"

"Nawsir."

"Does anyone else have a question?"

No one did.

"All right, open those books, and I want silence, and I mean silence."

I assigned Odessa Freeman primer and first grades; Irene Cole would teach second and third. Fourth graders opened their books to English grammar; fifth graders, geography; sixth, history. I told them I would test them later, if not this afternoon, then definitely tomorrow morning. I knew I would not be able to concentrate on teaching this morning, so I got my Westcott ruler and went outside.

It was a nice day. Blue sky. Not a cloud. Across the road in the Freemans' yard, I could see a patch of white lilies on either side of the walk that led up to the porch. An old automobile tire surrounded each flower. Behind the house was the sugarcane field. The new cane was about waist-high to the average man walking between the rows. Somewhere across the field I could hear the sound of a tractor. A white sharecropper must have been plowing the ground, since no colored people were working today. Even those who worked up at the big house for Henri Pichot or for other white people along the river had taken the day off. This had been discussed and agreed at church last Sunday. Those who were not at church were told what the others had decided, that he, Jefferson, should have all their respect this one day. Now, except for the sound of the tractor back in the field, the rest of the plantation was quiet. No one sat out on the porch, no one worked in the garden, no one walked across the yard or in the road.

I looked toward Miss Emma's house, farther down the quarter. My aunt was there, others were there, but they were all inside. The front door was shut, though the window was open to let in fresh air. I could see the white gauze curtain hanging limp in the window.

I went around to the back of the church. Like so many country churches, it was wood-framed, long and narrow, with a corrugated tin roof and a bell tower. Years ago, I was told, the church sat flat on the ground. Later, it was set up on wooden blocks. During the thirties, when I was a student here, the wooden blocks, which had rotted over the years, were replaced by bricks. A year or two before I started teaching, Farrell Jarreau and a couple of other men removed the bricks and put in cement blocks. But now even the cement blocks had sunk so low in the ground that a child losing a marble or a ball under the church had a hard time crawling under there to retrieve it.

I remembered playing ragball back here, the other children and I, using our fists as bats. We all tried to hit the ball out of the yard for a home run. I supposed I had done so as many times as anyone else, but the number of times was nothing to brag about.

Where were all the others now? Most had gone. To southern cities, to northern cities, others to the grave. Had Jefferson ever hit a home run? He was as big as anyone else, stronger than most, but to hit a home run off a ragball was a feat. Brute strength was not enough. Timing and luck were needed. You had to hit it just right, and that took timing and luck. Lily Green hit as many as anyone else, I supposed. But her luck ran out before she was twenty. Killed accidentally in a barroom in Baton Rouge. What a waste. Such a beautiful girl. All the boys loved Lily Green.

I started back toward the front. What about tomorrow? What happens after today? Nothing will ever be the same after today.

At five minutes to eleven, I was standing at my desk, facing the opened front door, when I saw the minister's car go up the quarter, with Harry Williams sitting in the passenger seat beside him. They were on their way into Bayonne. I told my students to put away their things quietly. Before letting them go, I reminded them that I didn't want any running or loud talking and that I wanted them all back at school no later than a quarter to twelve. When they had all gone, I sat down at my desk, facing the door.

I did not want to think. I wanted to sit there until I heard, but not to think before then. No, I wanted to go to my car and drive away. To go somewhere and lose all memory of where I had come from. I wanted to go, I wanted to— God, what does a person do who knows there is only one more hour to live?

I felt like crying, but I refused to cry. No, I would not cry. There were too many more who would end up as he did. I could not cry for all of them, could I?

I wished I could telephone Vivian, but there was not one telephone, public or otherwise, between here and Bayonne that I could use. I would see her tonight, though. I would definitely see her tonight. I need to see you tonight, my love.

But who was with him? Who is with you, Jefferson? Is He with you, Jefferson? He is with Reverend Ambrose, because Reverend Ambrose believes. Do you believe, Jefferson? Have I done anything to make you not believe? If I have, please forgive me for being a fool. For at this moment, what else is there?

I know now that that old man is much braver than I. I am not with you at this moment because—because I would not have been able to stand. I would not have been able to walk with you those last few steps. I would have embarrassed you. But the old man will not. He will be strong. He is going to use *their* God to give him strength. You just watch, Jefferson. You just watch. He is brave, braver than I, braver than any of them—except you, I hope. My faith is in you, Jefferson.

The children returned from dinner as I had asked them to do, and at ten minutes to twelve, I lined them up before the door. When the last one had marched into the church, I went to my desk to face them.

"In a couple of minutes it will be twelve o'clock. I will ask you to get down on your knees and remain on your knees until I ask you to get up. Are there any questions?"

Louis Washington, Jr., raised that grimy little hand again.

"Is you go'n bow down too, Mr. Wiggins?"

"The proper way to ask that question is, 'Are you going to bow down too, Mr. Wiggins?' "

"You go'n bow down too?"

"I'll be outside," I told the class. "Irene, you, Odessa, and Clarence are in charge. All right, please, on your knees. I'll tell you when to get up."

"We need to pray?" Louis Washington, Jr., wanted to know.

"Yes," I told him. "But quietly, to yourself."

Several of the larger girls knelt on scarves or handkerchiefs. I took up my Westcott and went out through the front door. I had no idea what I would do while I waited to hear from Bayonne, but I found myself out in the road and walking up the quarter. It was a couple of minutes after twelve, and I was trying not to think. But how could I not think about something that had dominated my thoughts for nearly six months? It seemed that I had spent more time with him in that jail cell than I had with the children in the church school.

Where was he at this very moment? At the window, looking out at the sky? Lying on the bunk, staring up at the gray ceiling? Standing at the cell door, waiting? How did he feel? Was he afraid? Was he crying? Were they coming to get him now, this moment? Was he on his knees, begging for one more minute of life? Was he standing?

Why wasn't I there? Why wasn't I standing beside him? Why wasn't my arm around him? Why?

Why wasn't I back there with the children? Why wasn't I down on my knees? Why?

At the mouth of the quarter, there was shade from a pecan tree in the corner of the fence surrounding Henri Pichot's yard. A shallow ditch ran between the fence and the road. The people from the quarter had sat under that tree as far back as I could

remember. Men had gambled there with cards and dice. Others
had stood or sat there to get out of the hot sun or the rain.
Before I had a car, I had stood there many times waiting for the
bus. The bus driver always blew the horn about a mile before
he got there, and I would have time to cross the highway to wave
it down. There would always be someone there, but today I sat
alone.

Behind me was Henri Pichot's gray and white antebellum
house, sitting on its foundation high above the ground. His car
was parked on the grass in the front yard. I figured that he would
be the first to hear, and maybe he would come into the quarter.
I looked back over my shoulder when I sat down, and I looked
back every minute or two afterward.

It must have been twelve-fifteen by now. I didn't want to look
at my watch anymore. Had it already happened? Or was he still
waiting, sitting on the bunk, hands clasped together, waiting?
Was he standing at the cell door, listening for that first sound of
footsteps coming toward him? Or was it finally, finally over?

Don't tell me to believe. Don't tell me to believe in the same
God or laws that men believe in who commit these murders.
Don't tell me to believe that God can bless this country and that
men are judged by their peers. Who among his peers judged
him? Was I there? Was the minister there? Was Harry Williams
there? Was Farrell Jarreau? Was my aunt? Was Vivian? No, his
peers did not judge him—and I will not believe.

Yet they must believe. They must believe, if only to free the
mind, if not the body. Only when the mind is free has the body
a chance to be free. Yes, they must believe, they must believe.
Because I know what it means to be a slave. I am a slave.

I looked back. But there was no movement at Henri Pichot's
house. It must have been close to twelve-thirty, but I refused to
look at my watch.

Several feet away from where I sat under the tree was a hill
of bull grass. I doubted that I had looked at it once in all the time
that I had been sitting there. I probably would not have noticed

it at all had a butterfly, a yellow butterfly with dark specks like
ink dots on its wings, not lit there. What had brought it there?
There was no odor that I could detect to have attracted it. There
were other places where it could have rested—there was the
wire fence on either side of the road, there were weeds along
both ditches with strong fragrances, there were flowers just a
short distance away in Pichot's yard—so why did it light on a hill
of bull grass that offered it nothing? I watched it closely, the way
it opened its wings and closed them, the way it opened its wings
again, fluttered, closed its wings for a second or two, then
opened them again and flew away. I watched it fly over the ditch
and down into the quarter, I watched it until I could not see it
anymore.

Yes, I told myself. It is finally over.

I waited another few minutes for Henri Pichot to come out,
but he did not. I stood up and stretched and looked across the
highway at the river, so tranquil, its water as blue as the sky. The
willows near the edge of the water were just as still, and no
breeze stirred the Spanish moss that hung from the cypresses. I
could hear the horn as the bus came around the big bend a mile
away on its way into Bayonne. I looked toward Pichot's house
again, and I started back down the quarter. I knew it was over,
but I would wait until I heard from the courthouse. I looked
back several times, but no Henri Pichot. I was the only person
in the road. Just me, and my gray car parked farther down the
quarter, in front of my aunt's house.

I took my time walking, and occasionally slapped my leg with
the Westcott. When I came up even with the church, I stopped
out in the road to look at Miss Emma's house again. The door
was still shut, the curtain hung limp in the window. I wondered
if she knew it was finally over.

Just before going into the churchyard, I looked back up the
quarter. And now I did see a car coming toward me. The driver
drove slowly to keep down the dust. It didn't look like Pichot's
car, and I knew it was not Reverend Ambrose's. I moved into

the ditch as Paul came up even with me and stopped. We looked at each other, and I knew he had come to bring me the news. I didn't go up to the car, as I was supposed to do; I waited for him to make his move. I saw him reach for something on the seat beside him, then he opened the door and got out. He had a notebook, just like the one I had given Jefferson. I waited for him to come to me.

"He wanted me to bring you this."

Paul looked directly at me, his gray-blue eyes more intense than I had ever seen them before. I took the notebook from him, and he continued to stare at me, like someone in shock.

"Do you have a minute?" he asked me.

"Yes. But I'll have to go inside first. I left the children on their knees. I'll be right back."

The children all looked at me as I walked up the aisle to the table. I told them to rise from their knees. When they had all sat down, some of them rubbing their knees before sitting, I told them I had to speak to someone, and I wanted them to remain quiet until I got back. I told them that Jefferson had sent a notebook to me, and I was going to leave it on the table, and later we would talk. I left Irene Cole in charge and went back outside.

Paul and I started walking down the quarter. We were both quiet. I waited for him to begin.

"It went as well as it could have gone." He spoke slowly as we walked abreast, he looking up ahead, I down at the ground. "There was no trouble. He was a little shaky—but no trouble."

Paul was quiet a moment, then suddenly he stopped walking. After going another step, I stopped, too, and looked back at him.

"He was the strongest man in that crowded room, Grant Wiggins," Paul said, staring at me and speaking louder than was necessary. "He was, he was. I'm not saying this to make you feel good, I'm not saying this to ease your pain. Ask that preacher, ask Harry Williams. He was the strongest man there. We all stood jammed together, no more than six, eight feet away from that chair. We all had each other to lean on. When Vincent asked him if he had any last words, he looked at the preacher and said, 'Tell Nannan I walked.' And straight he walked, Grant Wiggins. Straight he walked. I'm a witness. Straight he walked."

Paul stopped talking. He was breathing heavily. He was looking at me but seeing Jefferson in that chair. We started walking again. We were passing by Miss Emma's house, but Paul didn't know this. He had never been in the quarter before.

"After they put the death cloth over his face, I couldn't watch anymore. I looked down at the floor," Paul was saying. His voice was quieter, less intense now. "I heard the two jolts, but I wouldn't look up. I'll never forget the sound of that generator as long as I live on this earth."

We came to the end of the quarter and stood on the railroad tracks while gazing across the field at the rows of early cane. Paul got in front of me to look in my face.

"You're one great teacher, Grant Wiggins," he said.

"I'm not great. I'm not even a teacher."

"Why do you say that?"

"You have to believe to be a teacher," I said, looking at the rows of new cane. To the right of where we were standing were the tall pecan trees in the cemetery. There would be another grave there within a day or two.

"I saw the transformation, Grant Wiggins," Paul said.

"I didn't do it."

"Who, then?"

"Maybe he did it himself."

"He never could have done that. I saw the transformation. I'm a witness to that."

"Then maybe it was God," I said.

Paul continued to look at me. He did not like the way I had used the name of God. He came from good stock. He believed. But he didn't say anything.

"You're ready to start back?" I asked him.

"I didn't open his notebook," Paul said. We had turned and were walking up the quarter now. "I didn't think it was my place to open the notebook. He asked me to bring it to you, and I brought it to you. But I would like to know his thoughts sometime—if you don't mind."

"After I read it," I said.

"I suppose this has been very hard on everybody."

"Hard on the people here," I said.

"School is just about ready to end, huh?" Paul asked, after a while.

"Yes," I said. "We start a month later and get out two months earlier than the whites do."

"What are you going to do when school is over? Go on a vacation?"

"I don't know. It depends on Vivian. Whatever she wants."

"She's beautiful," Paul said. "You're a lucky fellow there, Grant Wiggins."

"Yes, I'm lucky," I said. "Some of us are."

"I'm sorry," Paul said. "I am very, very sorry."

We had stopped for a moment. Now we started walking again.

"If I could ever be of any help, I would like you to call on me. I mean that with all my heart."

We were passing by Miss Emma's house. Reverend Ambrose's car was parked before the door.

"Isn't that the preacher's car?" Paul asked.

"That's where Jefferson lived. That's his nannan's house."

Paul looked at the house as we went by. He looked at it again over his shoulder. We came up to the church and stopped at his car.

"Well, I better go in to the children," I said.

Paul stuck out his hand.

"Allow me to be your friend, Grant Wiggins. I don't ever want to forget this day. I don't ever want to forget him."

I took his hand. He held mine with both of his.

"I don't know what you're going to say when you go back in there. But tell them he was the bravest man in that room today. I'm a witness, Grant Wiggins. Tell them so."

"Maybe one day you will come back and tell them so."

"It would be an honor."

I turned from him and went into the church. Irene Cole told the class to rise, with their shoulders back. I went up to the desk and turned to face them. I was crying.

A NOTE ON THE TYPE

The text of this book was set in Simoncini Garamond,
a modern version by Francesco Simoncini of the type
attributed to the famous Parisian type cutter Claude
Garamond (ca. 1490–1561). Garamond was a pupil
of Geoffrey Tory and is believed to have based his
letters on the Venetian models, although he introduced
a number of important differences, and it is to him
we owe the letter that we know as old-style. He gave
to his letters a certain elegance and a feeling of movement that won for their creator an immediate reputation
and the patronage of Francis I of France.

Composed by ComCom, a division of
The Haddon Craftsmen, Inc.,
Allentown, Pennsylvania
Printed and bound by Fairfield Graphics,
Fairfield, Pennsylvania
Designed by Anthea Lingeman